Duty's Destiny

By the same author

Lady Hartley's Inheritance

Duty's Destiny

Wendy Soliman

ROBERT HALE · LONDON

ISBN-10: 0-7090-8138-3
ISBN-13: 978-0-7090-8138-8

Robert Hale Limited
Clerkenwell House
Clerkenwell Green
London EC1R 0HT

The right of Wendy Soliman to be identified as
author of this work has been asserted by her
in accordance with the Copyright, Designs and
Patents Act 1988

2 4 6 8 10 9 7 5 3 1

Typeset in 11½/14½pt Erhardt
by Derek Doyle & Associates, Shaw Heath
Printed in Great Britain by St Edmundsbury Press Limited
Bury St Edmunds, Suffolk
Bound by Woolnough Bookbinding Limited

Chapter One

CONCEALING a yawn behind his hand was the only effort that Felix, Viscount Western, made to disguise his boredom from Angelica Priestley, his beautiful, wild and often unpredictable mistress. Being aware that his punctilious manners were falling well short of the mark did nothing to shake off his distracted mood.

'Felix, you are a brute!' she declared with a pretty little pout, which would once have set his pulse racing and mind veering in the direction of further intimacies, but today left him unmoved.

'Angelica, m'dear, don't tell me you are you dissatisfied?' Felix flashed a challenging smile in her direction. 'I am devastated.'

'Of course not, my love, but you know my husband returns tomorrow. I cannot bear the thought of it.' She spoke with a calm indifference that belied her anxious words.

'If you are unequal to the reconciliation then you had best plead an indisposition,' Felix drawled, his mind already elsewhere.

'Huh, you do not care at all!' cried Angelica accusingly. 'Simon will be back and we will be unable to see one another for heaven knows how long and yet the prospect appears to distress you not one jot. I shall die without you!' she added dramatically, stretching out a hand to prevent Felix from leaving the bed. 'Stay a little longer, I beg of you, and . . . and talk to me.'

'You want to talk?' Felix was incredulous.

'Why not? We will not have another opportunity for intimate conversation for an age.'

'I am unable to oblige you, Angelica,' lied Felix smoothly. 'Have to see my father this afternoon.'

Angelica frowned moodily, observing Felix as he gracefully levered himself from the bed and reached for his clothes. He could feel her eyes devouring his naked torso and chuckled as he pulled his shirt over his head.

'I would not look at me like that at the duchess's ball tomorrow night, if I was you, m'dear, or you'll set the tabbies' tongues a'wagging for sure!' Felix's brown eyes twinkled with amusement.

'Huh!' Defiant, Angelica tossed her dishevelled blonde mane. 'What do I care? Felix, you are too cruel to leave so abruptly!' She leapt from the bed and plastered her naked body against his now fully clothed one. She wrapped her arms round his neck, sank her fingers into his thick mop of shiny brown curls, twining them playfully around her fingers, her blatant invitation a siren call that Felix had little difficulty resisting.

'Angelica, don't be such a widgeon! We have had some fun together, but you will be occupied with Simon's concerns now and we must proceed with caution.'

'Oh, do not remind me! Whatever possessed me to marry the man I cannot imagine.'

Felix grinned at his mistress. 'What indeed? You were debutante of the year two seasons ago, had the entire *ton* worshipping at your feet and yet you chose Towbridge.'

'Not the entire *ton*,' she reminded him, with another petulant pout. They both knew she was alluding to the fact that Felix and his best friend, the Earl of Newbury, were two of the few eligible gentlemen who had made no attempt to ensnare Angelica. Felix, knowing better than to comment upon that aspect of their amatory history, though, wisely ignored her words.

'Leaving aside the material gains to be derived from Simon's vast wealth,' he said, 'you married him because you wanted to be the Marchioness of Towbridge and benefit from the social privileges which accompany that elevated rank.'

In another of her abrupt changes of mood she smiled at him

sweetly, her heart reflected far too clearly in her eyes for Felix's comfort. 'Maybe so,' she conceded. 'But those privileges are already starting to pale. Simon is more than thirty years older than me—'

'You knew that when you married him.'

'Yes, but what I did not know was that he has no conversation and no interests other than hunting and serving the Prince Regent. He is a selfish lover and revels in parading me in front of his dreary friends, like some new addition to his wretched art collection, to be admired and drooled over, but never touched.' She threw back her head and prowled catlike around the room – totally at ease with her nakedness – picking up objects randomly and weighing them in her hands as she fought to control her fiery temper.

'Well, m'dear,' responded Felix, bored with a conversation that had been played out between them on countless previous occasions, 'you—'

'Oh, Felix, why could it not have been different? Before I met you I had no idea what I was missing and could endure Simon's attentions, but now. . . .'

Her voice trailed off and she fell into a chair and a sulk simultaneously. Felix watched her impassively, tired of her juvenile games. Angelica had been spoiled and indulged for her entire life: never more so than since meeting her doting husband. Felix had known as soon as he set eyes on her that he would never wish to marry such a creature and had simply watched from the sidelines, biding his time.

He may not have wanted to marry her, but there was no denying her quite exceptional beauty, and there had been another vacancy in his life that she had been more than qualified to fill. After six months of Simon's clumsy mauling he had sensed that she would be ripe for the picking and approached her. He could see straight away that her interest was piqued and her initial reticence had been more to do with lack of opportunity than any unwillingness on her part. It had not been long before Simon, as equerry to the Prince, had been obliged to travel to Ireland on behalf of his royal master. Felix grasped the opportunity and it was only then, after Angelica's sensuality had been properly awakened beneath his expert tutelage, that the full extent of her folly in marrying a man such as Simon, simply to obtain a position at Court, became apparent to her.

Felix ignored her and left her to her sulking: something the carefully selected band of sycophants she surrounded herself with would never presume to do. Left to her own devices though her mood changed again abruptly and she offered him a glittering smile.

'Anyway, I can manage Simon; I do not see why his return should mean that we must suspend our assignations.' When Felix made no reply, and showed no enthusiasm for her suggestion either, anger flared briefly in her eyes and a calculating expression spread across her lovely face. 'But what if rumours of our association should reach his ears?' she queried sweetly.

'If they do,' said Felix with deliberation, 'he will doubtless call me out and attempt to put a bullet through my head. Is that what it would take to make you happy?'

'Oh, darling, do not say such things! I cannot bear the thought of it. I will never reveal your name. Never! I swear I would die first! It is just that I love you to distraction and cannot bear the thought of being parted from you, even for a day.'

Felix hid his anger at her thinly veiled threat behind an attitude of casual indifference. 'Let us hope that it does not come to that then.'

'You do not love me at all!'

'No Angelica,' he replied, his anger giving way to amusement, 'I do not. But you certainly know how to entertain a man.' He winked lasciviously and pushed her away from him. 'Come, m'dear, needs must. Allow me to play the part of lady's maid.'

Felix assisted Angelica into her clothing, twisted her hair into a knot and hid the untidy results beneath her fashionable leghorn bonnet. He gave her a fleeting kiss and, having first checked that the coast was clear, ushered her from the rooms which he kept for the purpose of their assignations.

Breathing a sigh of relief at having escaped Angelica's ubiquitous clutches, Felix sauntered the length of Park Street and let himself into his father's residence. But his anger lingered: he did not care to be threatened. Their liaison had run its course; Angelica was turning into a dangerous liability and would have to go.

Felix heard female voices emanating from the drawing-room and suppressed a groan. His mother and sisters were entertaining again. Nothing unusual about that, but Felix had no desire to be drawn into their machinations and headed for the relative safety of the library, where he discovered his father already taking shelter.

'Ho, Father, another pilgrim seeking refuge from the fray, I see.'

'Absolutely!' agreed the earl with alacrity. 'Your mother is entertaining Lord Denby and his sister, amongst others. I dare say she is procrastinating, hoping for your return.'

Felix's only response was an elegant shrug. He headed for the decanter on the sideboard and held it up to his father. Receiving a nod of approbation Felix poured two glasses of Madeira and handed one to the earl.

'Thank you, Felix.' The earl sipped his wine appreciatively and the two men sat in companionable silence. Felix's thoughts dwelt upon the lessening of his interest in the lovely Angelica. He had entered into the liaison initially from a combination of boredom and an inability to resist the challenge she represented to every red-blooded male within the *ton*, a challenge that everyone agreed she would never risk acceding to. That she had capitulated readily had both surprised and delighted Felix and for a while she had held him in her thrall. But now? Well, now he was bored again. And not just with his mistress but with everything to do with life in the *grand monde*.

'I suppose we should join them,' said the earl, any enthusiasm he might feel at the prospect conspicuously absent from his voice.

'If we must.'

'Your mother will require you to charm Denby's sister, thereby leaving Denby free to pursue your own sibling,' the earl reminded Felix, his eyes alight with amusement.

'I have not the slightest doubt of it.'

'We both know, of course, that she intends Maria Denby for you.'

Felix's laconic response belied the fulminating anger that coursed through him as he contemplated his mother's attempts to manipulate his choice of bride. 'My mother's subtlety is a constant source of comfort to me. However, Denby is well able to offer for my sister without any assistance from me. Maria Denby is attractive enough, I suppose, but nothing exceptional and I now have reason to know that she has no conversation, no intellect and no particular interests in common with me.'

'I assume she will not become your viscountess then?'

'Your assumption is correct.'

'Your mother will be mortified.'

'She will get over it.'

'I know she is less than subtle in her machinations, Felix, but she does have a point, you know. Mothers are supposed to see their children through to good marriages. You are her only son and are now eight-and-twenty. She is right to be concerned about your dilatory attitude towards matrimony.'

'Not you too, Father?'

'Fear not, Felix, I will say no more on the matter. Just bear in mind though that two of your four younger sisters are already well married; Denby appears intent upon declaring for the third and the fourth will come out next year, when she will undoubtedly make short work of charming some suitable gentleman. Your mother has a right to expect you to settle down and produce a legitimate heir.' The earl paused and settled a meaningful look upon his son. 'As, too, do I.'

His father was right, of course. Felix was guiltily aware that he had been dragging his feet and vowed that he would, at last, commence the search for a suitable wife. A little intellect, a compliant nature and, naturally, some beauty, were his only requirements. Having found such a creature, Felix would dutifully beget a nursery full of heirs and continue to conduct his life as he saw fit, following his own father's excellent example. But he would find his spouse for himself, without any interference from his mother.

'I know that, Father, and you may rest easy in the knowledge that I will oblige you both before you are too much older. It is just that at the moment I—'

Felix, feeling increasingly uncomfortable in the wake of his father's unusually stern oration, had never been more relieved to have a conversation interrupted by a discreet knock. The butler entered and handed the earl a letter on a silver salver.

'This express was just delivered from Plymouth, my lord.'

'Thank you, Rogers.'

The earl broke the seal and read two pages covered in a close hand, frowning as he progressed.

'Trouble?' asked Felix.

'Possibly, it is from Smithers.'

'I see. And what does the Head of the Preventive Waterguard have on his mind?'

'He requires an urgent meeting with me: something about extreme and unusual smuggling activities.' The earl sighed, feigning reluctance. 'It would seem that I must return to Plymouth.'

'How tiresome for you,' sympathized Felix, grinning at his father.

Felix knew that his father would seize upon this very useful excuse to escape town and head to Western Hall, the family seat outside Plymouth, and not because he was particularly concerned about the revenue man's fears. That the smuggling was taking place was not in question, and as head of the eminent Western Shipping Line, a magistrate and squire of great influence in the South-West, such matters would routinely be reported to the earl. Felix did not doubt that a meeting to discuss this latest uprising could easily be postponed for another month or more, until the season came to an end. His father's sudden need to return to the country would undoubtedly have more to do with his desire to be reunited with the mistress he kept in Plymouth.

Felix was acquainted with the lady and could scarce blame his father for his impatience to return. The advancement towards her middle years was being smoothed by an innate elegance and quiet dignity. She possessed a sparkling wit, lively mind, was a gifted musician and amusing raconteur. She kept a good table and her home was comfortable and welcoming: a haven of tranquillity where, for once, no demands were placed upon Felix's father, other than those of the flesh.

An idea flashed into Felix's head. If his father could escape the madness of a London season in full swing then so too could he.

'Perhaps I should accompany you, Father?'

'There is no necessity for that, Felix.'

'Oh, but I believe there is.' When the earl looked set to demur, Felix forged ahead. 'Father, things have come to a pretty pass between my mother and me. If I do not get away then I fear I may say things to her that I will later regret. Her interference is becoming intolerable. When Luc fell prey to the parson's mousetrap, she could scarce conceal her glee, thinking that where one went another must surely follow.' Felix paused and smiled as he considered his friend's good fortune in having the beguiling Clarissa Hartley fall so conveniently into his path. 'Well, if another such as Clarissa exists in this world then she may just get her wish. But at the moment, the matrons are aiming their collective guns in my direction and showing no mercy. They are pushing chit after dreary chit at me and it is becoming altogether too fatiguing.'

It was true. Ever since his closest friend, Luc Deverill, the Earl of Newbury, had married Clarissa Hartley two months before, Felix's life had become intolerable. Not only did he miss Luc's company but also belatedly realized that there had been safety in numbers. What was more, without Luc's inventiveness there were no longer nearly so many amusing diversions to be had and he admitted to himself now that life within the *ton* had become one of boring predictability. He needed a diversion and an unscheduled trip to Plymouth could be just the thing.

'And what of the lovely Angelica?' enquired the earl, with a smile. 'Are not the compensations offered there worth the odd skirmish with your mother?'

'Angelica's husband is about to return from Ireland. What's more, she is starting to cling and is becoming less than discreet.' Felix spoke with casual indifference, not at all surprised to discover that his perspicacious father knew of the supposedly private arrangement he had with Angelica. 'She will have to go, I fear.'

'Hm, pity that.'

'Indeed, Father, but what about Plymouth? Am I to accompany you?'

Taking pity on his handsome and clearly restless son, the earl capitulated. 'But I will leave it to you to resolve matters with your mother.' The earl drained his glass and rose to his feet. 'Now, the least you can do is accompany me next door and be polite to Maria Denby for half an hour.'

Felix smiled in triumph. 'Under the circumstances, I will be happy to oblige you.'

Chapter Two

T HE following Monday found Colonel Smithers in the drawing-room at Western Hall. As Chief Officer of the Preventive Waterguard for the South-West his occupation was far from being easy. Customs men were universally disliked and Smithers' position was further complicated by the fact that smuggling in their part of the world was generally looked upon as a traditional profession, made respectable by the passage of time.

It was rare to find a man as honest and dedicated as Smithers and the earl held him in high regard. His litany of complaints was a common one though. Too few men to fight the smugglers, those that they did have being susceptible to bribery and intimidation. The long awaited peace following the end of the conflict in France saw the demobilization of 300,000 soldiers and sailors, but the gainful employment which the returning heroes felt they had the right to expect was not forthcoming. It was not difficult to persuade locals returning to the south-western coast to engage in some form of smuggling activity – albeit as lookouts, tubmen, flaskers and the like. Felix and his father knew that for one night unloading contraband cargo a man could expect to earn the equivalent of one week's pay from a legitimate profession. Furthermore, the smugglers had so many different places to unload their cargoes, and so many methods of so doing, that the chances of being detected were slight.

As befitted their elevated position within the locality, Felix and his father lent every assistance at their disposal to Smithers, promoting his struggle to control these illegal activities. But that didn't prevent them from privately entertaining a certain sympathy for the smugglers' plight when they expressed righteous indignation at being unable to secure legitimate work, having willingly risked their lives for King and country.

Colonel Smithers today most particularly wished to discuss a village by the name of Burton Bradstock, a key landing area for smugglers situated in the Lyme Bay area.

'Smuggling in that vicinity is getting out of control, my lords,' explained the good colonel. 'The area in question spreads across some seventeen miles, from Portland at one end of the bay to Burton Bradstock at the other. It would help no end if we could have coastal blockades, such as those that have just been erected along the Kent and Sussex coasts,' he added, more in hope than expectation.

The earl scowled. They had conducted this conversation on several previous occasions and Smithers was aware of the reasons why the blockages could not yet be erected on their part of the coastline. That being so he did not care to be the recipient of the Customs man's caustic barbs.

'Smithers, you forget yourself!'

Smithers bowed his apology. 'But in the meantime we are fighting an increasingly desperate battle. The men are ingenious when it comes to finding ways of landing their cargo and we are seldom able to obtain co-operation from any of the villages, since most of their inhabitants are involved.'

'What cargoes are in vogue nowadays, Smithers?' asked Felix.

'Good cognac is now coming out of France by the ankerload, my lord. Plus, naturally, the usual tobacco, wine, gin, silk and, of course, tea. They often "bury the cargo" at sea and collect it later. Or else it is landed by night and taken away by horse and cart, or buried in villagers' cottages and in caves. They are remarkably well organized and we always seem to be one step behind.'

'You have your work cut out for you, Smithers,' remarked Felix.

'Indeed, my lord, and it is not helped by the fact that so many types of people are now involved – even women!'

Felix hid his amusement with difficulty. That the fairer sex would consider active involvement in criminal activity clearly affronted the Customs man's sensibilities.

'In what respect, Smithers?'

'There was an incident recently in Gosport where a woman who was accustomed to supplying the crew of a boat with slops went out in a wherry to Spithead, when a sudden squall came down and sank the boat. All the watermen on board were drowned but the life of the woman was saved as she was buoyed up with a quantity of bladders, secreted about her person for the purpose of smuggling liquor into the ship.'

Felix and his father roared with laughter. 'A case of being buoyed up by good spirits, it would appear!'

The earl rose and refilled their glasses. 'All this is obviously frustrating for you, Smithers, but it is hardly anything new. What in particular has brought Burton Bradstock to your attention?'

'Well, my lords, the principal gang of smugglers situated near that village is, historically, the Northovers.'

'Yes, I have heard of them,' said Felix, who was elegantly slouched in a deep armchair, one booted leg casually draped across his opposite knee.

'It does not surprise me, my lord. But what you may not be aware of is that another family in that locality is also active in illegal transactions.'

'Who are they?' asked the earl, sensing that Smithers was at last getting to the point.

Smithers paused and pulled himself up to his full height. 'The patriarch is a Samuel Barker. His father owned a couple of fast luggers, and doubtless dabbled in a spot of contraband in his day, but Samuel has moved beyond such pedestrian activities. We have known about him for some time, but over the past couple of years his wealth appears to have increased disproportionately, arousing our suspicions. We discovered that he was not above running the French blockades during the war to get brandy out and we know that he took advantage of the war to run sugar out of the Indies, making vast profits.'

'Nothing illegal about that, the sugar I mean,' remarked the earl.

'Indeed not, my lord, but you will be aware that since the end of the hostilities the bottom has fallen out of the sugar trade.'

'Indeed.'

'But Barker's interest in the Indies has not lessened.'

'Explain yourself.'

'We strongly suspect that Barker has gone into the people smuggling business. Former slaves are being smuggled into this country and "sold" for phenomenal amounts into households that require, say, a black footman.'

'Good God!' exclaimed Felix and his father in unison.

A pause ensued, which was broken by the earl. 'I am having difficulty comprehending your precise meaning, Smithers. I assume you are quite sure of your facts?'

'Indeed so, my lord. The abolition of slavery has not proved to be quite the utopia that the abolitionists, or the slaves themselves for that matter, had hoped it would be.'

'It is not unreasonable to suppose that a period of readjustment might be necessary.'

'Indeed not, my lord, but unscrupulous people such as Barker are taking shameless advantage of the unrest which currently prevails. People in this country – quite often ladies, I regret to say – are anxious to have a black servant to show off to their friends and Barker is only too happy to oblige them. Greater profit for him and less risk involved than smuggling his normal contraband. He can run a ship full of legitimate cargo and easily stow away half a dozen Negroes at the same time.'

'How have you gathered this intelligence, Smithers?' asked Felix.

'We have suspected something of the sort for a long time but about a month ago we apprehended one such person. A landing in rough weather went wrong, our men intervened and one of the men being smuggled in was left for dead on the beach. He had sustained an apparently fatal gunshot wound during the skirmish, but happily he survived. Obviously though it suits our purpose for Barker to believe otherwise. The man knew little about who arranged his passage but, from what information we were able to glean, every avenue leads back to Barker. The only problem is that we are unable to produce proof and put an end to his despicable trade.'

'But I am still not entirely sure that I have the pleasure of following your reasoning,' said the earl, frowning. 'There is already a sizeable enclave of free blacks and mulattos in England. And I have seen any number of black servants in the various country houses I visit and so, if people are so anxious to obtain Negroes as retainers, why go to the trouble and expense and having them illegally shipped over?'

'The growing problem of poverty and destitution amongst Negroes in this country is appalling, my lord – ten times worse than that which exists for the white man – which may perhaps assist your lordships in appreciating the extent of their misery. The unfortunate blacks are the last to be offered honest work or Christian charity. Those not already employed are precluded from obtaining gainful employment due to poor health and debilitated strength. The government of the day back in '87 recognized the problem and attempted to solve it by sending three shiploads to Sierra Leone to set up a colony and become self-supporting.'

'Yes, I do indeed recall that there was something of a rumpus about it at the time,' said the earl, rubbing his chin thoughtfully.

'But to return to Barker's evil trade, my lords,' continued Smithers, 'the "purchasers" of the former slaves require young, strong and attractive men and women.'

'But if they have lived their lives as slaves then surely their health and strength will have suffered too?' reasoned Felix.

'Not to such a great extent. As in any sphere of life, the strongest survive, only to get stronger. And the procurers of the immigrants are artful. They select only the elite from amongst the young people and do so by integrating themselves in their communities and listening to them talk the dissatisfied talk of the young. That is how they identify their targets. Barker's "recruiters", it seems, fall into conversation with them, finding that many of them mention family already in England and speculate enviously about how much better their lives must be. Barker's men play upon this weakness and offer them the opportunity of a passage to England.

'It is only when they get here that they realize they will never see their families and are, effectively, slaves once again. Whoever purchases them must, of course, offer them board and lodging but they do not trouble themselves to pay their new servants a stipend, telling them instead that they must first work off the cost of their passage. And once they realize that their situation has gone from bad to worse it is too late for them to do anything about it, for although they are not physically restrained in their new masters' houses, they soon learn that they are unlikely to find another position without a good character. And many of the young women, sadly, find themselves swelling the numbers and choices of nationalities available to the clientele in the bawdy houses,' added Smithers, with obvious disgust, 'and so clearly there is no escape for them at all.'

'This is quite remarkable,' opined the earl quietly. 'So much evil, it makes one quite desperate. Clearly Barker must be stopped. What about the master of the vessel which brought the man in? Can he not be pressured to tell us more?'

'I was coming to that, my lord. It was in fact my main reason for coming to you with this story.' Smithers paused and coughed delicately. 'You see, the vessel was one from the Western Line.'

Felix and his father leapt from their chairs simultaneously. 'What?' spluttered the earl, spilling Madeira down his immaculate coat. 'Impossible!'

'I fear not, my lord. That is why I wished to discuss the matter with you in person.'

'Which ship and who was the master?'

Smithers told him.

'Impossible!' repeated the earl. 'That man has been with me for more than twenty years. I would stake my life on his honesty and loyalty.'

'I agree, my lord. We suspect that the boat upon which the slave was due to be transported was one that we have since discovered required extensive repairs before making the return voyage to this country. We think Barker must have been running out of time to deliver the person in question. Presumably even people involved in this sort of despicable trade have some code of honour,' he added scornfully, 'and so he engineered it that a new crew member on your ship, picked up in the Indies, was bribed to smuggle the man on board your vessel.'

'I suppose it would be possible,' mused Felix, looking at his father. 'Presumably the man was hidden in the hold with the cargo?'

'That is our understanding, my lord.'

'Well, there you are then. Damned uncomfortable, I should think, but I doubt if that caused the smugglers much concern.'

The earl looked angrier then Felix could ever before recall seeing him.

'I am not prepared to tolerate my vessels being used for such a purpose, however unintentionally,' he spluttered.

'That is what I expected you to say, my lord,' agreed Smithers evenly.

'So what can we do to take this Barker in charge and put an end to his foul trade?'

'Well, there lies the difficulty. He is very artful and carefully covers his tracks. He appears to work through a series of ever-changing intermediaries and thus no blame can be laid at his door on the present evidence. Believe me, my lords, I know, for I have investigated the matter most thoroughly.'

'So it would seem,' agreed the earl. 'But tell me more about the man himself. If we can understand him better then perhaps a method of defeating him will become apparent.'

'Samuel Barker, aged fifty, was married for twenty years to a lady of Russian extraction,' commenced Smithers, with the air of a man who knew his subject well. 'The marriage appeared to be happy and Barker's smuggling operation at that time must have been small, for it did not come to our attention. But his wife died about eight years ago and after that things changed drastically. He has two sons, both of whom work with him, but also appear to be completely cowed by his authoritative manner. He is a bull of a man, but is not without charm, when it suits his purpose. His weakness, if he has one, is his desire to be accepted into good society. He throws money in all the right directions and makes free with the names of his aristocratic connections, given the slightest opportunity. Both his sons married women of his choosing from good but impoverished families. They all live under Barker's roof at Southview Manor.'

Smithers paused to sip delicately at his drink before continuing. 'Barker also has a third child. His youngest is a daughter and, by all accounts, she was his favourite.'

'Was?' queried Felix.

'So I am given to understand. He was equally strict with her, but as she so closely resembled his wife he was also indulgent towards the girl – Saskia, I believe she is called. Her mother died when the girl was fifteen and not one year later Barker forced Saskia into a marriage with a Captain Eden, the master of a cutter which we suspect Barker wanted to add to his fleet – hence obliging his daughter to marry a man twenty years her senior.'

Felix and his father exchanged a glance. 'And is the marriage a happy one?' enquired the earl, already suspecting the answer to his own question.

'I know not, my lord, but I do know that it was exceedingly short. Not six months after it took place, Eden and his craft were lost in a storm in the Atlantic.'

'Good!' said Felix, although he was unsure why he cared.

'But this is the interesting part,' continued Smithers. 'Six months after that, Saskia gave birth to Eden's twins – a boy and a girl – and a mere three months thereafter she left Barker's house, quite without warning, apparently. No one can tell me why that was, but she went to live with her widowed aunt – Barker's sister, a Mrs Rivers – in her house in Swyre, three or four miles east of Burton Bradstock. That was six years ago and, as far as I can ascertain, she has had no contact with her father since that time.'

'Hm, interesting,' agreed the earl. 'What can have caused the rift, I wonder?'

'That I cannot say, my lord. I do know, however, that when Mrs Eden removed to her aunt's imposing home she, the aunt that is, was a lady of independent means. But since then her circumstances have undergone a change because her home, Riverside House, has been turned into an hotel. Mrs Eden and her aunt take in paying guests.'

'Good heavens!' exclaimed the earl. 'Are you telling me that this indulged young lady, who was presumably accustomed to the best of everything, is now reduced to being nothing more than a glorified landlady? And the father who supposedly loves her so much has done nothing to rescue her? How would that look to the local nobility, if he is trying to ingratiate himself with them, as you suggest?'

'I am unable to say, my lord, and neither can I ascertain that she has requested any assistance from her father.'

Felix, who had been lost in contemplation, found his voice again. 'But do you not see? That could be how Barker does it!'

'What do you mean, Felix?'

'Well, the aunt, taking in the daughter and opening up her house to strangers all of a sudden. Rather an odd thing to do, would you not say, unless the family was creating an opportunity for the daughter to act as a go-between, without exciting curiosity?'

'It is certainly a possibility,' agreed the earl.

'It seems perfectly obvious to me,' persevered Felix doggedly.

'Have a care, Felix,' cautioned the earl. 'There may be another explanation.'

'I concur with your observations, my lord,' said Smithers, with a bow in Felix's direction, 'and must confess that the idea had not previously occurred to me, as it most assuredly should have done.'

'Father, we cannot allow this despicable trade to continue and certainly cannot countenance the use of our vessels for such a purpose. Allow me to go to Swyre and register as a guest at Riverside House? Let me see what I can make of it first-hand.'

'Out of the question, Felix,' replied the earl curtly.

'But, Father, consider.' Agitated, Felix stood and paced the room. 'I cannot abide the thought of people profiting thus from such human misery. It is intolerable! But for a woman to involve herself – a woman who is a mother herself, moreover – is quite simply beyond the pale.' Felix's pacing became more and more agitated, lending proof to the depth of his feeling. 'We cannot, as gentlemen of principle, allow this evil trade to continue. You *must* permit me to do this, Father. I consider it to be my duty.'

The earl did not respond to this impassioned plea immediately. That his son's outrage was totally justifiable was not in question; but as to exposing his only son to the inherent dangers – well, that was altogether another matter.

'Your duty or your destiny, Felix?' he eventually queried quietly.

'I will take every precaution to ensure my own safety, Father, I do assure you.'

'Use your sense, Felix,' snapped the earl irascibly. 'Even if I were to permit it, you can hardly go barging into this place as Lord Western. Everyone there would know who you were in an instant.'

'Exactly, Father, and that is why I shall go as . . . now, let me see, who shall I be?' Felix paused, sensing that his father's resistance was weakening. 'I know, why not a Mr Beaumont, an "agent" from Bristol looking for, shall we say, certain "commodities" on behalf of my various wealthy clients? That should excite Barker's interest, if he is as keen on climbing the social ladder as Smithers believes to be the case.'

'Not in that coat, I think,' said the earl, his anxiety briefly giving way to amusement, as he ran his eyes over Felix's superbly-cut merino wool coat.

'I shall take Perkins with me,' responded Felix, undaunted. 'I am sure he will be able to find clothing more suitable for my purpose.'

But still the earl hesitated. 'I'm not at all sure about this, Felix. There can be no question that these men must be exceedingly ruthless.'

'Quite so, my lord,' put in Smithers. 'We believe the man we rescued was shot by Barker's own men when we intervened and he was unable to make good his escape.'

The earl and Felix both frowned at Smithers – for very different reasons.

'We must think of another way,' said the earl forcefully. 'I would not have you surrender your life, Felix.'

'But you already have my assurance that I will take the greatest possible care, Father.'

'Anyway, we do not know for definite that the daughter has any involvement at all,' remarked the earl. 'If that were the case, surely their meeting one another would not go unnoticed? So you would be risking your all for naught.'

'Possibly, but I for one find it hard to believe in such a convenient coincidence. It must, at the very least, be investigated. Do I have your approbation, Father?'

'If I give it to you, have you considered what am I to tell your mother?'

'When I miss Christina's betrothal party and the opportunity to escort Lady Maria into dinner, do you mean?' responded Felix, with a significant look.

The earl regarded his son for a long time. There could be no question that he had become restless since the nuptials of his best friend. He needed an opportunity to come to terms with his future responsibilities and this unexpected problem could be just the thing. The earl trembled when he thought about the myriad dangers involved with such a scheme – but since when did fiery young men allow such considerations to deter them?

'All right, Felix,' he said, 'but we must set up some form of reliable communication. I must know at all times what is going on and we must devise some method of sending you immediate assistance in the event that it becomes necessary.'

'Indeed we must!'

The earl was pleased to observe that Felix was already more alert, now that he had a difficulty of some import to wrestle with. The lethargy that had gripped him recently was evidently a thing of the past, and he was now bursting with righteous indignation, anxious to right a perceived wrong.

Chapter Three

TWO days after the meeting with Smithers, Felix and his valet, Perkins, undertook the journey to Weymouth. They travelled by post, not wishing to draw unnecessary attention to themselves by arriving in any conveyance connected to the Westerns.

Perkins, who had been with Felix for only a couple of years, and was not much older than his master, had been delighted at the prospect of participating in what he perceived as a famous escapade, dismissing, with youthful disregard for his safety, the likely dangers. Before their departure Perkins had managed to equip Felix with clothing suitable for a 'Gentleman Agent' and he was now the proud possessor of two valises full of such items.

At Weymouth, Felix and Perkins left the post and separated, giving no indication that they were in any way connected. Weymouth was bustling with activity, the constant arrival of vessels being largely responsible for the transient population. But Felix still considered it to be a relatively small community and someone as well connected in the area as Barker was likely to be kept informed of any unusual arrivals.

By prior agreement Perkins took himself off to an indifferent livery stable and hired a saddle horse. He was to ride direct to Burton Bradstock and take a room at the Dove Inn, a well known *rendezvous* for smugglers. Perkins was to pose as an itinerant and integrate himself with the customers on the pretext of looking for any type of work, making it clear that he was not too particular what it might entail. Perkins was both amiable and personable, as well as being young and strong, qualities that would doubtless be advantageous to his cause.

At Weymouth Felix called at a slightly superior livery stable and hired a curricle and two mediocre horses to convey him to Swyre. He set the horses to a leisurely trot and fell to contemplating the events of the past few days.

At the duchess's ball five nights previously he had danced one cotillion with Angelica, under the eagle-eye of her husband, but his behaviour had been impeccable and even the possessive Towbridge could find nothing to which to take exception. But, as Felix and Angelica joined hands to pass down the dance, Towbridge did not notice Felix whisper to his wife to meet him in half an hour on the terrace.

When the dance ended Felix slipped unnoticed through a side door. When Angelica appeared a few minutes later, Felix reached out and pulled her into a concealed alcove, out of sight of the other strolling couples.

'Darling, are you missing me already?'

Angelica wrapped her arms around his neck and snuggled close. That was not what Felix had in mind at all, but something about the feel of her body pressed against his, something about the warmth of the evening, the restlessness of his spirit, and the precariousness of their situation, stirred his blood. Wordlessly, he pulled her closer and kissed her. Even as he did so some part of his mind was screaming out a warning, telling him not to be so foolish. He was taking an absurd risk! But being mindful of the danger, of the likelihood of discovery, of his reckless folly, merely served to drive him on.

There were 400 people just yards away from them, on the other side of the wall which they were putting to such good use; there were dozens of people strolling the terrace mere feet away; there was one very possessive husband possibly, even now, searching for his wife. But still Felix, fuelled by heady passion, could not stop: he wanted her, right here and now.

With a superhuman effort, he resisted his baser instincts, pulled away from her and dispassionately informed her of his impending return to Plymouth. He was taken aback by the force of her protests, had never seen her so angry before. Her eyes blazed back at him, wild with fury. She opened her mouth to upbraid him, but before she could speak they heard her husband's voice calling to her.

'Go and lean on the balustrade. Tell him you needed some air,' Felix whispered in her ear, as he pushed her urgently away from him and concealed himself further within the murky depths of the alcove.

'Ah, there you are, my love!' Felix heard Towbridge say. 'What are you doing out here all alone?' He looked about him suspiciously, but the light was too dim, and Felix too well concealed, for Towbridge to be able to detect him.

'Just getting some air, my dear. It is so hot in there.'

'No particular reason for you being warm, is there?' asked Towbridge hopefully.

'None that I am aware of.'

'Oh well, pity that.' Towbridge was clearly disappointed. 'Never mind, we will just have to try a little harder.' Towbridge crudely grasped his wife's bottom and offered her a lewd wink. 'Now come, my dear, and make pretty with Lord Reagan for me. I need him to do me a favour for His Royal Highness.'

'Oh, Simon, must I? He is such an old goat. The last time I danced with him he kept pinching my bottom.'

Simon guffawed, obviously delighted that his acquaintances couldn't keep their hands off his wife. 'The devil he did! Ah well, it is probably your own fault, my love, for being so damned desirable. Now come on and do your duty by me in the ballroom and later, as a penance for allowing Reagan to take such liberties, there are some other things that you might do for me.'

Towbridge's suggestive chuckle faded away as he led his wife back inside. Felix smiled, well able to imagine the disgusted look on Angelica's beautiful face, and for once felt a smidgen of pity for her plight, self-inflicted though it might be.

Returning to the ballroom Felix danced one dutiful dance with his sister, Christina, who was so animated at having secured Denby that she appeared almost pretty, one more with Lady Maria, just to keep his mother happy, and then escaped to the card-room, in search of congenial male company.

As he later relived the events of the evening, Felix was aghast at his recklessness. Had his boredom really reached such levels that he was prepared to take such absurd risks? Had he actually permitted his rampaging instincts the free rein they so desperately sought, there could be no question that Towbridge would have caught them *in flagrante delicto*. The consequences didn't bear thinking about. It was probably just as well that he now had matters of greater import with which to occupy his mind, for had he remained in London his restlessness would eventually have overcome common sense and he could scarce have hoped for another such fortuitous escape.

Felix's mind turned to his meeting with his mother on the day after the ball. She had been furious when she learned of his plans and did not seek to hide the fact.

'But, Felix, what of Lady Maria?'

'What of her, Mother?' He did not intend to make this easy.

'Well, I thought . . .' The determined set of Felix's jaw had caused her words to trail off.

'Christina is now safely engaged to Denby: you need no further assistance from me.'

'But I thought that you liked Lady Maria.'

'Why ever would you think that?'

'But, Felix, be reasonable, she would be ideal for you.'

Felix had held on to his temper with the greatest of difficulty. 'Mother, I did your bidding in order to secure Denby for Christina, but I have no further interest in Maria Denby.'

'But you will return for Christina's betrothal party next week?' His mother's anxious entreaty had given Felix due warning that she did not intend to give up easily her matrimonial ambitions on his behalf.

'If Father and I have concluded our business by then you may rely upon my attendance.'

So saying Felix had left the room before his temper finally snapped.

Felix almost upon Swyre now, considered again what he was likely to encounter there. This led to thoughts of the enigmatic Saskia Eden, whose complicity in her father's exploits Felix did not doubt for a moment. In spite of his father's advice for caution, Felix was convinced that he knew better, and was determined to put a stop to the woman's evil exploits once and for all.

Saskia Eden's day had started badly and was getting progressively worse. She had arisen at her habitual early hour, only to enter the kitchen and find it completely deserted and as cold as the grave. Not only had that wretched new girl allowed the range to go out, in spite of Saskia's dire warnings as to the consequences if she were careless enough to permit such an eventuality, but she had obviously overslept as well. Saskia had to waste precious time riddling the damned range and coaxing it back to life. Then, stepping into the kitchen garden she had been horrified to discover that the coop door had been left unlatched and a fox had killed one of their precious hens. That new girl again!

Saskia had restored order, managing to hold on to her patience by dint of many years' practice, and breakfast had somehow been served on time. But now she was about to serve afternoon tea, only to discover that the new girl – trusted to bake scones on cook's one precious afternoon off – had carelessly allowed them to burn. It was the last straw and Saskia was seriously beginning to wonder if the girl had been planted in the house deliberately to exacerbate the demise of their business. Goodness only knew, her father had tried everything else, but surely he could not know how close he was to succeeding?

Saskia dismissed the idea almost at once, feeling slightly guilty. Betty was a little simple, that was all, and her family had been pathetically grateful that she had been given this chance of employment. Huh, what choice did they imagine that Saskia and her aunt had in the matter? After all, beggars could not be choosers. Saskia's father had effectively banned anyone half-decent from working at Riverside House and he wielded sufficient influence in the area to make people take his threats seriously.

Saskia felt ready to explode as she acknowledged this truth, a familiar feeling of injustice fuelling her anger. How petty-minded could one man be when it came to getting his own way? It was, Saskia acknowledged, hardly a question she needed to ask herself, being only too aware that he did not care to be bested by anyone, least of all his own flesh and blood, and she had long ago accepted that he was never likely to give up on her. It was her birthday soon. Doubtless she would receive the usual curt letter from him, asking if she was yet ready to beg his forgiveness and return home. Welcoming the renewed sense of purpose that surged through her, Saskia squared her shoulders. Never!

But was she being selfish? Look at the dire straights she had reduced her beloved aunt to with her stubbornness. She had burst uninvited into her well-ordered, comfortable household and turned it upon its head. But the older lady had never uttered so much as one word of complaint. What was more, she had refrained from asking Saskia any awkward questions about the circumstances surrounding her abrupt arrival, and her rift with her father. Instead she constantly reassured her niece that things would eventually improve. She would not hear of Saskia leaving and insisted that she adored having her niece and the twins in her house, claiming they made her feel young again. And in the early days, when Saskia's father had arrogantly assumed she would return home in defeat, Aunt Serena had been a tower of strength: robust, aggressive and protective as she had stoically rebuffed her brother's attempts to snatch the ailing Saskia away by force.

When Aunt Serena had subsequently been reduced to taking in paying guests, Saskia had thought to improve their income, and reduce her feelings of guilt, by taking on their guests' laundry and mending, meaning to attend to it herself. But that was not to be either. Aunt Serena seized upon the mending, saying it was just the very occupation she had been seeking: how clever of Saskia to think of it. She could sit quite comfortably in the window embrasure and not be the least put out. The woman was a saint!

And then there was the question of the twins. Yet another wave of guilt swept through Saskia as she contemplated the advantages she was depriving her children of by not dutifully returning to her father's household. Josh could be enrolled at a good school, whilst

Amy would benefit from the attentions of a governess. Saskia did not doubt for a moment that her father would provide unstintingly for her children's education. Was she being fair to deprive them in such a way? And, in her father's house, they would be assured of good clothing and . . . and what else?

Saskia continued to ponder the question as she worked swiftly, her economical movements punctuated by a lithe grace. The twins had schooling now, of sorts: quite sufficient for them at their age. And surely it was so much better for them not to be separated when they were still so young? And as for clothing, well Aunt Serena's needle was never idle. She was constantly making pretty new pinafores and petticoats for Amy, waistcoats and shirts for Josh. And in Aunt Serena's house Saskia was secure in the knowledge that her children were surrounded by an abundance of love and the freedom to grow, without the threat of someone else's will being imposed upon them.

Heartened by the knowledge that all the money in the world could never replace such comforts, and resolving anew not to permit her father to win, Saskia hastily knocked together a new batch of scones and was wearily removing them from the stove when the kitchen door flew open. The twins came bursting through it like a whirlwind, full of youthful energy, arms and legs flailing at seemingly impossible angles, disorderly red hair flying loose around Amy's shoulders and Hoskins, their wiry little terrier dog, leaping at their heels.

'What are you two doing in here?' demanded Saskia, hands on hips, trying to sound severe, but knowing that her face had softened at the sight of her adored children and that her stern tone was unlikely to deceive the little imps in the slightest. 'I thought I asked you to pick the beans in the kitchen garden for me?'

'Oh you did, Mama,' Josh hastened to assure her, 'but you see—'

'—we heard the front door and of course Mr Graham is not here today and—'

'—and so we went to see who it was.'

'And?' enquired Saskia, well used to her children speaking at the same time and finishing one another's sentences.

'It was a gentleman,' pronounced Amy importantly.

'And he requires a room.'

'We said you would go and see him.'

'His name is Mr Beauchamp.'

'No, Josh, it was Mr Beaumont.'

'Well anyway,' they finished together, 'he is waiting to see you. We showed him into the breakfast-room, just as you said we should whenever someone calls.'

'Take the scones into the drawing-room for me,' said Saskia, removing her apron and smoothing down her gown. 'And the cream and jam too. Carefully!' she screamed after their swiftly retreating figures.

As she moved towards the breakfast-room, Saskia was aware that she must look hot and flustered and that, as usual, long red curls were escaping from what was supposed to be an elegant chignon. She sighed resignedly, accepting there was little she could do to improve her appearance in the short time available, and trusted to luck that this stranger had a forgiving nature.

Chapter Four

SASKIA stepped into the breakfast-room into which Mr Beauchamp – or was it Beaumont? – had been shown by the twins. His back was towards her and Saskia paused, a little taken aback by what she saw. A young man, that much was obvious from his lean frame and upright stance. He was tall too, and well dressed. Whatever could bring such a person to sleepy Swyre? She was instantly alert, ever mindful of her father's increasingly artful attempts to undermine her.

Perhaps sensing her presence, the gentleman turned and Saskia found herself gaping. He was the most beautiful creature she had ever beheld, and she was not normally given to gawping at gentlemen. As the stranger looked in her direction, a polite smile on his lips, Saskia accepted ruefully that her face must be even redder than hitherto, with her uncharacteristically salacious thoughts written all over it as well, no doubt. She hastily dropped her eyes, only to be confronted by the strangely disconcerting sight of buckskin breeches fitting all too snugly against muscular, well-toned thighs.

Recovering her poise, Saskia offered the gentleman a brief curtsy and an economically professional smile. She still suspected her father's hand behind the appearance of this Adonis and was not about to let her guard down.

'Good afternoon, sir,' she managed to say evenly. 'I am Mrs Eden. How may I be of service to you?'

'Good afternoon to you, ma'am,' returned the gentleman, making her an elegant leg and offering up a smile as imperceptible as her own. 'My name is Beaumont and I am given to understand that lodgings are available in this dwelling.'

Saskia found herself taken aback by his beautiful manners and deep, gravelly voice and once again it took an effort of will for her to recover her air of detached politeness.

'That is perfectly correct, sir. I regret however that I have only one chamber available at present and, as it is our best, it is rather more expensive than the norm.'

'And pray what price do you require, ma'am?'

Taking a deep breath, Saskia named a figure, far higher than usual. If her father was trying to infiltrate the house then she might as well make some money from him. The gentleman raised a brow in surprise but did not immediately demur. Heartened by his response, Saskia boldly pushed ahead.

'I must also inform you, sir, that we do not let our rooms by the day or even by the week. All of our residents stay with us on a long term basis and I could not let the room go for a period of less than one month.'

'I see,' responded Felix, pretending to consider the matter. 'In that case perhaps I could see the room before making a decision?'

'By all means, sir. Please be good enough to step this way.'

Silently Saskia led the gentleman up to the first floor and to the room in the very middle of the front landing, the one which her aunt had shared with her husband for so many years but which she had refused to step foot in since his death. To love someone so completely that you could no longer bear even to look with equanimity upon the space you had once shared with that person? Saskia tried to imagine, as she always seemed to do whenever she enter this room, how glorious it must be to have experienced such a passion. Agony and ecstasy in equal measures, she suspected. Tiring, debilitating, exalting and . . . well, and something else that she had been wise enough to avoid.

Saskia reached for the door handle but Felix was there before her. His fingers brushed against hers, causing her to start violently.

'Allow me!' he offered, smiling at her. He opened the door and stood back, allowing her to enter in front of him. Surprised and a little gratified by his manners, Saskia observed Felix as he looked about him. He appeared surprised to discover that she had been telling the truth about the room. He must be aware that in most country houses this was the prime position occupied by the principal chamber. He could see for himself that it was exceedingly commodious. There was an enormous tester bed and all the usual furniture – a dressing table, armoire, escritoire – all of the finest quality. An enormous window, affording a spectacular view of the sea, dominated the front wall. A comfortable-looking sofa occupied the alcove in front of it.

Saskia felt an overwhelming urge to talk the man into taking the room, regardless of his reasons for being here. As he looked about him she crossed her fingers behind her back, silently pleading that he would find no fault with what he saw. If he would only take the room for one month then she would be able to pay the butcher's account for the last quarter. He was one of the few tradesmen who refused to be intimidated by her father and was willing to extend them credit and she was uncomfortably aware that they had exploited his goodwill on more than one occasion. They would be able to replace the lost hen as well and purchase more firewood. Oh, please, please take the room!

'If a month is more than you require then there is a reasonable inn in the village. Otherwise, in Burton Bradstock, there is the rather more commodious Dove Inn.' Now why had she said that? What was she thinking of, trying to talk herself out of a month's much-needed rent?

Felix turned and offered Saskia an engaging smile. 'The room is quite satisfactory, Mrs Eden, and I should be delighted if you would accept me as your guest for one month.' Without waiting for an answer he delved into his pocket, produced a pile of notes and peeled off the correct amount, forcing it into a stunned Saskia's hand. 'Now, about stabling for my horses?'

'I regret that there is none available here, sir,' responded Saskia, disguising her relief at his decision by employing the same distantly polite voice which she had used throughout their exchange, 'but there is a reasonable establishment in the main street. Swyre is a small village. You cannot miss it.'

'Excellent, I—'

The door flew open and the twins burst in.

'Are you going to stay with us, Mr Beaumont?'

'Indeed I am.'

'These are my children,' said Saskia, smiling in spite of the fact that she had lost count of the number of times she had warned them not to burst into guests' rooms uninvited. 'Joshua and Amy.'

The twins made a bow and curtsy respectively and offered up identical grins for Felix's inspection.

'We have already met,' remarked Felix, with a smile of his own.

'We are twins,' Josh informed him unnecessarily.

'Yes, so I observe.'

'We're six—'

'—and this is Hoskins—'

'—our dog—'

'—he can do tricks—'

'—yes, he jumps through Josh's hoop and he can—'

'Have you finished in the schoolroom, children,' asked Saskia severely.

'Yes, thank goodness,' they replied in unison.

'All right then, what about those beans you were picking for cook?'

'Oh yes, we had forgotten about that. Come on, Josh.'

And still full of chatter and good nature the children left the room as abruptly as they had entered it.

'My apologies, Mr Beaumont,' said Saskia, all business once again. 'They can be a little high spirited at times.'

'Not at all. They are delightful.'

'I hope you will still be of that opinion at the end of a month,' responded Saskia, with heartfelt sincerity. 'Now then, sir, tea is about to be served in the drawing-room and dinner is at six. We keep country hours.'

'I shall attend to my horses now and look forward to meeting the rest of your guests at dinner. Is there someone who could bring up my bags and unpack for me?'

'Of course!' agreed Saskia equably, wearily adding yet another task to her ever-increasing list.

As Felix entered the drawing room at Riverside House that evening, so seven heads turned in his direction, all conversation ceased and the occupants of the room eyed him with widely differing degrees of curiosity. After what seemed likes minutes frozen in time, during which nobody moved or spoke, Saskia detached herself from the group and approached Felix.

'May I introduce you to my aunt, Mr Beaumont?' she enquired, in the same politely detached tone she had employed earlier in the day. Without waiting for a reply she turned in the direction of an older, genteel-looking lady, who was seated beside the fire. 'Mr Beaumont, may I present my aunt, Mrs Rivers.'

'Your servant, ma'am,' responded Felix, offering the lady an elegantly proficient bow.

'Welcome to my house, Mr Beaumont,' responded Mrs Rivers, in a well-modulated voice. 'I trust that you are perfectly comfortable?'

'Indeed, ma'am, Mrs Eden appears to have thought of my every need.' He forced himself to offer Saskia an engaging smile, hoping to be rewarded with a lessening of the formally correct attitude she steadfastly displayed in his presence, but in that he was to be disappointed. Strange! His best *tonnish* smile had never failed him in the past and had been known to soften even the hardest of hearts. With the cold and callous Mrs Eden, though, it appeared to cut no ice whatsoever.

Felix exchanged small talk with Mrs Rivers for a few minutes, whilst covertly stealing glances at Saskia, attempting to fathom her. She was wearing an evening gown in pale blue batiste, which passed in this country drawing-room as being both elegant and modern: especially when compared to the attire of the other ladies present. But Felix knew it to be both poor in quality and several years out of date. He wondered if it was a deliberate ploy to avoid drawing attention to herself, much as her coolly detached attitude discouraged intimacy.

But why choose a gown that fitted her so ill? Just like the one which she had worn that afternoon, it was far too large for her exceptionally slim and unusually tall body and extraneous yards of fabric flapped uselessly about her as she moved. But whatever it was that Saskia sought to disguise, in one respect she was failing spectacularly, for Felix was uncomfortably aware that nothing could hope to conceal her spectacular breasts, which appeared all the more impressive when contrasted to the slenderness of the rest of her person. They fought valiantly against the confines of the batiste, making them impossible for a man such as Felix to ignore.

The neckline of Saskia's gown was exceptionally demure but her breasts rebelled against such attempts at modesty and displayed themselves to their best advantage in the soft candlelight. Predisposed as he was to dislike Mrs Eden, Felix could not prevent his eyes from falling upon her *décolletage* more frequently than politeness dictated: no more could he prevent himself from reluctantly admiring all that he saw.

The lady herself could hardly be described as beautiful. She had a profusion of the distinctive red hair which her children had inherited. This evening it was piled on top of her head, tendrils falling in long waterfall curls about her face, but lacked the combs, ribbons and other fripperies which Felix was accustomed to seeing deployed by the ladies of his acquaintance.

Saskia's eyes were arguably her best feature. Sparkling emerald green, they lit up her face, enhancing its strength of character. Her nose was a little too long and was covered with a dusting of freckles, which would have appalled any self-respecting society lady, but which somehow complemented Saskia's colouring and drew attention to her translucent skin. Her lips were full and sumptuous but would serve her so much better, Felix could not help feeling, if she smiled more.

Felix decided, almost against his will, that she was undeniably attractive, an impression only enhanced by her tranquil composure. Her demeanour engendered confidence in her abilities to handle anything life threw in her path and somehow made a man feel at ease when in her company. He was unable to put his finger on just what it was but there was something about her mannerisms, about the quietly efficient way in which she moved unobtrusively about the room, which attracted him. It was almost a fragility, which somehow excited his protective instincts, but why that should be when he had already seen for himself just how contained and organized she was, Felix could not say. What he did know was that he was seriously vexed for feeling any attraction towards her at all, determined as he was to entertain only contempt for the woman. Instead, he found himself imagining just how spectacular she would look if dressed in a fashionable gown and if she would only smile naturally, as he had thus far only observed her do once when addressing her children that afternoon.

Felix was snapped out of his reverie by the sound of Saskia's voice.

'May I introduce you to the rest of our guests, Mr Beaumont?'

'By all means!'

Felix followed her towards a tiny woman of indeterminate age. 'Mr Beaumont, may I present Miss Willoughby.'

The little woman trilled delightedly when Felix bowed before her but appeared a little alarmed by his size. She twittered, declared herself delighted, and fiddled distractedly with her shawls. A harmless creature and nothing to do with the foul goings-on in the Barker family, Felix decided at once.

'Miss Willoughby is an old acquaintance of my aunt's, Mr Beaumont, and is our longest standing resident. She has been with us ever since we opened our doors to guests.'

'And most comfortable you have made me, Saskia dear,' she declared earnestly.

A gentleman walked up to them. 'This is Captain Fanshaw, Mr Beaumont. He is engaged upon writing a Seafarer's Almanac.'

'Quite so,' agreed Fanshaw, shaking Felix's hand. 'Been a seafaring man all my life, sir, and would advise you most strongly not to believe all the rot that has been written upon the subject. Feel duty bound to set the record straight, you see; no choice in the matter. Do you know the sea yourself, Beaumont?'

'I cannot claim any particular knowledge of it,' lied Felix smoothly, turning his attention to the middle-aged couple whom Saskia was now waiting to introduce.

'This is Mr and Mrs Jenkins, who are spending the summer with us, Mr Beaumont. Mrs Jenkins has been indisposed and her physician has recommended sea air.'

'I trust you will soon make a full recovery, Mrs Jenkins,' said Felix, making yet another of his gallant bows.

'Oh, she will be fine,' her husband answered for her, his tone dismissive. 'Just a little rest and solitude will see her restored in no time.'

Mrs Jenkins did not appear capable of answering for herself, or of contradicting her domineering husband. Felix was glad of an excuse to turn away from them, as he awaited an introduction to the final person in the room, and the one who had attracted his attention almost as soon as he entered it.

'Mr Beaumont, may I present Mr Fothergill.'

Felix found his gaze focused upon a small, exceptionally thin man, whose head did not reach Felix's shoulder. His coat was threadbare, his neckcloth slightly soiled and he was wearing thin, badly fitting trousers rather than the more acceptable breeches which adorned the person of every other man in the room. His face bore the telltale signs of an imbiber, having broken blood vessels and unnaturally heightened colour. Felix noticed as well, when he shook his proffered hand, that it was slightly unsteady. As if to lend truth to Felix's suspicion, Fothergill helped himself, unbidden, to his second glass of sherry in ten minutes.

'Mr Fothergill is a schoolmaster,' explained Saskia calmly, seeming – or perhaps choosing – not to notice his rudeness in making free with her aunt's sherry, 'and currently has the task of teaching my children.'

'And they would learn well enough if only they were better disciplined,' declared Fothergill dictatorially, standing far closer to Saskia than politeness dictated, an air of propriety about his action. Saskia, Felix observed, frowned fleetingly at Fothergill's forthright statement but made no attempt to contradict him. 'Spare the rod and spoil the child was always the motto in my last school and I see nothing wrong with that!' Fothergill clasped his lapels, his stance supremely confident. He clearly believed that his opinion, expressed on a subject he felt well qualified to expound upon, would pass unchallenged.

'Indeed!' It was most annoying but Felix found himself wanting to defend Saskia and her delightful twins against this pompous oaf. 'I was of the opinion that such an attitude could be mistaken as an excuse for poor teaching.' Felix's expression was one of polite inquisitiveness, but he could have sworn that he was rewarded, just for a second, by the ghost of a smile on Saskia's lips. But when he looked at her again her features were arranged in their customary serene expression.

'My dear sir, I do assure you that is not the case. Mrs Eden has full confidence in my abilities and—'

The announcement by a butler, who must have been at least seventy years old, that dinner was served brought this discourse to a timely end. Felix considered it to be just as well. He was here to discover more about Barker and his daughter, not to fall out with the guests in Riverside House on his very first evening.

Approaching Mrs Rivers, Felix offered her his arm. 'May I have the honour to escort you, ma'am?' he asked.

She appeared taken aback but soon recovered herself. 'By all means, Mr Beaumont.' She smiled graciously, obviously not a stranger to good manners, but Felix suspected she had not seen any deployed in this house for quite sometime.

Felix settled Mrs Rivers in her seat at the head of the table and then, at her request, seated himself on her right-hand side. He was pleasantly surprised to find that the meal exceeded his expectations. Although plain and lacking the sophistication to which he was accustomed, it was nevertheless well cooked and plentiful. And the wines which accompanied each course were of surprisingly good vintage. Felix noticed, with interest, that Fothergill ate little but partook of a disproportionate amount of wine.

Of all the people at Riverside house, Fothergill appeared to Felix to be the only one, apart from Saskia herself, who could possibly be involved with Barker in any way. Although pompous, he clearly had an expensive habit to feed and, if Felix was any judge of character, he was not beyond selling any information he might glean – or acting as a go-between – if it was to his fiscal advantage. A single man of, supposedly, independent means could move about freely, whereas a widow living in a small community would surely excite unwarranted attention? His father had been right in that respect.

Just what was going on between Saskia and this popinjay anyway that she would be prepared to risk exposing her precious twins to his dictatorial teaching methods for hours on end? Surely there could be no intimacy between them? Felix shuddered as the thought crossed his mind. That was obviously the impression that Fothergill wished to create, but could she really be that desperate? Felix found he definitely did not wish it to be the case: after all, the twins deserved better than that.

Whilst fielding the inevitable questions about his own background, and his reasons for being in Swyre, by adroitly turning the subject back to the concerns of his questioners, Felix attempted to listen to the various conversations around the table and, at the same time, observe people's behaviour. Saskia's demeanour held his attention more than most. Without appearing to do so, it was obvious to Felix that she was minutely watching every course, ensuring that it was served in the correct manner. The ancient butler was in charge of serving but a young, backward-looking maid was assisting him and it was her actions, most of all, which Saskia appeared to be scrutinizing.

Dinner-table conversation was second nature to Felix and he maintained a polite and amusing discourse with Mrs Rivers and her neighbours, whilst closely observing everyone else. By the end of the meal he had discovered that the only person at the table who had eaten less than Cedric Fothergill was Saskia. Felix noticed Mrs Rivers surreptitiously casting significant glances in the direction of her niece, as course after course was removed from in front of her, almost untouched.

The meal came to an end and the ladies made to withdraw. Felix was instantly on his feet, assisting Mrs Rivers from her chair. The rest of the gentlemen looked rather taken aback, before belatedly struggling to their own feet. Once again, Felix could have sworn that a ghost of a smile graced Saskia's lips. It was clear that gentlemanly behaviour did not come as naturally to his fellow guests as it did to Felix. Reaching the door before the butler, Felix held it open for the ladies.

'Thank you, Mr Beaumont,' said Mrs Rivers, with an amused chuckle. 'I can see that I shall enjoy having you living beneath my roof.'

Saskia was the last of the ladies to leave the room. She thanked Felix absently but refused to meet his eye, contenting herself with sweeping regally past him. She looked almost angry and Felix would have given a very great deal to know what was passing through her mind at that particular moment.

Returning to the table, Felix accepted the decanter and was pleasantly surprised to find that the port was as good as the wine that had preceded it. He leaned back in his chair, content to listen to the gentlemen's conversation, aware that with the ladies absent they would naturally become less circumspect. It did not surprise him to find the proceedings dominated by Fothergill, who was holding forth once again upon the importance of discipline in education: something Felix suspected he had been temporarily unwilling to do in Mrs Eden's presence, following the incident before dinner. Felix felt as though Fothergill's remarks were being directed specifically at him, as if he wanted to regain lost ground following their initial skirmish.

'Those twins of Mrs Eden's are bright enough but not nearly as dedicated to their studies as they should be. Mrs Eden relies on my opinion to an astonishing degree, but she has a blind spot when it comes to her children. She is far too lenient with them but I will bring her round to my way of thinking, never fear. Now, left to my own devices. . . .'

Felix shut out Fothergill's humdrum voice, at the same time sparing a sympathetic thought for Saskia's feisty twins, who doubtless had to endure this man droning on for hours at a time. Eventually, though, even Felix could stand no more and brought Fothergill back to the present by asking him at what school he had previously taught.

Fothergill avoided a direct answer and adroitly changed the subject, which instantly piqued Felix's curiosity, making him all the more determined to elicit a response. When he could prevaricate no further, Fothergill admitted that he had taught French and Latin at a minor public school in Northumberland, the name of which Felix vaguely recognized.

More convinced than ever that Fothergill was the only person in the house who could link up with Barker or his agents without suspicion, Felix determined to find out more about him. Luc and Clarissa were currently on her estate in Northumberland. He would send word to Luc and see what he could find out about the circumstances surrounding Fothergill's leaving the school.

The gentlemen rejoined the ladies a short time later, but Felix deliberately hung back on the pretext of collecting something from his room. When he returned to the hall he was surprised to encounter Saskia herself wheeling the tea trolley into the drawing-room. Felix insisted upon completing the task for her – as surely any gentleman would? – and brushed aside her objections.

'I was merely saving Betty a job,' she explained, flustered out of her distant politeness.

'A natural enough thing to do,' agreed Felix suavely. But all the same he wondered what prompted Saskia to look so guilty when he chanced upon her doing this menial task; why she felt the need to offer any explanation to him at all and why, in so doing, she sounded so defensive.

Tea and coffee having been served, Saskia was called upon to play and seated herself at the piano. Felix was then to be truly astonished for the first time since entering the house. She played a well known Bach sonata with expertise, her interpretation so fresh and full of passion as to move him greatly. She was a superb musician and it was obvious to Felix that she lost herself completely in the music, allowing it to consume her and sweep her away to some private place of her own making, as she played from the heart. Felix, like his father, appreciated good music but had been obliged, over the years, to endure endless performances by young ladies keen to demonstrate their talent: hopeful of attracting his interest. None had ever come close to doing so. But Saskia? Well, anyone who could play like that could almost be forgiven any other defects of character.

Then Felix recalled his reasons for being at Riverside House and hardened his heart. Even so, at the conclusion of her performance, he congratulated her warmly.

'I think you must be a great music lover, Mrs Eden?'

'Indeed, sir, I consider music to be one of the greatest consolations in life. Without it I know not where I would be.'

'If one can play as passionately as you then I can readily understand that sentiment.'

'I don't know about passion, Mr Beaumont, I simply play what I feel.'

'In that case, m'dear,' Felix assured her languidly, 'you are certainly no stranger to passion.' His eyes burned directly into hers, compelling and intense, and for a moment she seemed unable to look away. She blushed slightly and Felix suspected that she was not accustomed to flirting. His gentle, mocking smile took on a predatory edge. He might not like the woman but some habits were difficult to break.

Mr Fothergill bustled up to them, spoiling the moment, and launched upon a long explanation as to why Saskia's performance was not quite up to par.

'You play yourself then do you, Fothergill?' Felix enquired casually.

'Well, no, but that does not mean that. . . .'

And this time there could be no doubt that Saskia offered Felix the merest hint of an amused smile.

Chapter Five

L ATER that same evening, Felix sat on the sofa in his chamber's
window embrasure and threw the window open wide. The
familiar sound of the waves crashing against the shore a short distance
in front of him, repetitive and soothing, acted as the balm he had been
unconsciously seeking to overcome his restlessness. Feeling strangely
at one with nature, he gazed into the inky blackness of the night,
breathing in the clean air and tasting the salt that stung his lips,
driven by the sea breeze that assaulted his face.

Smoking a cigar, Felix considered all he had seen since arriving at
Riverside House. Grinning wryly, he made a mental note to inform
Perkins that in spite of his best efforts to 'dress him down' he was still
by far the most elegantly attired man in the house. Perkins would be
highly gratified.

Felix mulled over the characteristics of the people he had met that
evening, convinced now that if Saskia was communicating with her
father then she could only do so with the help of an intermediary. If?
Surprised at the unexpected turn his thoughts had taken, he sat a
little straighter. Since when had he entertained any doubts as to her
complicity?

Mrs Rivers, he was entirely certain, had nothing to do with her
brother's ghastly trade and knew nothing whatsoever about it. The
bird-like Miss Willoughby could be dismissed also: she was afraid of
her own shadow and completely harmless. Captain Fanshaw? No, if
Felix was any judge then he was exactly what he said he was: totally
wrapped up in the history of seafaring and no threat to anyone. Mr

and Mrs Jenkins were also absolved by Felix from having any involvement in wrong doing. They had only been at Riverside House for a month and would be leaving again at the end of the summer.

That just left Fothergill. Felix disliked the man, and his arrogant air of self-aggrandizement, but was determined not to allow his personal feelings to sway his judgement. But still, there could be no question but that he was the most likely candidate. He had been at Riverside House for almost as long as Miss Willoughby and it seemed that he owed the favour of his residency there, unfortunately for the twins, to his willingness to educate them. He was a little too fond of the potations: Felix had seen the signs in far too many men to misinterpret what he had observed of Fothergill's habits and, if he received no stipend for his teaching duties, then how did he support his addiction? Whatever Luc was able to discover about his history at Farmouth School was likely to make interesting reading.

Finally, Felix turned his thoughts to Saskia Eden, conceding that he could not make her out. That she had closely guarded secrets was not in question. She was no stranger to prevarication either and had treated his mild enquiries about her circumstances in an evasive manner too polite for him to take exception to. Her remoteness, however, left him in no doubt that she was wary of him and would prefer him not to be at Riverside House. The price she had extracted from him for this very room had been ridiculously high and obviously intended to discourage him. When he had asked to see the room anyway, she had immediately launched into a description of the other establishments in the area which offered accommodation and which might better suit his requirements. His eventual agreement to her terms stunned her and she was most reluctant to accept his money: he had literally had to force it into her hand.

Felix could think of only two reasons why she would not want a stranger in the house: either she was fearful that his presence would interfere with her communications with her father, or else she suspected him of being linked to the authorities. Felix grimaced. How right she was to be on her guard!

*

Saskia breathed a heartfelt sigh of relief as another day drew to a satisfactory conclusion. She climbed the stairs to the top of the house
slowly, almost too tired to put one foot in front of the other, and
opened the door to the twins' room. She smiled, maternal pride
temporarily overcoming all weariness, at the sight of the two tousled
heads. Amy's hair had escaped its braid – much as her own had always
done at that age – and was spread all over the place beneath her. Josh,
as usual, had pushed his covers aside and lay curled on his right-hand
side, facing his sister's bed, as though he had fallen asleep whilst in
mid-conversation with her. Saskia would not be in the slightest bit
surprised to discover that had been the case. Amy, curled on her left,
thumb firmly fixed in her mouth, faced her brother. Hoskins, loyal-
ties clearly divided, was stretched on his back between the two beds,
all four legs pointing heavenwards, and snoring softly.

Saskia stealthily adjusted her children's covers, careful not to wake
them, as she enjoyed this most precious of moments when she could
drink in the sight of her twins; safely asleep, silent for once, and
mercifully young enough still not to have a care in the word. She
kissed each head in turn and left the room, closing the door silently
behind her.

In her own tiny room next door to the twins, Saskia climbed into
her lonely bed but for once did not fall immediately into an exhausted
sleep. Instead she contemplated their new guest and wondered anew
what had brought him to Swyre. She had noticed how easily he
brushed their naturally curious questions in that respect aside and
that, as much as anything else, set her on her guard. The fact that he
had paid so much for a room was also a worry. She could see that he
knew he was being overcharged but he did not once query the fact.
Why?

There could be no doubt that Mr Beaumont was going out of his
way to be charming. His manners were faultless, intuitive and
elegant; far superior to anything she had ever known before. Saskia
could see that her aunt appreciated the fact as well. She was used to
good society, but it was a long time since she had been exposed to
such punctilious attentions. If nothing else, Saskia was grateful that

this man had brought some pleasure into her aunt's humdrum existence. That he was impossibly handsome did not harm matters either and, whatever his reason for being in Riverside House, Saskia could not help being grateful for the way in which he had handled the insufferable Mr Fothergill earlier. Saskia smiled as she recalled the look of outrage on Fothergill's flushed face when Felix dared to question his motives and teaching methods.

Saskia was mindful of the fact that she really must do something about Fothergill before too much longer. He was becoming intolerable, taking more and more liberties and blatantly ignoring her instructions in respect of the twins' education.

When Saskia finally fell into an exhausted sleep, it was interrupted by visions of compelling brown eyes, set in a dangerously handsome face, which sported a mockingly intimate smile: a smile which she had steadfastly ignored for the whole evening but which, alas, her subconscious did not seem willing to disregard quite so readily.

After a substantial breakfast the following morning, at which neither Saskia nor her aunt put in an appearance, Felix set about exploring his new environment. Swyre was indeed as small as Saskia had given him to understand. A rocky path led from the gardens of Riverside House to a small, shingle-covered bay, which this morning was deserted. A steep climb from the other end of the cove led to a coastal path and half-a-mile further on lay the village itself. It sported the inn that Saskia had already told him to expect, the livery stable which had charge of Felix's hired cattle, a general store and not much else.

In the mood for exercise, Felix strode out of the village and, rejoining the coastal path, made his way towards Burton Bradstock. He discovered it to be an attractive village, with pretty thatched cottages clustered around the fifteenth-century church. Perkins's new residence, the Dove Inn, occupied a central position, but the most unusual aspect of the village was the two watermills built to swingle and spin flax. Felix took an interest in them and was treated to a lecture as to their purpose by an elderly villager, who appeared both proud of the structures and pleased to be able to pass the time of day with an interested visitor.

Felix was aware that several eyebrows were raised in curiosity as he sauntered the main street in Burton Bradstock. He was a stranger and was clearly exciting interest amongst the locals, especially when he rushed to the assistance of two ladies leaving the circulating library, arms loaded with books. He made an elegant leg and held the door for them. Knowing he could do no more without first being introduced, he had nevertheless made the most of the opportunity. His gentlemanly conduct had made an impression upon the women and doubtless Barker would know of his presence in the village before the end of the day, just as Felix intended that he should.

Felix met up with Perkins a little later and learned that he was already comfortably ensconced in the inn and making contacts amongst the clientele: not to mention a favourable impression upon an attractive young barmaid.

'Just remember why we are here, Perkins. I do not wish you to be distracted from your purpose.'

'Naturally, my lord, but if I am to gain the trust of these people fully, then I cannot afford to ignore any opportunities that come my way, can I now?' Perkins's wide-eyed innocence and apparent dedication to duty would have been quite convincing had not Felix been well aware of his predilection for the fairer sex and had his statement not been accompanied by a devilish grin.

Felix chuckled with amusement. 'Just take care, Perkins.'

'Of course, my lord, but this gal seems to know everything and everyone and you know how women like to run on.'

'When they're on their backs you mean?'

'My lord!' Perkins affected an injured expression.

'Meet me at the same time tomorrow, Perkins, but this time on the dunes. In the meantime arrange for this letter to be sent to the Earl of Newbury.'

'At once, my lord.'

Returning to Riverside House, with a half-hour to spare before luncheon, Felix strolled through the French doors leading from the drawing-room to an attractive honey-coloured stone terrace. He was surprised to observe that weeds were growing between the terrace slabs and the benches and stone urns were covered with green lichen. The lawns, which sloped gently down towards the sea, were overdue for cutting and the flower borders, although artfully arranged to resemble a wild country garden, were in fact overgrown and in need of urgent pruning. Weeds were encroaching upon the paths in places and the entrance to one walk was completely obscured by brambles.

Felix was wondering why this should be, adding it to the list of anomalies he had already noted at Riverside House, when an explosion of noise alerted him to the presence of the twins, Hoskins leaping about them and sharing their relief at having escaped the schoolroom.

'Hello, Mr Beaumont, we have just finished our lessons for the morning—'

'—thank goodness!'

'Mr Fothergill is beastly to us—'

'—but we have several hours off now—'

'—he likes to walk into Swyre before luncheon—'

'—and when he comes back his breath smells funny!'

'Yes,' added Amy sombrely, 'but at least we don't have to do many lessons in the afternoons—'

'—sometimes he slurs his words or falls asleep—'

'—hope he does today and then we will not have to—'

'Oh yes, I had forgotten.'

Felix smiled at them, glad of their company. So, Fothergill was unable to get past luncheon without first calling at Swyre Inn. Interesting! Amy's voice, resonating with indignation, brought him back to the present.

'We have to congregate—'

'—we have to know how to say *être* by heart or he will punish us—'

'—and it is very hard and we cannot remember it.'

Felix was thunderstruck. Good God, what in the name of Hades was wrong with Fothergill? Six-year-olds conjugating French verbs! His heart went out to them and, before he could think the better of it, resolved to offer them his help.

'Well you know, when I was at school I did not care for French either but I found a way to do it that made it easy.'

'What was that?' asked two eager voices in unison.

'Well now, let me see. Try this!

Je suis, came to tea
Tu es, couldn't care less
Il est, is the best
Nous sommes, tiddly pom
Vous êtes, Hoskins' a pet
Ils sont, is all we want!'

The twins giggled, delighted at the prospect of an engaging game. 'Can we say it with you, Mr Beaumont?'

'Most assuredly.'

Amy slipped her hand trustingly into Felix's, making him feel absurdly privileged. He placed his other arm around Josh's shoulders, which appeared to please the boy, and the three of them strolled the lawns, calling out Felix's ridiculous rhyme at the top of their voices: the twins declaring that it actually made learning French fun. By the time the luncheon gong sounded, Felix was confident that they would be word perfect for the wretched Fothergill that afternoon.

'We have our luncheon in the kitchen with Mrs Graham,' explained Josh, as they headed together towards the house.

'She says she doesn't think it's right to have Hoskins in there but then she pretends not to see him and drops things on the floor for him.'

'Goodbye, Mr Beaumont,' they chorused, waving happily as they skipped around the side of the building. 'Shall we see you later and tell you how it went?'

'I wish you would.'

Felix sat alone in the drawing-room after luncheon. He had not been at Riverside House for a whole day yet but already he was starting to have doubts about Saskia's involvement with her father. There were so many things which did not make sense; the first of which was her clothes. He could think of no reason why a lady would dress so badly through choice. Even if she was keeping up some sort of pretence at having nothing to do with her father, surely she could still clothe herself more appropriately without exciting comment?

And then there was the state of the gardens, which he had so recently witnessed at first-hand. He had seen no sign of any gardeners, or come to that, any male staff at all, other than the ancient butler. There were no footmen, boot boys and the like: at least none that Felix had encountered. There was Mrs Graham, the cook whom the twins had mentioned, who was married to the butler. They had, apparently, both been at Riverside House for more than forty years. Apart from that, Felix had seen the vacant-looking girl who had helped to serve dinner the evening before and a slightly brighter one who had performed the same service at luncheon today, but no one else.

This was not a large house by Felix's standards. But still, it must require a vast number of staff, certainly more than he had observed, to maintain it at a satisfactory level? Reviewing the layout Felix knew that apart from the best room, which he occupied on the first floor, Mrs Rivers had two rooms for her private use on one side of him and Mr and Mrs Jennings occupied the large room on his left. Fothergill had a room of his own at one end of the corridor, which interlinked with the schoolroom and Miss Willoughby and Captain Fanshaw had the only remaining rooms on that floor.

The twins, presumably, slept on the top floor – as must the servants. But what of Saskia? Surely she was not relegated to the top floor as well? If she was acting purely as her father's go-between, why endure such privations? Twice that day he had come upon her carrying out menial tasks herself and, just as when he had found her wheeling the tea trolley the previous evening, she became flustered, insisting defensively upon offering him unnecessary explanations for her actions.

Felix was trying to make sense of it all when the door burst open in a manner which he was already starting to recognize. The twins were upon him in seconds, claiming that the French had gone well and that Mr Fothergill had been very surprised. But they were uncharacteristically subdued and would say nothing more on the matter.

'Well,' said Felix, rising from his chair, 'I am off to the bay to do a little fishing. I met a man in Burton Bradstock today who has arranged to meet me there and supply me with tackle.'

'Oh, that will be Mr Evans—'

'—he persuades everyone who is new here to fish our river—'

'—the River Bride, it is called,' offered Josh helpfully.

'Indeed, so I understand. Do you like to fish, twins?'

'Mama does not allow it.'

'What does Mama not allow?' asked Saskia, noiselessly joining the group.

'For us to go fishing.'

'It's dangerous for children on their own, Josh, as you are very well aware,' Saskia explained gently.

'But if we went with Mr Beaumont—'

'—he would look after us.'

'Has Mr Beaumont invited you to join him?'

'Well, no but—'

'But I was about to, with your permission, Mrs Eden.' Felix offered her a mildly expectant and perfectly courteous expression.

'Well, I am not sure.'

'Oh, Mama, please!' Naturally this was said in unison.

'You may rest assured that I will take the best of care of them and would welcome their company,' said Felix, replacing his courteous expression with a disarming smile.

Saskia hesitated for a long time, valiantly attempting to ignore the turmoil which his blasted smile caused within her, especially since it appeared to deprive her temporarily of her wits. She was uncomfortably aware that the twins received far too little of her attention and were seldom permitted to leave the confines of Riverside House. But still, she was suspicious of this glamorous stranger, who had so unexpectedly appeared in their midst, seemingly intent upon charming them all.

But then Saskia focused on the eager faces of her children, upturned expectantly towards her, full of an excitement that prevented them from standing still, and could not bring herself to deny them the pleasure they would derive from this simple fishing expedition. Whatever this man's reasons for being here, she somehow understood that he would never allow any harm to come to her beloved twins.

'Well, all right then,' she agreed with a smile. 'But you are to do whatever Mr Beaumont asks of you without question, children, and are not to be any trouble. Do you understand me now?'

'Yes, Mama!' But they were already leaping around, narrowly managing to avoid tripping over Hoskins, who was dashing about in tight circles, chasing his tail and generally adding to the mayhem.

Two hours later, Felix carried a sound-asleep Amy through the doors of Riverside House. Josh was at his side, valiantly attempting to conceal his yawns. Saskia came rushing up to them, her face ashen.

'What has happened? What is wrong with her? Is she harmed?'

'Calm yourself, Mrs Eden. She is merely asleep. Too much excitement and fresh air, I fear,' Felix assured her, indicating the yawning Josh with his eyes.

Saskia breathed an audible sigh of relief. 'Well, at least I will not have the usual struggle to get them to bed tonight. Thank you, Mr Beaumont, I can take her now.'

'I would not hear of it; you might wake her. I will carry her up for you.'

'I can manage.'

'I dare say, but not as easily as me.'

Giving her no time to demur, Felix carried Amy up to the first floor and, at receiving a nod from Saskia, continued on to the second. Saskia opened the door to the twins' room and Felix laid Amy gently on her bed.

'Girls aren't as strong as us men, are they, Mr Beaumont?' said Josh, sinking on to his own bed, with an exhausted sigh, inordinately proud that he had managed to stay awake. Saskia and Felix shared the first amused smile of their acquaintanceship.

'You must always take care of your sister, Josh,' said Felix.

'Of course, sir!'

'Have you thanked Mr Beaumont for his kindness, Josh?'

'Yes, Mama. And we caught lots of fish, but Mr Beaumont said we had to throw them back because they were too small to eat. Amy did not care to put the worms on the hook but girls don't like doing that either, do they, Mr Beaumont?'

Leaving Josh chattering away to no one in particular, Felix moved towards the door and whispered to Saskia, 'Ask Josh what happened to his knuckles.'

The twins had remained subdued for much of the afternoon and Felix realized, after a while, why that must be. Josh had angry red marks across the back of his knuckles. Felix and Luc had received a ruler across their own hands during their school days far too often for him not to recognize the signs. But this attack upon Josh had been particularly vicious. It was not Felix's business, of course, and he knew he should not permit himself to be distracted from his purpose, but it was already too late for that. He had developed a special rapport with these delightful children and suspected that if Saskia was not capable of upbraiding Fothergill for his undoubtedly drink-fuelled brutality against a helpless six-year-old then, in all probability, he would feel compelled to do so in her stead.

Felix soon discovered that he need not have doubted Saskia's mettle when it came to protecting her children. He was leaving his room that evening, on the way to dinner, when he heard raised voices coming from the schoolroom. Naturally he stopped to listen.

'Calm yourself, Mrs Eden, and allow me to worry about the children's discipline whilst in the schoolroom,' Felix heard Fothergill saying, his oily voice oozing patronage.

'Mr Fothergill, I wish to know precisely what it is that my son did to cause you to beat him so viciously.'

'He was rude about his French verbs,' said Fothergill shortly.

'In what way? Had he not studied, as you asked him to?'

'He was word perfect.' Fothergill made this concession with obvious reluctance.

'Then I do not understand the problem.'

'The problem, my dear lady, is that the twins were making fun of learning and I regret to inform you that your new guest was entirely responsible for this latitude.'

'In what respect?'

'My dear, he taught them to conjugate a verb by making up ridiculous rhymes! They thought it was fun.'

A penetrating silence greeted this statement but when Saskia spoke again Felix could have sworn that she was attempting to keep the amusement out of her voice. 'Let me see if I have got this right, Mr Fothergill. Mr Beaumont was good enough to assist the twins with work that I consider to be far too advanced for them – but then you are already aware of my views on that subject. But, anyway, Mr Beaumont managed to get them to learn their verb, and to enjoy doing so, and yet you considered this to be a reason to punish my son violently!' Her voice had risen again, resonating with undiminished anger. 'If that is how you reward good conduct, Mr Fothergill, I dread to think what could be in store for my children if they fail to learn their lessons.'

'But Saskia, my dear, he undermined my authority and must be taught to respect his elders and betters.'

Felix grunted aloud, unable to believe that even Fothergill could be so pompous.

'It is Mrs Eden to you, sir!' Felix could easily imagine Saskia breathing deeply as she attempted to keep her temper under control. When she did continue to speak her words were punctuated with a firm determination. 'Now, Mr Fothergill, let us understand one another right well. You will never again, I repeat never, strike either of my children without my express permission. If I find that you have done so, then you will leave this house immediately. Immediately, sir! This is your last warning, Mr Fothergill! I trust we understand one another?'

'My dear, you do not understand these things.' Fothergill was back to his patronizing best. 'You cannot run this house and expect to keep control of the children as well. You must allow me, at least, to shoulder that burden in your stead. You know that I am exceptionally well qualified as a teacher and you really must permit me to know what is best for them. I would, my dear, as I have told you on any number of occasions, happily shoulder all of your burdens and remain faithfully at your side as your consort.'

Felix, still eavesdropping shamelessly, had to clench his fists and dig his fingernails into his palms to force himself not to intervene. But it appeared that Saskia had no need of his assistance and Felix smiled to himself as he listened to her carelessly dismiss Fothergill's presumptuous proposal.

'Mr Fothergill, you forget yourself!'

Felix silently applauded her handling of the situation but suspected Fothergill thought too well of himself to detect the disdainful contempt beneath her words.

'Your father would be so distressed to see you reduced to dealing with such matters as your son's discipline on your own,' Fothergill remarked deviously. 'Only a man can be expected to undertake such a task.'

A further deathly silence ensued. Felix held his breath. It seemed that he was about to discover the true nature of Fothergill's residence in this house, and his relationship with Barker's daughter rather sooner than he could reasonably have expected to be the case.

'What do you know of my father?' enquired Saskia suspiciously.

'Only that you had some kind of stupid quarrel with him and are too proud to apologize. But I am sure he would welcome you and your children back, if only you would admit that you were wrong and behaved in future as a dutiful daughter should. Everyone around these parts knows what a good and forgiving gentleman Mr Samuel Barker is.'

'Mr Fothergill!' Saskia, in command of herself once more, sounded imperiously detached. Felix could only imagine the haughty tilt of her chin and the anger blazing in those remarkable eyes of hers. 'My relationship with my family is not your concern. The education of my children however is.' She paused, before issuing her next warning in a frosty tone. 'At least for the time being. I give you due notice however, Mr Fothergill, and you would do well to heed my words. One more example of the cruelty which you have exhibited and you will be out of this house before the end of the day. I trust you understand me, sir?'

The door flew open but Felix hardly needed to conceal himself. Saskia swept out, her eyes glinting with a mixture of suppressed fury and unshed tears, and marched away from Fothergill's room, looking neither to left nor right.

Chapter Six

SASKIA did not appear in the drawing-room until shortly before dinner was announced. When she did make her entrance her features were calmly composed, with no sign of the tears that had been so close when she left the schoolroom. She made a brief apology to the assembled company for her tardiness and, passing close to Felix a short time later, quietly thanked him for pointing out Josh's injury.

'I am relieved that he felt he could confide in you.'

'He did not exactly confide.'

'Then how did you know?'

'The twins were unusually subdued this afternoon and when I noticed Josh's hand I realized at once how he must have sustained the injury.' Felix offered her a puerile grin. 'I was the recipient of similar punishments when I was a boy. But not,' he added, his features hardening, 'when I was six years old and certainly not anything like as severely.'

'Indeed, sir, we are of one mind on the matter. It is a deplorable state of affairs but I have dealt with it and am confident it will not recur.'

'I am relieved to hear you say so.'

'And I understand, Mr Beaumont, that I also have you to thank for assisting the twins with their French verbs.'

He smiled at her again, willing her to lower her guard and offer some sort of response. 'Not at all! I enjoy *congregating* verbs.'

To his delight Saskia did return his smile, and held his gaze as well, just for a second or two, before moving away and conversing with others. Felix was left with the impression that she had been momentarily tempted to confide in him further. Her manner towards him was entirely different from that of the previous day but there was still a reserve about her which discouraged intimacy and kept people at a distance.

Felix observed Saskia as she moved about the room, putting her guests at their ease with her gracious manner and quiet competence. She was wearing a lavender-coloured muslin gown and this too was ill-fitting and dated: insufficient reasons in themselves to prevent Felix's mind from dwelling upon the delightful prospect of the body beneath the garment, which it made such poor work of disguising. But this crowded room was clearly not the place for lascivious thoughts. Disciplining himself to behave, Felix turned, with a charming smile, to Mrs Rivers and entered into conversation with her.

Felix anticipated that Fothergill's manner would be truculent, following the events of the afternoon, and that he would place the blame for his disagreement with Saskia squarely at his door. The fact that his behaviour was completely the opposite, his manner veering towards obeisance, supplied all the proof that Felix required to confirm his suspicions. There could no longer be any question that Fothergill was in the pay of Barker and placed in this house to act as his spy.

When the ladies had withdrawn and the port was circulating, Fothergill held court, much as he had the previous evening. Tonight however he spent an inordinate amount of time stressing the need for a permanent masculine presence in Riverside House. He did not see how two genteel ladies could be expected to run such an establishment unaided. It was true, of course, that they relied upon him to an inordinate degree and he was more than willing to lend them any assistance within his power but, should he decide to take another position in a school – he was, needless to say, constantly turning offers down: after all, experienced schoolmasters were in short supply nowadays – then he could not say how Mrs Rivers, and Mrs Eden in particular, would manage without him. Those twins of hers were permitted to run almost wild and had no idea how to behave. Were it not for him, he dreaded to think how they would turn out. Really, Mrs Eden was far too tender-hearted for her own good.

Captain Fanshaw and Mr Jennings nodded vigorously in agreement with him, the latter mumbling something about children being seen and not heard. Felix was not about to give him the satisfaction of voicing an opinion. Instead he lent back in his chair casually, savouring his port, and remained silent. He listened to Fothergill's discourse with studied nonchalance and made no contribution to the conversation.

Discovering at length that he had said all he could upon the subject, Fothergill turned to Felix and asked detailed and very pointed questions as to his reason for being in Swyre. Felix had half expected as much, satisfied as he now was that Fothergill must be acting upon instructions passed on to him at the Swyre Inn before luncheon. Felix answered readily enough, giving deliberately tantalizing descriptions of the wealthy clients for whom he was commissioned to purchase certain items: items which he had been given to understand were available in the vicinity of Burton Bradstock, provided one knew where to look. Fothergill listened intently, nodding his vigorous agreement, doubtless trying to store in his drink-befuddled memory everything that Felix said.

In the drawing-room there were no melodic Bach sonatas from Saskia this evening. Instead she poured her heart into a Beethoven concerto, hammering out the chords with fury and passion, giving vent to her pent-up emotions in the process. Even so, her performance, if anything, exceeded that of the previous evening. Her fingers expertly ran across the keyboard, interpreting the composer's work with an intensity and fervour which left Felix in no doubt that there was still a well of anger to be expunged from her in the wake of Fothergill's harsh treatment of her son. To Felix she was a compelling mixture of pride and insecurity, determination and vulnerability, tough resourcefulness and beguiling femininity. He could already tell that her nightly sojourn at the piano was a means of giving public vent to her anxieties; her choice of composer a useful tool by which to gauge her mood.

Felix had no further opportunity for private conversation with Saskia that evening and so withdrew to his chamber when the rest of the household retired. Once again he occupied the window-seat and mused upon the progress he had made that day. There were three things which he now definitely knew about Saskia Eden: she had no contact with her father because of some sort of disagreement; she was not in league with him in any way that he could detect; and she was almost certainly deeply afraid of him.

Fothergill, on the other hand, was definitely in Barker's employ. His singularly shabby attire alone lent proof to his impecunious state. This fact, added to the other compelling evidence that Felix had collated, only served to reinforce his conclusion. Could that be why Fothergill was so smugly confident about his own expectations and felt empowered to disregard carelessly Saskia's attempts to determine the direction of her children's education? Could Felix detect the twins' grandfather's hand behind the teacher's *modus operandi*? This notion had an unsettling effect upon Felix and he found himself fervently hoping that he was wrong.

As far as Felix had been able to ascertain, Fothergill was a schoolmaster of decidedly mediocre ability. He enjoyed no rapport with his pupils, did not appear to be seeking one, and was only able to keep their attention through threats of punishment: threats which he appeared prepared to carry out if given the slightest provocation.

Despite his protestations to the contrary, Felix was sure there was no likelihood of Fothergill ever being offered another position in a quality school. Furthermore, how could a man from a supposedly purely academic background, with no exposure to matters of business, have known to question him quite so intuitively about his reasons for being in Swyre? Unless, of course, someone had specifically advised him what form his questioning should take and what information he should attempt to obtain.

Taken altogether, there could be no doubt of Fothergill's complicity. He was a greedy and ambitious man who, having failed in his chosen profession, was left feeling bitter and resentful. He was not above taking money from a man who had doubtless persuaded him that his only concern was for the welfare of his daughter and grand-children.

Felix gave a shudder of distaste and turned his mind to other matters pertinent to Riverside House. There was still much that he did not comprehend. If Mrs Rivers had lived comfortably before Saskia's arrival, then she must have an income of sorts, for surely her late husband would have provided for her financially? So, why the need to take in lodgers? Why did that necessity arise only after Saskia's removal to the house and, more to the point, why did Saskia herself need to work so hard?

Felix needed to find out more. His intention to get to Barker through his daughter was now looking increasingly unlikely to succeed. It might be necessary to consult with his father before deciding upon his next step. But first he intended to get to the bottom of things here at Riverside House. He had noticed today that Mr and Mrs Jenkins went driving for the entire morning and only returned for luncheon. He understood that it was their custom to spend all of their mornings thus occupied. Fothergill, of course, was in the schoolroom, Captain Fanshaw spent every morning out of the house, researching his almanac and Miss Willoughby, apparently, was inclined to sit with Mrs Rivers in her private apartment, sewing, drinking tea and gossiping about the old days. With the whole house-hold occupied in various ways, the mornings would obviously be the best time for him to make a private exploration of Riverside House.

The next day Felix met with Perkins, who assured him, with a rakish smirk, that he was making satisfactory progress with his barmaid at least as rapidly as with his other contacts. He then returned to Riverside House early and unobtrusively let himself in. As he had expected, no one was about. His first destination was the top floor. Just as a matter of curiosity he wanted to see for himself where Saskia slept. He entered the room next to the twins' and let out an astonished oath. It was little more than a cell: a small trestle bed, armoire, one chair and no room for anything else. All was neat and tidy and there could be no doubt that it was Saskia's room. But why was she forced to live in such conditions? What could have happened between her and her father that she would prefer this kind of life to the comparative luxury of his residence?

Felix strolled to the tiny window and looked down at the kitchen garden, mulling the question over in his mind. Preoccupied as he was, it took a moment for him to register the scene below. A lineful of washing had fallen on to the muddy ground and would need to be redone; an untidy pile of logs lay uncut beside the block, outside an almost empty log shed; a long line of empty pails stood beside the pump waiting to be filled and it appeared that a whole row of lettuces had been roughly half-pulled out of the ground by someone or something, and left where they were to rot.

Amidst all this disarray, Saskia sat on the ground, head in her hands, weeping so despondently as to move his heart. Felix contemplated her plight, attempting a detachment he no longer felt, his mind already seeking ways to assist her.

Things could hardly get much worse before she and her aunt were forced to give up Riverside House, Saskia knew. Her emotional state had progressed way beyond despair, but somehow, giving in to a rare bout of self-indulgence and having a good cry, had made her feel more composed. She squared her shoulders, her emerald eyes glinting again with the light of battle. She would not be beaten, she simply would not! Somehow she would find a way to make things work.

If only that damned boy from the village had turned up today, as promised, to cut the logs and tidy the garden. Doubtless her father had managed to get to him as well and they would, yet again, be reduced to looking for help elsewhere. Saskia herself could turn her hand to most tasks, but even she could not chop logs: that was definitely men's work. Still, the washing had been redone. She would hang it out again now, making sure the rope was properly secured this time, and take advantage of the weak afternoon sun. Then she would see what wood she could salvage from the rapidly dwindling pile for this evening's fires. At least the weather was co-operating, since it had remained mild and they would be able to get away with smaller blazes.

Encouraged by this thought, Saskia stepped through the scullery door, washing basket under her arm, and stopped dead in her tracks as an astonished, '*Oh!*' escaped her lips. A man had his back to her and was swinging the axe through the air as easily as though it were made of matchwood, slicing the logs cleanly in two each time he made contact with them. The man was tall, naked to the waist, and in possession of an abundance of thick curly brown hair, which he had tied back with a kerchief. Saskia could see the shimmer of perspiration on his naked torso and the flexion of the muscles in his arms and back, which rippled smoothly in time with his seemingly effortless labours. She found herself rooted to the spot in rapt fascination, unable to move since her legs refused to co-operate with the commands issued from her befuddled brain. Her mouth had gone dry; she was having difficulty drawing breath and her stomach was lurching in a most peculiar manner.

The twins were there too, stacking kindling a safe distance away from the flying splinters of wood, whilst Hoskins charged about in crazy circles with a stick in his mouth, wagging his stumpy tail and generally getting in the way.

Sensing her presence, her children shouted a greeting.

'Mr Beaumont is cutting the logs, Mama.'

'He has done loads—'

'—and we are helping—'

'—look how much we have done already.'

Felix turned to look at her and Saskia heartily wished that he had not done so. If the prospect of his naked back had been unsettling, it was nothing to the sight of his disconcertingly broad chest, which was fascinatingly covered with wiry brown hair. She could hardly prevent herself noticing that his muscular shoulders appeared so much more impressive from this angle, as too did his lean torso. His waist was narrower than she would have imagined possible and the fact that his close-fitting breeches clung very firmly to well-defined thighs was an observation impossible to ignore, given his lack of a shirt. Saskia gulped and averted her eyes.

Felix wiped the perspiration from his brow and smiled at her. 'Good afternoon, Mrs Eden,' he offered, bowing elegantly. It should have looked ridiculous, of course. If any other gentleman of her acquaintance had attempted to bow whilst half-dressed it doubtless would have done so, but with him . . . well, Saskia did not attempt to analyse what was happening to her senses at that precise moment: she was too occupied trying to avoid looking at him, whilst seemingly unable to drag her eyes away. He was an unconscionable rogue sent here deliberately to overset her. Well, she was completely indifferent to urbane and charming gentlemen with compelling brown eyes, seductive smiles and broad, disconcerting chests, was she not? She simply would not allow this one to have any effect upon her and would continue to treat him with polite disdain.

Fortified by this resolve, and with her emotions once again under close guard, she addressed him.

'What do you think you are about, Mr Beaumont? Guests are not permitted in the kitchen garden.'

She pulled herself up to her full height and spoke as severely as she knew how, but it did nothing whatsoever to diminish the impudent light in his eye. The twins were dancing about all the while, full of themselves and clearly enjoying every moment that they spent with this engaging but irritatingly urbane man. In the face of their delight and the absurdity of the situation, Saskia found it difficult to maintain her scandalized pose and only narrowly avoided smiling.

'My pardon, ma'am,' offered Felix smoothly. 'The twins mentioned that your garden boy had not reported for work today. I had nothing particular to occupy me this afternoon and felt the need for exercise. This seemed like a neat solution to both our problems.'

'So I see.' She collected herself with difficulty, searching frantically for the dignity that had chosen a most inconvenient time to desert her. 'I am obliged to you, sir, but your intervention was quite unnecessary.'

Felix didn't contradict her but simply stood beside his neatly chopped wood and smiled that wretchedly enticing smile of his. His attitude flustered her, causing her to attempt a justification she knew was unnecessary.

'I was aware, sir, that the garden boy would not be here today, but I have the situation under control.' The lie might just have convinced him, had she not blushed quite so deeply. 'I am, however, in your debt,' she murmured reluctantly, lowering her gaze only to find it focused squarely in the centre of that damned chest of his: an unfortunate circumstance which served to rouse her anger. She did not want to be beholden to this man. He was dangerous, she could sense that much, and he wanted something from her too, of that she was equally certain. Was this crude exhibition of his masculine strength meant to impress her? How shallow did he imagine she was?

'Indeed you are, Mrs Eden, and I fully intend to call in that debt.' His quiet voice intruded upon her introspection, causing her to draw in a sharp breath as his eyes raked her face with impudent familiarity.

'Pray, what is your meaning, sir?' she demanded in alarm. 'I did not ask you for assistance.'

'Nevertheless, you just owned that you are indebted to me.'

'You want payment?' Saskia placed her hands on her hips and glowered her displeasure.

'Indeed not, m'dear, I had a far more pleasant form of reward in mind.' His eyes held an amused expression: his voice languid yet strangely compelling. 'You see, I noticed whilst in Burton Bradstock this morning that there is to be a public ball held there on Saturday. Dare I hope that you would consider favouring me with your company?'

'Indeed not, sir, it is quite out of the question!'

'That is exactly the response I expected from you.'

'Then you can hardly claim disappointment.'

Saskia turned deliberately away from him but not before he had picked up the axe again and she was treated to a frontal view of his chest and those rippling muscles as he swung effortlessly at the log on the block and cleft it cleanly in two. '*Damn!*' she muttered to herself, as she turned her attention to her washing and attempted to retie the rope.

Struggling to do so she collided with a solid obstruction: an obstruction with taut muscles, warm flesh and a distinctly masculine aroma: a combination of soap, perspiration and outdoor activity. A heat swept through her, pooling in the pit of her stomach. She felt the blood rush to her face, even as her heart leapt wildly within her breast. His dangerously close proximity deprived her of the ability to think rationally once again and her mind was reduced to a chaotic jumble of conflicting emotions. She felt as though she had jumped several feet in the air and moved away from him so fast that she almost lost her footing.

Felix caught her arm to steady her, the affect of his urbane smile spoiled by a knowing look in his eye that Saskia did not care to interpret, especially when it broadened into an unmistakably mocking challenge. She felt herself blushing even more deeply and cursed her inability to keep better control of her reactions.

'Allow me,' he said, taking the rope from her hand and tying it firmly in place, testing the result with the palm of his hand. 'That will hold,' he assured her, his smile now distinctly predatory.

'Thank you!'

She turned away from him and fled to the comparative safety of the kitchen, feeling his eyes boring into her retreating back as she did so.

Felix entered the drawing-room slightly before six that evening and enjoyed the satisfaction of discovering Mrs Rivers there alone.

'Ah, Mr Beaumont!' she exclaimed, her expression welcoming.

'Your servant, ma'am.' Felix offered her a graceful bow.

'I understand we are indebted to you, sir, for the very fire that warms us this evening?'

'Indeed, ma'am, I am surprised that your niece took the trouble to mention such a trifling matter to you.'

'She did not.'

'The twins, I can only assume?'

'Quite! But anyway, Mr Beaumont, I wished to thank you in person.'

'There is no need. It was the work of a moment,' responded Felix with a casual shrug.

'Ha, that is not the case, I feel assured. But I must confess too,' she added with a mischievous smile, 'that I would have enjoyed witnessing the event. No matter, you have my thanks, Mr Beaumont, and you may be assured that if there is anything I can do for you in return that you have but to name it.'

Felix suppressed an amused grin. The old lady was flirting with him! But she was also playing straight into his hands. Or was she? Felix was unsure as to her motives, or if she even had any, but continued to play the part he now half-suspected Mrs Rivers had intended for him all along.

'Indeed, ma'am, there is one trifling matter with which I would crave your interference. I did ask your niece if she would honour me with the pleasure of her company at a ball in Burton Bradstock on Saturday evening, but, it seems, she has a disinclination for dancing.'

Mrs Rivers chuckled. 'Rejection is not something you are accustomed to, I am prepared to wager, sir.'

'Is there any particular reason why Mrs Eden would prefer not to attend a ball?' asked Felix, ignoring the jibe.

'Several.'

Mrs Rivers contemplated Felix for some time without speaking. Felix was content to allow the silence to stretch between them, making it work to his advantage.

'You must have already discovered that my niece has a father who resides in Burton Bradstock. Indeed, if you have frequented the village you will not have been able to avoid hearing his name mentioned, for he wields considerable influence in these parts. He will also be aware of your presence in this house by now, for nothing that happens here is too trifling to escape his notice. Saskia's father is my brother, Mr Beaumont,' she said, pausing for emphasis, 'my twin brother.'

Felix raised a brow in surprise. He had not known that. 'But it would appear that you are estranged?'

'Sadly, that is the case. But when we were children we were as close as Josh and Amy are now.'

70

'Would it be improper for me to enquire what happened to cause your estrangement?'

'Samuel was sent away to school, whilst I was educated at home, but we were still bound together by that invisible tie peculiar to twins. Then we grew up. I married and moved here. Samuel married as well: a beautiful lady of Russian extraction, hence Saskia's exotic name. My brother and I were both very fortunate in the choices that were made on our behalf, for we were enamoured with our respective partners and enjoyed happy lives with them, and Sam and I remained on the most intimate of terms.

'My brother was being groomed to take over our father's shipping business. But our father was a bully and a tyrant, just as Sam has become since his wife died and he lost her restraining influence. I could not countenance his behaviour towards his own children and told him as much, but he would brook no interference, even from me, and although still on speaking terms, I made my feelings known by calling upon him far less frequently. But my nephews, and especially my niece, knew that they could always come to me if they had difficulties which they were unable to resolve.'

Mrs Rivers's words tailed off on a regretful sigh. Felix, sensing that she was now considering whether to confide further in him, moved to the sideboard and poured her a glass of Madeira, which she accepted gratefully. 'My niece arrived at this house at seven o'clock one morning, with the three-month-old twins clasped in her arms. She had walked five miles, in the middle of a storm, to get here. She was, as you will easily be able to imagine, exhausted. Her feet were swollen and bleeding, she was suffering from hypothermia and fainted clean away as soon as I took the twins from her.'

'Dear God!'

'She had other injuries, Mr Beaumont, the nature of which I am not at liberty to disclose. She was seriously ill for three weeks and at one stage we feared she would not recover.'

'Happily,' said Felix, silently willing Mrs Rivers to reveal more, 'it is clear that she did.'

'Indeed, we were blessed by having her restored to us. But I know not why she left my brother's house in such an abrupt and drastic manner, Mr Beaumont, for I have never asked her and she has never felt the need to explain herself. My brother holds me responsible for keeping her from him however: hence our estrangement. Samuel has never relaxed his efforts to persuade his daughter to return to him. He adores her, you see. She was always his favourite, resembling her mother as closely as she does. But Samuel is not used to disobedience; it reflects badly upon him to have a rebellious daughter and we both think that he is unlikely ever to relax his efforts to get her back. He does not hesitate to use every method at his disposal to wear us down and, as I mentioned earlier, he has influence hereabouts, which he exploits shamelessly if he thinks it will help him to persuade Saskia to return. You have seen for yourself today just how close he is to succeeding in his endeavours. We are living very close to the edge. My niece works like a Trojan and is sometimes close to exhaustion, but she never complains and infinitely prefers her lot here to the only other option available to her, which is returning to a life of comparative luxury which she knows she could once again claim beneath my brother's roof at any time of her choosing.'

Felix paced the room, alarmed and perplexed in equal measure by all he had heard, yet anxious to learn more. But it appeared that Mrs Rivers had said all she intended to say on the subject and Felix knew he could not, in all politeness, raise the many questions he would like answers to. Questions such as, where had all her money gone? Why take in guests? Why not simply sell Riverside House and move somewhere more manageable? Why was Mrs Rivers herself accepting the downturn of her fortunes with such apparent equanimity? Did she love her niece so much that she would continue to put up with it when, presumably, if she insisted that Saskia return to her father's house, then everything would once again be as it was before?

It was frustrating in the extreme to be unable to raise these matters. Felix consoled himself with the knowledge that he had only been at Riverside House for three days and in that time he had already learned far more than he would ever have thought possible.

'Are you saying,' asked Felix with a frown, 'that Mrs Eden does not wish to go to a ball in Burton Bradstock in case she encounters her father? Whatever could occasion such a degree of fear, I wonder?'

'I have my suspicions, but that is all they are and I am not ready to share them with you.'

Felix bowed in acknowledgement of the old lady's right to secrecy. 'But do you not consider that it would do your niece the world of good to have an evening for herself: to dance and worry about nothing more taxing than her own enjoyment for once?'

'Indeed I do, Mr Beaumont. She used to be inordinately fond of dancing.'

'Then may I rely upon you to persuade her? You may rest assured that no harm will befall her whilst she is in my care and if her father should be anywhere near the ball, then he will most certainly not be given the opportunity to address her, unless she wishes it.'

Mrs Rivers looked at Felix, registering the firm set to his jaw, the determined light in his eye. 'I have no doubts on that score. My niece is fortunate to have attracted the attentions of a gentleman such as yourself.'

Felix made another slight bow in acknowledgement of the compliment. 'Thank you.'

'You *are* a gentleman, Mr Beaumont, are you not?'

'I certainly hope so, ma'am!'

'Hm, well, on that score, at least, we are agreed. But I think there is a very great deal more to you than that, Mr Beaumont.'

Felix feigned ignorance in what he hoped was a convincing fashion but was more than a little disconcerted by the knowledge that one perspicacious old lady could so quickly entertain doubts about his carefully constructed alias.

'I do not understand your meaning, Mrs Rivers.'

The old lady chuckled. 'Oh, I think you do, but no matter, I am confident you represent no threat to my niece and so I will be happy to ally myself with you in an effort to persuade her to attend the ball. You are certainly correct to suggest that she deserves a little pleasure and I am sure that dancing with you, Mr Beaumont,' she continued, twinkling at him, 'will provide her with an abundance of that.'

73

'Mrs Rivers!' Felix affected a pose of mild outrage, which did not seem to deceive the old lady in the slightest, since it only served to make her chuckle even more heartily.

'Your niece will doubtless claim that she must be excused on the grounds that she has nothing suitable to wear for the occasion,' suggested Felix.

'Hah, I have her there! I have a bolt of changeable silk that I have been waiting for years to put to good use: and just the right colours for her too. Now then, today is Tuesday and the ball is on Saturday, you say?' Felix nodded. 'Fine! If Eleanor Willoughby and I set to first thing tomorrow then we can run her up a gown before then.'

'I take it then, ma'am, that you will be able to persuade her?'

'Just leave her to me, Mr Beaumont.'

Chapter Seven

As usual Saskia was the last person to retire. As soon as she had seen the last of their guests climb the stairs she lost no time in making her way to the kitchen to commence her customary late night tidying, first ensuring that the range was still alight.

Even by her own standards Saskia was exceptionally tired this evening, the extraordinary events of the day having left an indelible mark upon her exhausted person. Every bone in her body ached, screaming out the need for repose. But before she could surrender to that need she must finish her chores. She was in the midst of doing so when the door opened behind her, causing her to start violently.

'I thought I would find you here.'

'All is well, Aunt, and I was just about to retire.'

'Come up to my apartment first, child, I would speak with you.'

Saskia hid her dismay behind a sunny smile of acquiescence. Her narrow trestle bed had never before seemed more enticing, but she knew she could not ignore such a direct request from her aunt.

'What did you wish to discuss with me, Aunt?' asked Saskia, as she sank gratefully into the soft cushions offered by her aunt's commodious sofa, a few minutes later.

'You have had a difficult day, my dear,' said Mrs Rivers sympathetically. 'I just wish I were strong enough to give you more assistance.'

'Oh, Aunt Serena!' Saskia was appalled. She was responsible for reducing her aunt to this sorry state of affairs but the older lady felt the need to apologize to *her*. She was too good! Saskia's tiredness became shrouded in guilt and regret. 'I can manage perfectly well, Aunt. Pray, do not make yourself uneasy on my account.'

'As you managed the logs today?'

'You know about that?'

'The twins.'

'Ah, yes!' Saskia rolled her eyes.

'It was very kind of Mr Beaumont, Saskia.'

'I expressed my thanks,' she responded defensively.

'I have no doubt that you did.' Mrs Rivers smiled at her niece but said nothing more. She had a disconcerting habit of knowing when silence would serve her purpose more eloquently than words. Never had she put the trait to better use and Saskia knew she was blushing under the older lady's close scrutiny.

'You like Mr Beaumont, do you not, Aunt?' It was a statement as much as a question, which Mrs Rivers answered in the affirmative, without the slightest hesitation.

'Very much.'

'Do you think that is wise? I mean, we know so little about him. He makes me uneasy, although I admit that I would be hard-pressed to say why. But there is just something about him. He is dangerous, I think.'

'And handsome?'

'Yes,' agreed Saskia, with a sigh, 'he is most assuredly handsome.'

'But not handsome enough to partner you in a dance?'

So that was what this was about. He had enlisted her aunt's help to persuade her to attend that blasted ball. Fiery anger flashed briefly in Saskia's eyes. 'He frightens me, Aunt,' she said, avoiding a direct reply.

'Is it Mr Beaumont who frightens you, Saskia, or are you afraid of your own feelings?'

'Aunt Serena, what a thing to suggest!'

'Or,' the older woman suggested, her voice speculative, 'perhaps it is the thought of being observed in Burton Bradstock that is unsettling you?' Without waiting for an answer, Mrs Rivers continued to speak her mind. 'Saskia, my love, I worry about you. You work much too hard; you are far too thin; you spend all your time worrying about the twins; about our future in this house and . . . oh, about everything. You are still young but you never find the time for diversions.'

'Huh, what need do I have for them?'

'Oh, Saskia, everyone deserves to have a little time for themselves. Mr Beaumont, whatever his motives for being here, is first and foremost a gentleman. You will come to no harm with him and I have his assurance that he will not let anyone connected to your father anywhere near you.'

'You have discussed my father with him?' Saskia's question was expressed sharply, her tone disbelieving. She could not comprehend her aunt's incautiousness and was furious with her for her uncharacteristic lack of discretion.

'Only in the most abstract way, be not alarmed. I could hardly discuss specifics with him, even if I wished to do so, for you have never enlightened me as to the reason for your estrangement from your father. Mr Beaumont merely wishes to take you to a ball and it would give me the greatest possible pleasure to see you accept his invitation.'

The anger drained out of Saskia as quickly as it arrived. Saskia had lived with her aunt for almost six years and never once before in all that time had she attempted to persuade her to do that which she would prefer not to. So how, in all conscience, could she deny the simple request she was making of her now?

Dancing! It was an age since Saskia had graced the floor but she recalled just how much she had once enjoyed it. But with Mr Beaumont? She shivered as she imagined him holding her; almost certainly closer than he should. She anticipated that mocking smile of his and blushed as she thought of the challenging look that would undoubtedly accompany it. She could already imagine the envy on the faces of the other ladies present, for Felix Beaumont was most assuredly a cut above the type of gentleman who would normally be expected to attend such a parochial assembly.

No one had ever unsettled her before in quite the way that Mr Beaumont was able to manage. He was unquestionably dangerous and she heartily wished she had never set eyes upon him. She wished also that she had gone with her first instincts and told him that they had no rooms available.

'Yes, Aunt, you are right,' declared Saskia with spirit, suppressing her doubts and smiling graciously. 'I would happily accept Mr Beaumont's kind invitation, if you wish me to, but it is quite impossible since I have nothing suitable to wear.'

She sat back, smugly aware that her aunt could have no answer to that, only to discover that she had been wrong-footed once again. Her aunt chuckled and ordered her imperiously to report to her straight after breakfast the next morning for her first fitting.

Felix saw little of Saskia over the next few days, apart from at dinner, when he was disappointed to detect no marked change in her manner towards him. It remained as polite and formally correct as it had always been. No mention was made of her being compelled by her aunt to attend the ball, but it appeared that she was exacting her revenge by deliberately giving Felix the minimum attention that politeness dictated. No matter, Felix was content to bide his time. On Saturday he would have her all to himself and was determined that when that time came he would make it impossible for her to continue ignoring him.

Of the twins Felix saw rather more. If he was at Riverside House when they were released from the schoolroom they sought him out and joined him in whatever activity he was engaged upon. They rode with him in his curricle, went fishing for a second time and even persuaded him to help them fly their kite.

Felix occupied his time by driving out in his curricle to the villages surrounding Burton Bradstock, where he made verbose enquiries of various traders on behalf of his fictitious clients. That his activities were being observed soon became apparent when he noticed the same two men, on separate days, loitering in the street as he drove by, trying too hard not to pay him any attention. But they made basic mistakes: appearing wherever he happened to be, often in different villages on the same day, seeming to imagine that their presence would go undetected.

Saturday evening arrived and, dressed in the most formal attire that Perkins had considered appropriate to his reduced circumstances, Felix entered the drawing room before the usual hour. Saskia too was punctual, arriving a very short time after him in the company of her aunt and a beaming Miss Willoughby, the twins giving vent to their excitement by frolicking about them like puppies.

Mrs Rivers's changeable silk was of emerald green and turquoise, living up to its name by altering hue as she moved beneath the soft candlelight. The gown was gratifyingly simple: a smooth sheath caught beneath her breasts with an emerald ribbon, and floating about her long legs in a manner that illustrated their slenderness far too graphically for Felix's comfort. There was the tiniest scrap of sleeve and a disappointingly high neckline, edged with a little Flemish lace, displaying only a modest amount of Saskia's impressive *décolletage*. Her hair had been piled into a heap of loose curls, some of which fell about her face, enhancing her fragile beauty.

Felix suspected, from the amused chuckle which Mrs Rivers and Miss Willoughby exchanged, that his lascivious thoughts must be clearly visible upon his features. That did not prevent a smile of admiration from gracing his lips: a token of his appreciation which he stubbornly refused to remove. Beautiful ladies, dressed for special occasions, deserved to be admired and he sensed that the confidence of this one, in particular, would receive a much-needed boost from the knowledge that she had secured his regard.

'M'dear,' he drawled on a long breath, picking up her gloved hand and kissing it, 'you look ravishing!'

'Thank you, sir.'

'The same could be said of you, Mr Beaumont,' remarked Mrs Rivers capriciously.

Felix had not worn this particular attire before at Riverside House and the ladies clearly considered his plum-coloured formal coat, contrasting silk waistcoat, immaculately tied neckcloth and cream wool breeches to be superior. If only they could see what he would normally have worn for such an occasion!

'Why, Mrs Rivers,' said Felix, arching a brow in mock surprise. 'I do believe that you would wish to accompany us.'

'Ah, if only I were a year or two younger, Mr Beaumont.' She sighed with regret.

The door opened to admit Fothergill and the rest of the guests. They were talking amongst themselves but stopped abruptly at the sight of Saskia.

'Mr dear, Mrs Eden!' exclaimed Fothergill. 'To what do we owe the—'

'Mama is going to a ball—'

'—with Mr Beaumont—'

'—and Aunt Serena and Miss Willoughby—'

'—made her a new gown.'

'Is this right, Mrs Eden?' snapped Fothergill.

Saskia inclined her head.

'My dear!' Fothergill took her arm and led her aside. 'Do you consider this to be expeditious? I mean, my dear, you hardly know the man. Had I known you had a predisposition for dancing I would gladly—'

'Thank you, Mr Fothergill,' said Saskia, detaching her arm forcefully from his grasp. 'I am perfectly at ease with the arrangement I have made.'

'You look really nice, Mr Beaumont—'

'—like a prince—'

'—do you like dancing?'

'What are the twins doing in here at this hour?' demanded Fothergill, transferring his anger onto them.

'Mama said we could see her dress—'

'Speak when you are spoken to!' boomed Fothergill. 'Off to bed with you now.'

'Mr Fothergill, you forget yourself.' Saskia glowered at him. 'Again!'

Felix hid a smile, impressed by the composed manner in which Saskia had handled the much deserved put-down. Fothergill though pretended not to have heard her and returned his attention to the twins.

'Did you hear me, you two?'

'The whole room heard you, Fothergill,' said Felix, with deceptive calm. 'Now then.' With casual deliberation he turned his back on Fothergill and crouched down to face the twins. 'Who wants to be carried up?'

'Me please!' cried Amy, running into Felix's outstretched arms. Felix laughed at her, ruffled her hair and swept her from the floor. 'You are a little too big now to be carried, don't you think?' he asked of Josh, winking at him.

'Oh yes!' Josh assured him. 'But it's all right for girls.'

'I do not think that you should be—'

'Of course it is,' agreed Felix, ignoring Fothergill's interruption. 'Now then, say goodnight, children. Would you like me to take them up for you, Mrs Eden?'

'Yes, please, sir. I will follow directly, children, to listen to your prayers.'

And for the first time that evening Saskia smiled, in gratitude, at Felix.

'Well, I do not know about the rest of you,' declared Fothergill over dinner, 'but now that I think of it, the notion of dancing rather appeals to me.'

Felix ran his eyes scathingly over Fothergill's shabby coat but said nothing.

'It is an age since I last graced the floor,' remarked Mrs Jennings wistfully.

'Always enjoyed treading a measure myself,' conceded Captain Fanshaw.

At that moment the last of the plates were removed and the ladies made to withdraw. Felix rose with them and offered Saskia his arm.

'Ready, m'dear?' he asked her. She nodded. 'In that case we will wish you all a good evening,' said Felix, casually ignoring the not-so-subtle attempts of the rest of the party to be invited to join them. 'Good evening to you, Mrs Rivers.'

'And good evening to you, sir. Pray take care of my niece and enjoy yourselves.'

Felix assisted Saskia with her evening cape and opened the front door for her. His curricle was drawn up in front of the house, the horses being held by a lad from the livery yard. Felix flipped a coin at the boy, who caught it deftly, doffed his cap and disappeared. A groom from the same yard was waiting beside the conveyance and would be up behind them. At a country ball Felix could get away with appearing with Saskia unchaperoned, but to drive alone with her at night could compromise her reputation. Felix had not lost sight of his reasons for being in Burton Bradstock and did not wish to destroy his credentials in the eyes of her father before they even met.

Assisting Saskia into the conveyance, Felix took up the ribbons and encouraged his cattle forward. As he did so he was aware of Fothergill's face, pressed against the drawing-room window, rigid with fury. Felix raised his driving whip in an ironic salute.

The assembly room was already crowded but a momentary hush fell upon the proceedings as Saskia entered on Felix's arm. He tightened his muscles beneath her fingers, a gesture intended to offer encouragement. In response she lifted her chin and looked about the room, for all the world perfectly at her ease, appearing as though she did this sort of thing every day of her life. Felix, understanding her fears and some of the reasons for them, admired her mettle.

They had not proceeded many paces before they were descended upon by a matron, whose round face was wreathed in smiles.

'Saskia, my dear! I am delighted to see you here.' The lady smiled encouragement at Saskia and looked, with undisguised interested, in Felix's direction.

'Good evening, Mrs Watkins. May I present Mr Beaumont, a guest of my aunt? Mr Beaumont, this is Mrs Watkins, our rector's wife.'

Not surprisingly, Felix's elegant bow sent the lady into spasms of delight.

'You are most welcome, Mr Beaumont, especially as you have been clever enough to persuade Saskia to show herself in public again. We had all but given up on her ever doing so,' she added, giving Saskia's arm an affectionate squeeze.

'It was not easy, ma'am, I do assure you.'

'I have no doubt, but I can perhaps understand why she was tempted,' said Mrs Watkins, with a glint in her eye that Mrs Rivers could not have bettered.

The first dance was about to form up when a commotion behind them heralded the inevitable arrival of Fothergill, Fanshaw and the Jenningses. Felix hid his irritation behind a languid mask of indifference. It would, if nothing else, give him an opportunity to observe Fothergill in a public forum and it would be interesting to see if he risked approaching any of Barker's men.

'We made the decision to follow your good example,' said Fothergill, who was still clad in his dreadful puce-coloured coat. 'Ah, Mrs Eden, the first dance. Shall we?' And without giving Saskia the opportunity to refuse he swept her bossily on to the floor.

Saskia was surrounded by a number of gentlemen, all of whom she appeared to know, at the conclusion of each dance. Felix kept a weather-eye on her from whichever part of the room Mrs Watkins had led him to. She introduced him to a seemingly endless supply of curious matrons and their blushing daughters, most of whom were, quite literally, lost for words in the presence of such an imposing sophisticate, the likes of which they had only ever previously dreamt of encountering. He danced with one or two of the girls, much to the delight of their avaricious mothers, all the while biding his time.

Just when he had given up hope of it ever happening, the final dance before supper struck up and Felix recognized the opening stanza of a waltz. Saskia was still surrounded, but Felix strode between her admirers, something about his purposeful determination causing them to scatter, mumbling their complaints, as he bowed before her.

'I believe the pleasure is mine, Mrs Eden?' he said in a velvety drawl, smiling up at her.

Saskia hesitated for a fraction of a second, before making a graceful curtsy and returning his smile. 'I believe, sir, that you are correct.'

Ignoring the disappointed expressions on the faces of several of the gentleman surrounding her – principally Fothergill's – Felix led Saskia to the floor and swept her into his arms. She waltzed beautifully, moving with instinctive grace wherever his feet led. Her body in his arms was feather light and a smile of genuine pleasure graced her features, the likes of which he had not observed her adopt for any of her other partners throughout the entire evening. She was enjoying herself at last but not, he was surprised to discover, nearly as much as he was.

'You waltz very well,' he remarked quietly.

'Thank you, sir, as do you.'

It was no less than the truth. Felix held her tightly but not, Saskia was surprised and possibly a little disappointed to discover, any closer than he should.

'You enjoy dancing, I think?'

'Yes, indeed, but it is a long time since I last had the opportunity.'

'You have lost none of your skill.'

Saskia blushed and averted her gaze.

'Who is that person leaning in the corner? His attention has been concentrated upon you for the entire evening. Not,' continued Felix, with a gentle smile, 'that I can blame him for that. You put every other lady in attendance to shame.' And now he did pull her a little closer. Any number of the men in the room had cast covetous glances at Saskia during the course of the evening and Felix was suddenly taken with an overwhelming urge to have her to himself. As she looked in the direction which Felix had indicated, the smile left her face with such abruptness that he regretted his question.

'My father's steward,' she answered succinctly. 'His name is Johnson.'

'And you do not wish him to address you?'

She shuddered. 'I do not wish to have anything to do with him. Or anyone else here this evening who is connected to my father.'

'Then he shall not be given that opportunity.'

Saskia's smile of gratitude was all the reward that Felix could have asked for.

The dance came to and end. Felix raised Saskia from her curtsy and offered her his arm, for all the world as though he was about to escort her into supper. As he did so he noticed Johnson heading in their direction.

'Mrs Eden!' He raised his hand in greeting. 'A word, if you please.'

At the same time Fothergill and his entourage were approaching them from the other side of the room. The desperation in Saskia's eye was in direct variance to her expression of pleasure when waltzing with Felix. He had had more than enough of her every movement being dogged by half the men in the room, and suspected that she felt the same way. He understood better now her reluctance to attend this gathering in the first place and blamed himself for compelling her to do so and thus exposing her to such unwelcome attention.

'Do you wish to take supper here?' he asked her quietly.

'Not any more!' she declared emphatically.

'Then come with me.'

She nodded and raised not one objection.

Using the surging crowd as cover, Felix dexterously guided Saskia towards the door. He made her stand in the shadows as he retrieved her evening cape and then ushered her into the evening air. He called up his curricle and within minutes they were alone, the services of the livery yard groom having been dispensed with. To hell with appearances!

Without saying a word Felix took the road which would lead them towards the dunes, and guaranteed solitude.

Chapter Eight

FELIX slanted sideways glances at his distracted companion as they drove away, but said nothing, giving her the opportunity to gather her thoughts and regain her composure. The horses trotted along at a steady pace, the rhythmic sound of their hooves and the gentle swaying of the curricle soothing its occupants. A light breeze worried at Saskia's hair but she appeared oblivious to it.

After ten minutes Felix halted the curricle at the spot he had chosen for that very purpose on the previous day. They were close to the sea, in a slight cove in the dunes, which would afford them some protection from the elements. Still without speaking, Felix alighted from the conveyance, removed the travelling rug which he had placed over Saskia's knees and helped her down. Looking about her she spoke at last.

'What are we doing here?'

'Having supper. You did not imagine that I would allow you to go hungry, surely?'

'Mr Beaumont, I do not think it entirely appropriate that you should—'

'Shush, just trust me.' His voice conveyed conviction, his smile reassurance, as he led her to the rug, now spread on the ground, in the lee of the cove. 'Your table, madam!' he declared with an exaggerated bow.

Laughing in spite of her doubts, Saskia allowed herself to be swept along by Felix's spontaneity.

'Now, if madam will excuse me for just one moment?'

Felix went to the trunk of his curricle and returned almost immediately with a large hamper. Saskia looked at him in disbelief.

'I rather think you planned this diversion all along.'

'No, but I did anticipate that Fothergill *et al* might attempt to follow our example this evening and I had no wish for their company. And,' he added lightly, 'upon reflection I rather thought that the ball might prove to be more of a trial for you than a pleasure. It seems I was right on both counts.'

Felix set two candles within protective lanterns into the sand. They cast an eerie glow and elongated shadows across the cove, adding an air of intimacy to their clandestine supper. Felix delved into the hamper and produced a bottle of champagne: perfectly chilled, naturally. He opened it with swift proficiency and filled two flutes.

'What shall we drink to?' he asked her, handing her a glass.

'You choose.' She looked at him but could not meet his eye.

Felix returned her look with a smile of encouragement. There was wariness in her expression but he took heart from the fact that she did not appear especially alarmed at the prospect of their unconventional *al fresco* supper. In the dim illumination provided by the candles her features were partially hidden, but he could detect enough of them to appreciate that she was distracted. There was a melancholy about her and tenseness underlined her every movement: a situation which Felix silently vowed to rectify.

As Felix regarded her, sitting there in her simple emerald gown, making no effort to secure his attention, he felt the first stirrings of something he had never before experienced. It momentarily confused him, but also served to strengthen his resolve. The heightening of his interest necessitated that he discover what it was that had frightened her so. In short, he intended to learn what had happened to her in her father's house.

Saskia was looking at him, a question in her eyes, and he realized he had made her no answer in respect of their proposed toast. He rallied and offer her a curling smile.

'Why do we not drink to the loveliness of nature?' he suggested lightly, encompassing with an outstretched arm the moonlit sea lapping gently against the shore; the undulating dunes, eerie and mysterious in the lantern light.

'To nature then,' she agreed, raising her glass to his.

Felix unpacked the hamper. That Perkins would have done him proud was not in doubt. There was cold chicken and ham, tiny quails' eggs, cheeses, pickles, fresh crusty bread and every delicacy that the limited resources of Burton Bradstock had been able to produce. Felix spread a crisp white napkin over Saskia's knees and commanded her to eat: all the while topping up her glass.

Much to his surprise she did eat: more than he had ever seen her do during his time at Riverside House. For once she had no one else's needs to consider but her own.

'Thank you, Mr Beaumont,' she said, as she consumed the last fragments of ham, 'that was most thoughtful of you.'

'You are welcome, m'dear,' he assured her, packing away the remnants of food and filling her glass again.

After a brief silence Saskia addressed him. 'I believe I owe you an apology, Mr Beaumont.'

'And why would that be?'

She hesitated. 'Because . . . well, because I overcharged you for your room.'

'I know.'

'You know! Well, if you knew, why did you take the room?'

'Why did you overcharge me?'

After another brief hesitation, and perhaps emboldened by the champagne, she spoke the truth. 'Because I thought you had been sent by my father to spy upon me.'

Felix showed no surprise at this admission. 'But you no longer consider that to be the case?'

'No,' she said softly, 'I do not.'

'Thank you. And you are quite correct. You have my assurance as a gentleman that I have never met your father, nor do I have any connection with him.'

'Yes, I realize that now, but I must confess that I am still curious as to why you would take a room at a price which is far too high?'

'I will tell you soon, I promise, but first will you not tell me what it is that frightens you so much about your father?'

'It is complicated,' she responded, alarm flaring in her eyes.

Felix realized then that he had grossly underestimated the extent of her fear. Her voice trembled, her hands were unsteady and, if she could have taken flight and run from him, Felix did not doubt that she would have done so.

'We have plenty of time and there is no one here to overhear us,' he assured her, waving his arm in a circle to emphasize their solitude. 'But if you would prefer me to return you to Riverside House, if I am alarming you in any way, you need only say the word.'

Felix waited, knowing better than to try further persuasion. After what seemed like an eternity she started to speak in a low emotionless voice.

'My mother died when I was fifteen. I loved her very much, and so did my father. We were all devastated by her untimely demise but, of course, life had to go on. But my father changed after her death. He had always been a strict disciplinarian but without her restraining influence his desire to dominate and control everything and everyone was free to run riot, for there was no one else who would dare to try to reason with him. I confess that I was a little scared of him even then, although I always fared better than my two brothers, whom he would routinely beat when they were boys, at the slightest provocation.

'Anyway, about a year after my mother's death, when I was sixteen, my father informed me that he wished me to marry.'

'And you had no say in the matter?'

'Heavens, no! That was how it had been for my brothers and I had always known it would be the same for me. He would want me to marry someone who could be of assistance to him in some way, I knew that. Mr Eden was twenty years older than I and owned a cutter which my father wanted to include in his fleet. I was the bargaining point in their negotiations,' she said calmly, 'and I knew there was nothing I could do about it.'

'But did you like Eden? Was he kind to you?'

'Not really to both of your questions, but fortunately I saw little of him. He was at sea for much of the time and six months after we were married his ship foundered and was lost with all hands, including its captain.'

'I am sorry,' said Felix, not knowing what else to say.

'There is no need to be. He was a brute of a man. I was but sixteen, Mr Beaumont, and completely innocent. But he spared no thought for that and forced himself upon me every night when he was at home.'

Saskia was silent for a moment, relieving those dreadful days: days when he would enter her room night after night, his breath smelling of stale tobacco and port. He would leer at her and, without any pretence at tenderness, bluntly order her to do her duty. She shuddered with distaste. God, how she hated the very sound of those words! She remembered how she felt as she lay there trembling and praying that, just for once, he would not come that night. He always did so eventually but sometimes only after she dared to allow a glimmer of hope to surface: to imagine that he might be intoxicated, or embroiled in a game of cards with her father. It was almost as if he had understood her fear and fed upon it; enjoying the power he wielded over her; emphasizing his total domination of every aspect of her life.

'I knew nothing of what to expect from the marriage bed,' she continued in a bland tone, 'and my husband made no effort to teach me. He simply brutally took his pleasure, hurting me so much that sometimes I could not prevent myself from crying out. That seemed only to encourage him, however, and I soon learned to bite my tongue and suffer in silence. It lasted for less time that way.' She stopped speaking and looked at Felix for the first time, unshed tears shining in her eyes.

'Oh, Saskia!'

Powerless to prevent himself he slipped his arm around her shoulders and pulled her towards him. She was crying gently now, moved to tears by his compassion. Felix said nothing and simply allowed her to give vent to the emotion that had lain dormant for far too long.

When at last her tears were exhausted he silently passed her his handkerchief and watched as she mopped her face. He kissed the top of her head, causing her to look up at him, a mixture of fear and curiosity in her expression. Her body trembled.

'You are cold, m'dear,' said Felix, removing his coat and placing it about her shoulders.

'No, I am fine!' She offered him a watery smile. 'It is just that I have never told anyone about my husband before and was wondering why I should choose this moment to speak of it. More to the point, why I should choose to tell you? After all, I hardly know you and it is not a fitting subject for a lady to discuss with anyone, much less a stranger.'

'Sometimes it helps to talk about matters to someone who is unlikely to be falsely judgemental. But tell me how you felt when you knew your husband was gone forever.'

'Relieved, may God forgive me.' She looked him squarely in the eye. 'It is an unChristian reaction, of that I am well aware, but it is no more than the truth, for all that. The only thing he ever gave me that I cannot regret is the twins.'

'Ah yes, the twins!' He smiled at her. 'They are indeed a blessing.'

'You like my children, I think.'

'Indeed I do, they are engaging company and I cannot imagine anyone finding a reason to dislike them.'

'Mr Fothergill would likely disagree with you.'

'Fothergill is an idiot!'

'Well, I do not know about that, but I do know the twins are quite besotted with you and it irritates Mr Fothergill excessively.'

'Good! But what of their mother?' he asked her flirtatiously. 'Dare I hope that she is just a little besotted too?' He shifted his position, pulled her a little closer to him, tilted her chin upwards and placed a very delicate kiss on her lips. She made no objection, neither responding nor drawing away. Encouraged by her passiveness he kissed her again, a little more firmly this time, probing a question with his tongue. He was rewarded with a gentle sigh as she leaned a little closer, but it was clear that she did not have any notion of how to go on. She had spoken the truth when she claimed that her husband had not concerned himself with the trifling business of educating her in the ways of intimacy.

Felix was glad, imagining the pleasures in store for him if he chose to teach her himself. Her innocence appealed to him, arousing him yet making him sensible as to her vulnerable state. He had never felt the need to possess anyone more urgently: desire streaked unchecked through his body and he knew he was closer then he had ever been before to losing control.

But Felix also knew that this was neither the time nor the place. He broke the kiss, whilst he was still in command of his faculties, and put her gently away from him.

'I am sorry, Saskia, if you consider that I have taken liberties. It was not my intention.'

'There is no necessity for apologies, sir.' She spoke in a voice rendered hazy with passion.

'Address me as Felix, if you will,' he invited.

She smiled at him. His arm was still draped loosely around her shoulders and, returning her smile with an intimate one of his own, he asked her the question which was uppermost in his mind.

'Will you tell me what happened to make you estranged from your father?'

'I cannot!'

'Why?'

'Because I have never told anyone: not even my aunt. Because it is shocking, terrible and I would prefer to forget all about it.'

'But you cannot forget it, can you? Not when you are living so close to him and he is doing everything he can to ruin you and your aunt. If you were to trust me, to confide in me, then if nothing else it would at least make you feel better, I can promise you that much. But it may also put me in a position to be of service to you. But I cannot know that unless you choose to tell me it all.'

Felix had said all he could upon the subject and fell silent. After several minutes Saskia slowly nodded her head.

'Very well,' she said softly. 'I am not convinced that it will do any good but I will tell you anyway.' She drew a deep breath and began her narrative.

'After my husband died I soon realized my condition and was glad that I would have a child of my own to love, even if Eden was its father. It was during that time I first noticed a deterioration in my father's behaviour. I am afraid to say that he was adding debauchery to his growing list of unsavoury habits. He started taking . . . well, liberties, with some of the housemaids. One did not appear to mind but the other was quite distraught. She could not tell me what ailed her, of course, but I guessed. I tried to reassure her, and felt dreadfully sorry for her, but in actuality could do little to help. I could scarce confront my father, and the girl could not risk telling me the truth, in case she was discharged without a character.'

'It does sometimes happen, Saskia,' said Felix quietly.

'Yes, I suppose so. But you have yet to hear the worst of it.' She drew another fortifying breath but her next words were a long time in coming.

'Go on,' he prompted.

'I have two brothers Mr Beaumont, er . . . Felix.' The sound of his name falling from her lips aroused Felix and only by exercising the severest self-control did he resist taking her in his arms and kissing away her concerns. 'My brother, Gerald, contracted scarlet fever when he was young and we feared that he might die. Happily he survived but it left him permanently debilitated. He is small in stature and has little physical strength. But what he lacks in brawn is more than compensated for by his agile brain. He keeps my father's paperwork in order and is exceedingly efficient.'

'You are fond of Gerald?'

'Oh yes! He is five years older than I but we have always been close. He is married to Henrietta. She is the youngest daughter of a shipping magnate whom my father was keen to cultivate. She is perfect for Gerald and they are very happy together, in spite of my father's constant interference in their affairs. Henrietta is an expert botanist. She can tell you anything you wish to know about the flora and fauna hereabouts. She is a gentle and steadying influence in my father's household. Gerald and Henrietta had one daughter before I left home and have since then have been blessed with another. I regret though that I have never seen the new baby.'

'Your brother does not visit you at Riverside House?'

'Henrietta used to at first: until my father forbade it.'

'I see.' Felix did see and did not care for the view one little bit. 'But what of your older brother?'

Saskia's expression darkened. 'Charles is ten years my senior. He has little intellect and is, to boot, both a gamester and imbiber. He has all of the physical strength which Gerald lacks and will, when my father is gone, follow seamlessly in his wake. I do not, as you must by now have surmised, like my elder brother.

'The only person Charles will defer to is my father. Charles is married to Elsbeth, the daughter of a prominent squire in Weymouth. Unlike gentle Henrietta, Elsbeth is both beautiful and an impossible flirt. I do not like her either! When my mother died Charles and Elsbeth had been married for five years but the union had been childless, which I knew was a great disappointment to them, as well as to my father. He wanted his elder son to produce a son and heir of his own, you see.

'Anyway, one day I chanced to walk past Charles and Elsbeth's room in the middle of the afternoon. The sounds I could hear from within could only be interpreted in one way. I thought it strange, knowing that Charles was away on business for my father, but assumed he must have returned that afternoon. I was soon to find out my mistake,' she added, after a pause, 'since the door opened and my father came out of the room.'

'Ah, I see. So your father was making free with his son's wife then?'

'Yes, and much as I disliked Elsbeth I own I felt a moment's sympathy for her plight, since once my father sets his mind to something, few people have the courage to stand up to him. I thought he had forced himself upon her.' Saskia sighed. 'But I soon discovered just how wrong I was. She followed him to the door, threw her arms around his neck and begged him not to leave her.'

'Dear God!'

'Yes.' Saskia recalled the scene as clearly as if it were yesterday and shuddered with distaste. 'My father chuckled, grabbed at Elsbeth's body in the crudest fashion imaginable and told her she now knew what it felt like to have been bedded by a real man. Elsbeth still clung to him and my father pulled her into his own chamber, where he claimed there was less chance of their being discovered.

'I can only assume that their liaison continued for Elsbeth's whole attitude changed after that. She knew me to be my father's favourite and we had, until that time, maintained a polite charade of friendliness, even though we did not like one another. But after I witnessed that scene, Elsbeth kept chipping away at my role as my father's housekeeper, countermanding orders I gave to the servants and grasping every opportunity to undermine my authority. And she was becoming increasingly familiar with my father in public as well, pushing herself forward to the point where it became embarrassing. My brother was powerless to do anything about it and took comfort instead from the bottle. It was altogether a degrading spectacle, disgusting to watch.

'A few months after I suspect she and my father first became intimate, Elsbeth jubilantly announced her condition. She has given birth to three daughters over the past six years, two of whom did not survive, and all of whom I suspect are my father's progeny.'

'It must have been torture for you to have to live with such an awful secret and have no one in whom you could confide your fears.' Felix pulled her a little closer and smiled his sympathy. 'I suspect, however, that it is not why you left your father's house.'

'No indeed. I was still my father's favourite and that infuriated Elsbeth; I could see that much, for no matter what she did she could never see in my father's eye one-tenth of the love for her that he entertained for me. And when I gave birth to the twins, giving my father his first much-wanted grandson in the process, I thought she would go demented with jealousy.'

'What happened then?'

'My father used to come to my chamber every evening after dinner and talk to me. I was most embarrassed, as you can imagine. After all, it hardly seemed an appropriate location for a conversation, but I did not dare ask him to leave. I was not even sure if I was being too modest, for I had no way of knowing if his behaviour was any way out of the ordinary. I had never seen him more relaxed than at those times: he was almost the way he had been when my mother was alive. He would talk to me about her; about how much he missed her still and how proud she would have been of me and the twins. He was full of plans for their futures, especially Josh's, and I had never known him to speak with such compassion before.

'When the twins were three months old, my father came to my room as usual, but on that particular night he went on endlessly about how attractive I had become, how motherhood suited me, and what an asset I could be to him. Then he said he had a Mr Benson coming to dinner the following evening, who could be very helpful to him, and that I was to wear a new gown he had just bought me and be pleasant to the man. I thought it to be rather improper, since I was still supposedly in mourning for my husband, but did not dare to refuse.

'Mr Benson must have been sixty if he was a day. He was a small, wizened man who never stopped leering at me the whole evening. He made outrageously suggestive remarks but my father simply laughed at them and did not once rebuke him. Even Elsbeth's overt flirting did not seem to register with Mr Benson and it was obvious from the first that he was enamoured of me.' Saskia faltered and fell silent.

'Go on,' prompted Felix gently.

'That night, when my father came to my room, he said he was very pleased with the way I had behaved at dinner and told me I was to be married again. To Mr Benson.'

'Good God!'

'That was precisely my reaction. If Eden had been bad enough he was nothing compared to Benson. Well, something snapped within me at that moment. I was not prepared to be used in that manner a second time and said that I would not do it. I can still see the surprised look on my father's face. No one had ever dared to defy him before and he appeared momentarily nonplussed. But unfortunately for me that was only a temporary condition. He attempted to reason with me, telling me that Benson was exceedingly rich and well connected in the maritime business; that I would want for nothing. But still I refused.

'Well, then he got angry. I have never seen him half so mad before: at least not with me. He told me there was no place in his household for undutiful children. I tried to make him understand how I felt but my continued disobedience just seemed to fuel his anger. He grabbed hold of me, put me across his knee, tore away my under-garments and beat me with his leather belt until I bled.'

'Saskia, m'dear, whatever did you do?'

Saskia's gaze was fastened on the horizon and she displayed no emotion as she relived the shame and humiliation of the moment. 'Then he told me it was my fault, I only had myself to blame. I should know better than to go against his wishes and to flaunt myself in front of him. He said he had promised me to Benson, I would marry him and that was the end of the matter. And if I still refused, the same thing, or worse, would happen to me every night until I came to my senses and remembered where my duty lay. I understood then what he meant. I suspected what had occurred between him and some of the maids, and knew for a certainty that he and Elsbeth enjoyed an intimate relationship. I could also see how much beating me had excited him.' She looked up at Felix through eyes rimmed with tears. 'I was not prepared to marry that old man, and was too scared to remain beneath my father's roof. . . .'

'And so you took the twins and walked to your aunt's house in the middle of a storm.'

'Yes. There was nothing else I could do. Something changed in me that night and I knew I would put up with anything rather than endure my father's abuse, or marriage to yet another horrible old man. My aunt simply took me in, nursed me back to health and has never once questioned me as to my motives.

'My father came after me as soon as he realized I was missing. He knew there was only one place I could go. But Aunt Serena kept him away from me until I was well enough to decide whether I wished to see him.'

'And did you see him?'

'Yes, but I kept him waiting for three weeks, apparently.'

'Good for you!'

'Well, I was not aware of the fact at that time for I was delirious with fever. Anyway, I had no desire to see him, but I knew he would not go away until he heard it from my own lips. He appeared subdued, ashamed of what he had done and fearful of my ensuing illness. But still, he did not believe for a moment that I would have the strength to continue defying him. When he realized that I really did not mean to go back to him he got angry and started the vendetta against my aunt and me that you have witnessed.'

'Poor Aunt Serena,' remarked Saskia fondly. 'When I think of what chaos I have caused in her life: what privations I have forced her to endure, what indignities, what inconvenience. But, you know, she has never once asked me for an explanation and never once suggested that I should return home.'

'She is a good woman and loves you and the twins very much, I think.'

'Indeed she is. But my father, as you have observed, continues to plague us and will stop at nothing to achieve his end. He has intimidated the locals so that almost no one dares to work for us, has cut off my aunt's stipend and generally does everything he can to force me to go back. He does not like to be bested and, as things stand, it looks increasingly likely that he will succeed. I know not how much more we can tolerate but, when I am tired and at my lowest ebb, the one thing which stops me admitting defeat is the thought of what might happen to Josh and Amy under that roof. My aunt and my father were as close as my twins are now when they were children but look what happened to them. I could not bear it if Josh were to be influenced by his grandfather and become like him, or if Amy's safety was threatened in any way. It is that thought alone that gives me strength to continue resisting him.'

'Has your father ever admitted he was wrong and apologized to you?'

'Not precisely, and no more would I expect him to. But when he saw me that time at Aunt Serena's there could be no doubting that he was shocked by my condition. He said then that when I returned home nothing more would be said of the matter and that I would not be required to marry Benson. That was as close to an apology as I have ever known him to come. But it was not enough for me. I will never go back to him! Somehow I will find a way to survive without him, no matter what I must do.' She gave a defiant tilt of her chin and fell silent.

Felix stood, pulled her to her feet and into his arms. His kiss was designed as a deliberately tender caress. When he met with no resistance he pulled her more firmly against him, continuing to offer her comfort, and she responded by resting her head on his shoulder and closing her eyes.

'Thank you, Saskia, for telling me. It cannot have been easy for you.'

She smiled at him. 'No, but do not forget that I am a mother and I discovered that night just what lengths a mother will go to in order to protect her children.' She moved slightly away from him and he could hear the smile in her voice. 'Anyway, talking about it at last has liberated me, I think, you were right about that. If anything, I am now more determined than ever to resist his ubiquitous clutches. I am reminded that he is, after all, only human and therefore fallible.'

'And we will overcome him, I promise you.'

'We? This is not your fight, Felix. I am not asking you for assistance.'

'Do you imagine, now that you have honoured me with this explanation, that I will allow you to fight him alone?'

She looked up into eyes rendered dark with passion but, unsure now as to his motives, said nothing more.

'Come, my dear. It is late and getting colder. I think I should return you to Riverside House before your aunt accuses me of abducting you.'

'Yes, indeed. But first, you have not yet told me why you took a room with us when you knew it to be too expensive.'

He kissed the end of her nose. 'I will tell you, I promise, but not until tomorrow.'

Suddenly, he was wary about revealing his true identity, as he knew in all honour he now must, as well as his original suspicions about her involvement in her father's schemes. Her opinion mattered to him now and he knew that however carefully he phrased his admittance, she would be angry and hurt by his assumptions as to her culpability. 'Tomorrow, after luncheon, what say you that you, the twins and I go for a drive? I will tell you it all then.'

'You make it sound very mysterious but yes, all right, it would be pleasant to take an outing with the children for once. I cannot be absent for too long though, I have many tasks to attend to.'

'Perhaps your fortunes are about to change and unexpected help will come your way?' suggested Felix innocently.

'I hardly expect that is likely. I gave up believing in miracles six years ago.'

Chapter Nine

SASKIA woke from her first good night's sleep in a twelve month, feeling as though a great burden had been lifted from her shoulders. Curled on her side in her narrow bed she hugged herself, relishing the warm glow that spread slowly through her body, as she recalled the events of the previous evening. She could scarce believe that she had spoken to a virtual stranger about that which she had never intended to reveal to a living soul. She waited for regret to overtake her but found instead that she was already benefiting from the feelings of relief that traditionally followed in the wake of troubles shared.

Felix would keep her confidence: that much she instinctively understood. Her opinion of him had undergone a marked change as well and she was now able to admit to a respect and admiration for his noble conduct, which even as recently as yesterday she would not for a moment have entertained. He had listened to her shocking revelations with no discernible evidence of disgust; tolerating her ensuing lachrymal state with composure and a surprising degree of empathy. The fact that she had slept so soundly, and felt so much more in command of herself today, only went to prove how right he had been to persuade her to be candid.

Feeling a surprising lack of fatigue, in spite of the lateness of the hour at which she had retired, Saskia washed and dressed quickly and prepared to face the day in a buoyant mood. Nothing of a material nature had changed, it was true, but she felt stronger now and invigorated by a fresh determination to keep her father at bay.

Saskia chuckled as she recalled the chaotic scene that had reigned in the drawing room when she and Felix returned home. Fothergill, in a state of righteous indignation, was attempting to rouse a perfectly calm Mrs Rivers to show some concern for her niece's welfare. About to enter the room, Felix had stayed her by placing his hand on her arm and, smiling at one another, they listened to Fothergill droning on.

'She disappeared from the ball, with Beaumont, before supper and no one has seen anything of her since then. Surely you comprehend my meaning, madam? I really think you should send word to her father's house that she is missing? After all, we cannot know what has become of her, and Beaumont is not at all to be trusted, in my opinion. I am rather surprised, Mrs Rivers, that you permitted the arrangement in the first instance.'

As Felix opened the door and ushered Saskia through it in front of him, they discovered that, predictably, Aunt Serena was having none of it and, living up to her name, continued to sit calmly in her chair beside the fire, refusing to be goaded into an action which she deemed entirely unnecessary.

'Ah there you are, my dears!' she exclaimed brightly, smiling at Saskia and Felix.

'Where have you been?' demanded Fothergill rudely.

'I beg your pardon?' Saskia used the tone she usually reserved for the twins, when they had been up to mischief. It had the desired affect upon Fothergill, causing him belatedly to remember his manners.

'Your pardon, my dear, but it is very late and you left the ball so suddenly,' he said, moderating his tone. 'We were all most concerned for your welfare.'

'And why would that be, I wonder, when you knew that Mrs Eden was in my care?' Felix had asked with becoming languor, causing Aunt Serena to chuckle with mirth.

'Well, I really do not see what else we could have thought? It is, after all, so late and. . . .'

He blanched under Felix's basilisk gaze and wisely refrained from sharing more of his cogitations with the company. Instead he cast a beseeching glance in the direction of his fellow guests, all of whom were still in the drawing room, delaying their retirement until they had witnessed for themselves the outcome of this diverting battle of wills. Not one of them spoke up on Fothergill's behalf.

'Well, no matter,' he said brightly. 'You are here safe and sound but I was most disappointed, my dear, not to have the opportunity to dance with you a second time.'

'You are predisposed then,' drawled Felix, who had arranged himself in an impossibly elegant pose against the mantelpiece, 'to imagine that Mrs Eden would have accepted you as a partner again?'

Aunt Serena had coughed loudly at that point and Saskia, glancing in Felix's direction, was the recipient of a curling smile and complicit wink.

Fothergill tried hard, by means of artfully disguised questions, to discover where Felix and Saskia had been for so long and at such a late hour, but at the end of fifteen minutes knew no more than he had at the first and was forced to retire unappeased.

After breakfast the next day, Saskia responded to a persistent knocking at the kitchen door and was confronted by a respectable-looking young couple, who claimed to have been directed to Riverside House after making enquiries for work at the Dove Inn. Saskia could hardly believe her luck! It appeared that Molly and Jed Peters had worked for some years as parlour maid and gardener respectively at a large house outside Weymouth. Unable to suppress their passion they had secretly married without their mistress's permission, causing her to throw them out without a character. They were therefore willing to work for not much more than their keep, if only they could remain together.

Saskia would have thought that the gods were finally smiling upon her, had not Felix made that casual remark last night about her staff problems perhaps being at an end. She knew somehow, as she tried not to show too much enthusiasm about engaging the young couple, that he was behind their sudden appearance and she was determined to know just what he thought he was about. He would have a lot of explaining to do when they took their drive that afternoon.

*

Felix drove his curricle to the front door, with the enthusiastic assistance of the twins, and helped Saskia into the seat. The twins piled in between them, with Hoskins sitting upon both of their laps at once. Again, Felix observed Fothergill's distraught features pressed against the drawing-room window, but even he could hardly object to such a harmless outing on a Sunday afternoon, with the twins present and the livery-yard groom once again up behind.

Felix drove for half an hour, singing songs with the twins, which they persuaded Saskia to join in with. Laughing together they finally pulled up at a pretty spot beside the river. Josh and Amy demanded that Felix play games with them. Saskia sat and watched, laughing, as her children tumbled all over him like excited puppies. Felix felt rather like an overgrown boy himself as he tussled with Josh and helped Amy to find ingenious places in which to hide from her brother and the groom.

Eventually Felix left the children flying their kite, with the aid of the groom, and flopped down next to Saskia, stretching himself out to his full length, one elbow propped on the grass for the purpose of supporting his head.

'Whew!' he exclaimed. 'I am getting too old for all this.'

'Nonsense, the children adore you and you are very good with them. You will make a fine father one of these days.'

'Perhaps.' Felix's tone was vague, discouraging further comment.

'Now then, sir, it is your turn for an explanation.'

'I know.' But Felix was uncharacteristically hesitant.

'What is wrong?'

'I do not want to tell you what I know I must for fear of oversetting you.'

'You are oversetting me already with all this mystery. Pray, just tell me. It surely cannot be a matter of any great import.'

Felix would have done anything to retain her trust for he knew now, with disheartening certainty, that what he was about to disclose would spoil the air of intimacy that was growing between them. There could be no avoiding the fact that he had deceived her: not only about his identity but also about his reason for being in Swyre, and that alone would be sufficient for Saskia to view his actions as duplicitous. But when she learned that he had initially suspected her of being in league with her father, Felix knew she would be furious and doubted that she would be able to forgive his perfidious behaviour.

Felix had spent a largely sleepless night trying to decide how much to reveal to her. Did she need to know it all? Could he devise a means to spare her feelings? But Saskia was looking at him now so expectantly, an inquisitive expression lighting her emerald eyes, that Felix knew she deserved the entire truth. Whatever the result might be upon their fledgling relationship he could not, in all conscience, honour her with anything less.

Sitting up and turning towards her, Felix took her hand in his. 'Saskia, what I have to tell you will be a surprise and, I suspect, is likely to overset you. All I ask is that you listen to everything I have to say before forming a judgement of me.'

'But of course!' But there was a wariness about her now. Felix suspected that she had been so often let down in the past that she was already steeling herself for unpleasantness.

'Firstly I must apologize for deceiving to you as to my identity. I am not Felix Beaumont—'

'What the—'

'My name is Felix Western.' He hesitated. 'Viscount Western.'

'Good God!' She was momentarily nonplussed. 'But, my lord, why pretend to be who you are not?'

'I thought we agreed you would call me Felix?'

'That was when I thought we were equals.'

He squeezed the hand which he still held in his. 'We will always be equals, Saskia, nothing has changed there. My father is Earl Western of the Western Shipping Line.'

'So this has been about my father all along! She snatched her hand out of his grasp. 'I should have known.'

'Why do you say that?'

'Ships,' she responded succinctly.

'Yes, ships. Permit me to explain.'

And he did. He related the whole of the conversation he and his father had had with Smithers, leaving nothing out. Saskia was aghast that her father could be implicated in anything quite so abhorrent but, interestingly, did not attempt to deny the possibility.

'I did not realize that he had sunk quite so low,' she mused, her expression reflective. 'But that still does not explain your residency in my aunt's house under an assumed name.'

'Yes, I know.' This was the part Felix was dreading the most. 'When Smithers told us of your abrupt departure from your father's house six years ago I jumped to a rather erroneous conclusion. You must understand, Saskia, that I did not know you at the time, but Smithers was adamant that you and your father had been very close so why would you leave him so precipitously? The only conclusion we could draw was that you were somehow in league with him.'

Saskia stood up, eyes blazing with anger, hurt and – hardest of all for Felix to bear – disappointment. 'How could you think such a thing of me?'

'Saskia, if it is any consolation to you, I had not been in Riverside House for one day before I realized that you were completely innocent of any duplicity. But you must see how it looked to us from the outside?'

'I see nothing, sir, but an arrogant assumption based solely upon a false premise.'

'You are right to be angry and I most humbly beg your pardon.'

'And I suppose all that last night, persuading me to tell you my innermost secrets relating to my father, was just your way of gaining further information.'

'No; I appreciate that you are seriously distressed but I must beg to you believe me when I assure you that that is not the case.'

'Please do not try to tell me what I should believe,' she retorted, her anger rising in direction proportion to her temper.

Felix was momentarily nonplussed. He had expected her to be angry, but nothing could have prepared him for the scale of her affront. 'I was already well aware by last night that you and your aunt have no involvement. Our evening together on the dunes was just what it seemed to be.' He looked into soulful green eyes, glittering with disillusionment and unshed tears, and would have done anything at that moment to restore the trust they had so recently shared. 'I wanted to be alone with you, Saskia,' was all he could think of to say.

'Now that I am aware of the extent of your mendacity I do not see how you can expect me to believe anything you say.'

'Because, once again, I offer you my word as a gentleman.'

Saskia's only response was a quelling glance. He could see that she knew he would not make such a vow lightly and dared to hope that she might find it in her heart to understand his motives. It was a forlorn hope though; he realized that as she turned the full force of her fury upon him.

'Thank you for the timely reminder,' she said to him, her voice dripping with sarcasm. 'You have just offered me reason a'plenty to never believe anything a gentleman says. You forced your way into our house, ingratiated yourself with my aunt. Heavens, you even cultivated a false friendship with my children in order to get close to me. And that,' she said, glowering at him with icy contempt, 'I will never be able to forgive.'

'Saskia, you know that is not so!' He placed his hands on her shoulders to prevent her from pacing angrily in front of him but she brushed them aside.

'Do I? How can I believe that? Just leave me alone. Do not presume to touch me, sir.' She swung away from him.

'Saskia, please listen to reason. You must believe that my regard for your children is entirely genuine as,' he added softly, looking directly into her now suspiciously moist eyes, 'is my regard for you. Were it not the case then what would I have to gain from revealing the truth to you: or continuing with this conversation?'

'Stop it, I do not wish to hear it.'

'I know.'

For the moment, Felix admitted defeat. His spirit was crushed and he had never disliked himself more. He looked into eyes that now flashed resentment and were full of wounded pride.

107

'I will take you back to Riverside House now and I will leave your establishment first thing in the morning. I will find another way to complete my business here.'

'As you wish.'

They drove back in silence and even the twins, presumably sensing the emotionally-charged atmosphere, were unusually subdued.

An hour before dinner Mrs Rivers sent word to Felix that she would like to see him in her private apartment. When he arrived he was not surprised to find Saskia there also.

'Ah, Mr Beaumont, or should I say, your lordship?'

Felix bowed to both ladies. 'You have my apologies for deceiving you, Mrs Rivers,' he said with transparent sincerity. 'I have already informed your niece that I will leave first thing in the morning but, if you wish to be rid of me before that, I dare say it can be arranged.'

'I knew you were not what you claimed to be!' crowed Mrs Rivers, as though he had not spoken. 'Those manners, that air about you. No matter! My niece has told me of your reason for being here. It saddens me more than you can possibly be expected to understand that my brother has sunk so low. I suppose there can be no doubt?'

'Unfortunately not.'

'I see. My niece has also told me what I believe she told you last night, as to her reasons for leaving my brother's house.'

Felix looked at Saskia in surprise but she would not meet his eye. He could see that she had been crying and was still upset. He felt like a first-rate churl.

'What will you do now, *Mister* Beaumont?'

'Find another way to put a stop to your brother.'

'But your original intention was to approach him through the good offices of my niece?'

'Yes. To my great shame I must own it. I was hoping she would introduce us, thereby making it easier for me to lure him into a trap. But no matter, I shall return to Western Hall tomorrow and confer with my father. We will devise some other method.'

'No!' Saskia spoke for the first time. Her voice sounded unnaturally brittle but she appeared more composed than hitherto and her determination was evident from the defiant tilt of her chin.

'What do you mean?'

'If you attempt to approach my father about such a delicate matter he will immediately be suspicious. He is far too wily to be taken in by such a ploy. The only way you can hope to get to him without attracting unnecessary attention is through me.'

'No, I will not hear of it. You have not spoken to him for six years. Why would you do so now without arousing his suspicions as to *your* motives?'

She still would not look at him. 'He will know all about you; especially since the ball yesterday. He probably even knows about our little sojourn on the dunes last night,' she added contemptuously.

'Maybe so, but I do not think—'

'I will call upon him, displaying a suitable amount of contrition for my past behaviour, naturally, and admit there is a guest in this house for whom I have developed a *tendresse*.' She spoke the word as though it was contaminated with the plague. 'I will say that this gentleman has requested an introduction to him, with a view to discussing some business matter, the details of which I am naturally not a party to. I believe he will be so pleased that I have gone to see him that he will grant my request without recourse to his habitual caution.'

Felix sat beside her and took her hand, mindless of the sudden interest that Mrs Rivers took in the gesture. 'No, Saskia, I will not permit it. It is too dangerous and, besides, it would be too humiliating for you to go crawling back to him after everything he has forced you to endure.'

'I have no intention of crawling, my lord,' she countered, snatching her hand away from him, 'or of humiliating myself either. But talking about what happened has made me realize that I must stand up to him if I am ever to be free of his tyranny. I am doing this for my sake as much as that of law and order.'

'No, no, there must be another way.'

'If Saskia feels so strongly then I think she should be permitted to have her way,' said Mrs Rivers decisively. 'Whatever else he does, my brother will never harm her.' Saskia and Felix, who were glaring at one another with widely differing feelings, had forgotten her presence and turned towards her in surprise.

'Why do you say that, ma'am? Surely he has harmed her enough already. I will not hide behind her.'

'It is not a question of hiding and it is, after all, a decision which I believe that only she is qualified to make. And surely, if she merely affects an introduction there can be no danger in it for her?'

Felix stood and paced the room. 'I still do not like it.'

'It is not your decision.'

'So you have already said, but still I—'

'My mind is made up upon the matter.' Saskia tossed her head and Felix, already starting to recognize the gesture, reluctantly accepted that he was beaten.

'All right!' He threw his hands up in surrender. 'But we must proceed with extreme caution. And it is not safe to speak openly in this house. You realize, of course, that Fothergill is in your father's employ?'

'What!' cried Saskia and her aunt simultaneously.

'There can be no doubt, I am afraid. I was immediately suspicious of him and not just because I did not like him.' Felix was rewarded with a flicker of a smile from Saskia. 'But I did consider it to be something of a coincidence, a teacher conveniently seeking accommodation so soon after you took in guests; and coincidences always make me suspicious. Why would an impecunious teacher seek lodgings at such a superior establishment unless he knew he was about to find a way of working off the cost? And besides, a teacher who favours your father's strict ideas of discipline would be an ideal choice for his grandchildren, surely? If you still doubt my opinion, consider his expensive habit which requires his presence in the Swayle Inn every day: a most convenient location to meet your father's representatives and pass on any information he may have gleaned, do you not think?' The ladies shared a horrified glance. 'There can be no doubt about it, I fear.'

'I can see it all now,' said Mrs Rivers bitterly. 'What fools we have been, Saskia, to allow ourselves to be thus taken in. That is how Samuel always knew when to put on more pressure. He knows when we are at our most vulnerable and therefore when to prevent the servants from coming to work . . .' Her words trailed off and she fell into gloomy contemplation at this latest evidence of her brother's deviousness.

'To think,' said Saskia slowly, 'that all along I have been playing into his hands and allowing my children to be educated to his order.' She was so angry that when she picked up an ornament and weighed it absently in her hand Felix was concerned that she might actually hurl it through the window, or at him. He gently removed it from her grasp.

'Indeed! My valet, Perkins, is established at the Dove Inn, attempting to infiltrate your father's organization. I sent him to the Swayle Inn today and he reported that Fothergill had a long conversation with your father's steward; the one we saw at the ball last night.'

'When do you want me to go and see my father?' asked Saskia, with stoic determination.

'We must consult with Perkins first.' Felix looked towards Mrs Rivers for permission and then rang the bell. Molly answered it with alacrity.

'Ah, Molly!'

'Sir?' She looked confused.

'It is all right, Molly, these ladies now know who I am. But have a care, for no one else in the house does, and neither must they.'

'Very good, my lord.' She curtsied to him and awaited his instructions. Felix saw Mrs Rivers and Saskia exchange a significant glance. Now that they had observed one of his servants, treating him with a deference that he accepted as a matter of course, it seemed the enormity of his true identity was at last taking a hold. For the first time since entering the room he could sense a slight lessening in Saskia's hostility towards him.

'Get word to Perkins, Molly. Have him come to the house at eleven this evening. You and Jed must let him in through the kitchen door

111

and get him up here.' He paused, looking to Mrs Rivers for her approbation, which she gave with a nod. 'Without being detected. Do you think you can do that?'

'Just leave it to us, my lord.'

'All right, Molly, thank you.'

'So we must thank you for the gift of our new servants as well, must we?' asked Mrs Rivers in a resigned tone. 'It was too much, I suppose, to imagine that fortune was smiling upon us, for a change.'

'They are on loan from Western Hall,' responded Felix smoothly. 'I trust you will not take offence. They really are respectably married and entirely discreet and dependable.' He turned towards Saskia, looked her straight in the eye and smiled at her in such a captivating manner that she could be left with little doubt as to his sincerity. 'I just could not bear the thought of you having to work so hard,' he said.

Chapter Ten

DINNER at Riverside House that evening was a fraught affair. Saskia was distracted: still outraged at the discovery that Fothergill had been educating her children according to her father's dictate and was having trouble looking at him with anything other that the vilest dislike. Perversely, Fothergill was being especially charming to her and, for once, his pompous and supercilious traits were nowhere in evidence.

Saskia did not once look in Felix's direction and, when addressed by him, answered concisely and with the minimum of civility. Felix knew that such treatment and was no more than he deserved but minded about it far more than he could have anticipated. His only consolation was that Molly served the meal with such efficient expertise as to leave Saskia with at least one less concern.

Shortly before eleven o'clock, Felix entered Mrs Rivers's private apartment and found the old lady there alone. She smiled and bade him sit beside her.

'Well, my lord,' she began brightly, 'I know not how you normally live your life but you have been in my house for not much more than a week and I can assure you, with absolute authority, that life has certainly not been dull during that time.'

'I am sorry to have wreaked so much havoc, Mrs Rivers. I would that it could have been otherwise.'

'That someone else could have informed me of my brother's iniquitous trade? Yes, I daresay you do, and I have tried to persuade Saskia to that point of view.' She sighed. 'I am sure she will come to see things that way eventually and I, at least, can appreciate that you had no alternative but to act in the way that you did. Give Saskia time and she will come round, especially as you did us the service of exposing Fothergill's hidden agenda.'

'For my own part I must accept that Saskia's opinion of me is, in her eyes, well-founded. I wonder though if I could prevail upon you to persuade her not to confront her father? I fear for her safety.'

'No, sir, I shall not attempt to dissuade her. She must do it, for her own sake. I am relieved that she has finally spoken about her reasons for leaving her father's house. I must confess to being shocked by what she had to say, shocked and deeply upset. I guessed, of course, when she arrived in such a state something of what had happened to her but still my mind was reluctant to acknowledge the awful truth.' Mrs Rivers paused to collect herself. 'That my brother could act in such a manner saddens me deeply.'

'It is unspeakable!' declared Felix, with passion. 'But—'

Mrs Rivers interrupted him without apology. 'My niece is fragile, Lord Western. She works as hard as she does partly of necessity and partly, I suspect, to keep her mind occupied and memories of her unhappy past buried beneath her fatigue. By forcing her to face up to those memories, and demonstrating just how closely her father still manipulates her, you have unwittingly destroyed her peace of mind. She must now do what she feels is right: for her own sake as well as that of the twins.'

'I can see that, of course, but—'

Mrs Rivers cut him off for the second time and looked him squarely in the eye. 'You must give me your assurance that you will never hurt her,' she said quietly. 'It would destroy her if you did.'

Felix did not pretend to misunderstand her and simply bowed in silent acquiescence.

Felix and Mrs Rivers spoke of general matters then, Mrs Rivers again lamenting the need for her niece to work so hard, thus presenting Felix with his opening.

'How has your brother managed to reduce your circumstances

thus, may I enquire, Mrs Rivers? I understood that you owned this house.'

'No sir. It is entailed to my late husband's brother, since we were not blessed with a son of our own. I have tenure for my lifetime only.'

'I see. But surely, ma'am, if you will pardon the indelicacy of my question, your late husband must have made financial provision for you?'

Mrs Rivers's smile was laced with irony. 'Indeed he did. But whom do you imagine is the executor of his will?'

'Your brother.'

'Precisely! And the attorney who looks after the matter is the only one in Burton Bradstock. I need hardly tell you who controls him.'

'But have you done nothing to try to restore the income which is rightfully yours?'

'Yes, I tried it once when Samuel first cut it off. But the attorney merely advised me that the payments have been made to my brother's account, in the accepted manner, and that I should take the matter up with him. The poor man is terrified of Samuel and I know that if I go to him, cap in hand – which is, of course, precisely what he is waiting for – then his price to restore what is rightfully mine will be the return of his daughter and grandchildren. I am not prepared to make that sacrifice.'

Felix, who already held Mrs Rivers in high regard, found his respect for her increasing ten-fold, and told her as much. She simply smiled at him, saying she had everything she could wish for in her life and was not about to give in to bullying. As Saskia herself chose that moment to join them, Felix was unable to offer his assistance in respect of the restoration of her income, which he felt assured, given his connections, could be easily managed. Instead he rose gracefully to his feet and made to assist Saskia with her chair but she moved to sit beside her aunt and studiously ignored him. Any embarrassing lull in the conversation, which this deliberate slight might have occasioned, was obviated by the timely arrival of Perkins.

'Ah, Perkins, there you are,' said Felix, glad of occupation and purpose at last.

'My lord.'

'Perkins, these ladies are Mrs Rivers and Mrs Eden.'

'Your servant, ladies.' Perkins's bow was almost as elegant as his master's, causing Mrs Rivers to let forth with an amused chuckle.

'You look as though you are set for dirty deeds,' remarked Felix, casting an amused eye over Perkins's attire, which was of workman-like quality and almost entirely black.

'I am to be at Burton Bradstock beach by midnight, my lord. One Jeremiah Gladstone requires my assistance this evening with the unloading of certain "commodities",' declared Perkins, with a cheerful grin. 'It seems my services on their behalf last night passed muster and they have asked for me again this evening.'

'Gladstone is one of my father's men,' remarked Saskia. 'He is second only to Johnson.'

'Indeed, ma'am.'

'I am glad you have infiltrated yourself so readily, Perkins.'

'Ah well, you know me, m'lord, always ready to lend a willing hand.'

Perkins was incorrigible and even Saskia could not prevent herself from smiling at his indefatigable attitude.

'Just have a care, Perkins,' warned Felix. 'This is not a game.'

'Certainly not, my lord.' Perkins adopted an injured expression. 'But since Captain Smithers has declared immunity in the event that I am captured, I have naught to fear.'

'Except the wrath of my brother's men if they discover who you are.'

'Quite so, ma'am.' But Perkins was clearly not deterred by this thought.

'Now,' said Felix, taking control again, 'what have you been able to ascertain with regard to incoming slaves?'

'They're a bit reluctant to say much in front of me, but after we finished unloading last night and were sampling an anker or two of the booty, if you understand my meaning, ladies, they loosened up a bit. Seems Barker is getting a bit cocky and I gather a cutter is expected imminently, containing more of the poor so-and-so's than they have

116

ever dared to bring in at one time before.'

'Do you know when and where, Perkins?'

'No, milord, but what I do know is that they do not have customers for all of them.'

'Excellent, our timing could not be better! Saskia,' he continued, looking significantly in her direction, 'the sooner we can approach your father, the better it will be.'

'I am more than ready to play my part.' She regarded him steadily, but her expression was guarded, her true feelings impossible for him to interpret.

'Are you still determined?' He spoke in a whisper, frantically willing her to demur.

'Yes!'

Felix sighed in defeat. 'Very well! Perkins, I had best send word to warn the earl.'

'Oh heavens, my lord, I almost forgot.'

Withdrawing a letter from inside his singlet he handed it to Felix who, recognizing the handwriting of his friend, Luc Deverill, tore it open and began to read.

'I asked Luc to look into Fothergill's background at the school he taught at in Northumberland,' he explained to the ladies as he continued to read. 'Good lord! Luc and Clarissa are on their way south and plan to stop in Weymouth tomorrow, at the Grand Hotel. He will impart his news to me there.'

'Does that mean you will be in a position to wear a decent coat again, m'lord?' enquired the irrepressible Perkins.

'Since I am still supposed to be Mr Beaumont, obviously not.'

'Ah well, that one will give Lord Deverill a right laugh.'

'Remember yourself, Perkins. And had you better not get going?'

Perkins bowed to the ladies and left the room as silently as he had entered it.

'Sorry about Perkins, ladies, he is something of a law unto himself, but an excellent valet and so I make allowances. Now then, Saskia, will you accompany me to Weymouth tomorrow?' She looked up in surprise. 'We must purchase you a new travelling gown.'

She raised a disdainful brow in his direction. 'So, am I to deduce that my clothing fails to meets your exacting requirements, along with everything else about me?'

'Saskia, you could go to your father's house dressed in rags and it would not change my opinion of you. But I think it best that you approach the forthcoming interview from a position of strength. He will expect you to be downtrodden and beaten. Appear before him in smart and fashionable attire, with head held high and dignity intact, and it will give him pause for thought. After all, he will already have received intelligence of your attending the ball in a lovely new gown. Appear before him in another and he will wonder if his tactics to wear you down have been working aright.'

Saskia wished to argue with him but could, annoyingly, appreciate his logic and satisfied herself with a succinct, 'Very well!' She was too preoccupied to notice the complicit glance which Felix and Mrs Rivers shared.

'And after visiting the modiste I will take you to meet my friends in the Grand Hotel.'

'I cannot be away from the house for that long.'

'Yes, you can: Molly and Jed, remember?'

'Very well,' she said irascibly for the second time and, leaning to give her aunt a gentle kiss, she left the room without further acknowledgement of his presence.

When Saskia and Felix left the modiste's in Weymouth the following morning she was attired in a new, pale-blue velvet travelling gown; complemented by a matching bonnet and gloves. Felix was carrying two further packages containing a turquoise evening gown in the finest muslin and a day-dress in Bengal stripes of green and cream. Saskia was unsure quite how she finished up adding to her wardrobe in such an extravagant manner but knew it must all be Felix's fault. He took over as soon as they entered the establishment, charmed the modiste and her assistant with his *laissez-faire* attitude, and persuaded Saskia to try several outfits: just in case.

He declared the three he chose to be indispensable. When she quibbled about the ruinous cost he reminded her of their purpose and said that if, at the end of it all, monies due from her late husband's estate were not restored to her then doubtless the Revenue would be glad to take on her expenses, in view of the pivotal role she would play in bringing her father to justice. He was so charmingly and elegantly persuasive, dominating the tiny establishment with his commanding presence, that she found it difficult to concentrate upon formulating a riposte. And when she appeared before him arrayed in his different choices his eyes softened in that now familiar way of his and an appreciative – albeit shockingly inappropriate – smile crept across his features, making it suddenly seem unimportant who was paying for the garments, or why she even needed them. Felix approved; it felt wonderful to wear something new and fashionable for a change and she would worry about the propriety of allowing a comparative stranger to bear the cost of it all at some other time.

Now that Saskia had had time to digest all that Felix had revealed to her, and had calmed down a little, she reluctantly conceded that in his position she would most likely have drawn the same conclusion. She knew he spoke the truth when he swore that he had absolved her of any involvement within one day. She had angrily accused him of cultivating a friendship with the twins, in order to further his nefarious plans. She knew that accusation had hurt him, it had shown in his eyes, and at the time she had been glad to reap this petty revenge. But she knew now that her accusation had been unfounded.

Saskia understood the true reason for her anger with Felix and was honest enough to admit it, at least to herself. Felix had awakened something in her that evening on the dunes, something that had lain dormant all her life; of the existence of which she had lived in blissful ignorance. It had only taken the brush of his lips against hers though to set her heart racing and bring her alive in ways she had never before realized were possible.

Now that she knew who he was though – what an exalted position he occupied and what high expectations there must be for his future – it was blindingly obvious that she could be nothing to him. This realization hurt far more than she cared to admit. Females everywhere doubtless sighed over him: he must be accustomed to such behaviour. Saskia, understanding the hopelessness of her situation, vowed not to let her partiality show and covered her hurt with a show of mild indifference.

Entering the Grand Hotel a short time later, Saskia was relieved that Felix had persuaded her to wear her new travelling gown. The ridiculous feather in the bonnet covered half her face and, hiding behind it, she felt reassuringly equal to her elegant surroundings. To begin with she found confidence in the admiring glances she saw directed her way but by the time they reached the door to the earl's suite her courage again faltered. Felix, comprehending her fears, smiled his reassurance in such an intimate manner as to give her fresh heart; at the same time it reduced her insides to mush.

The door was opened by a maid and Saskia found herself in an elegantly furnished sitting room.

'Luc!'

Felix crossed the room in two strides and embraced a gentleman even taller than himself: one who was at least as handsome as Felix and equally self-assured.

'Good God, Felix!' returned Luc. 'What in the name of Hades are you wearing?'

Saskia smiled briefly. Up until now Felix had been the best-dressed gentleman she had ever encountered, and she had wondered what Perkins could have meant by his jibe the evening before. Now she understood! Compared to Lord Deverill's attire, Felix looked third rate. Saskia's smile faded abruptly as she comprehended the truth. What she had previously considered to be a gap between their respective status now appeared more as an unbridgeable chasm.

'Ah, Clarissa!' A tall lady of exceptional beauty, dressed simply in pink sprigged muslin, stepped forward to embrace Felix.

As one the tableau turned to look at Saskia. Felix moved back to her side and placed her hand on his sleeve.

'The Earl and Countess of Newbury, may I present Mrs Eden.'

Saskia curtsied to them and watched the earl's eyebrows disappear in what she supposed must be surprise and, she was gratified to realize, a degree of appreciation as well. Casting a curious glance at Felix, Luc raised her from her curtsy, took both of her hands in his and assured her that he was charmed to make her acquaintance.

'Mrs Eden,' said the countess, stepping up in her turn, 'how delightful! Do come and sit over here with me by the fire.'

Saskia was fussed over by Luc and Clarissa, who succeeded in putting her at ease without appearing to try. Felix had told her that they were charming people, who did not give themselves airs and had, ever intuitive, hinted that Clarissa's background was as ordinary as her own. Saskia had not, until now, believed him.

When they were all seated, Felix asked Luc what brought them to Weymouth.

'Your mother.'

'My mother?'

'Yes, the unseasonably warm weather persuaded many families to leave the *ton* early, your mother amongst them. It seems she is anxious to win the race to be the first hostess to hold a summer house party. We received our invitation about the same time as I received your letter. Your mother is most insistent that we attend,' continued Luc amiably, but Felix knew him too well to take his words at face value. Felix's mother had always been less than enthusiastic about his friendship with Luc. The fact that she so ardently sought his company now could only mean that she hoped Luc's attendance at her party would ensure that Felix was also there: for Maria Denby's benefit, no doubt.

Felix sighed. 'I see.'

'Thought you would,' responded Luc cheerfully.

'But that still does not explain the detour to Weymouth. Bit out of your way I would have thought.'

'Indeed it is, but how could I resist when I received such a mysterious request from you, asking me to look into the background of a country schoolmaster. And,' added Luc, his black eyes alight with interest as they regarded Saskia, 'I can see now that I was right. Now, come on, Felix, out with it, what are you up to that requires you to dress so appallingly? Not,' he added with amusement and a wickedly suggestive smile in Saskia's direction, 'that the involvement of a beautiful lady surprises me.'

'Oh, ignore them, Mrs Eden!' exclaimed Clarissa, glaring at her husband. 'These two are always the same when they are in one another's company.'

Saskia could not prevent herself from blushing beneath the force of Luc's extravagant compliment. The predatory look in his eye reminded her of her aunt's words on the subject of Luc and Felix the previous evening. An avid reader of the social columns, she was able to inform her niece that before Luc's marriage he and Felix were renowned within the *ton* for their escapades. Many a matron had long since given up hope of securing either of them for their daughters and it was only when Luc fell captive to the beguiling Clarissa that they began to entertain hopes that Felix would follow suit. Saskia could already tell from their ease with one another – not to mention the impressively handsome figure they cut – that the stories were very likely true. It served to remind her also that any hopes she herself might briefly have entertained in respect of Felix were unrealistic. It was a timely reminder and she vowed anew that she would come out of it all with her dignity intact and her true feelings under close guard.

Felix had told Luc nothing of his reasons for being in the area in his correspondence but did so now, omitting all mention of Saskia's reason for leaving her father's house.

'Oh, my poor Mrs Eden!' exclaimed Clarissa, clutching Saskia's hand. 'Do please assure me that Felix did not actually believe you capable of involvement in such a despicable business?'

'Not once I had met her I did not,' declared Felix, looking distinctly uncomfortable.

'Huh, nevertheless! Have you forgiven him yet, Mrs Eden?'

'I have not yet decided.'

'I should think not. Felix, how could you?'

Felix smiled engagingly at Clarissa but it appeared to cut no ice with her and Saskia wondered if one became immune to such charm when exposed to it on a continual basis.

'That does not explain the schoolteacher,' Luc reminded Felix.

Felix explained about the twins and Fothergill's residence at Riverside House.

'Hm, well his cruelty does not surprise me,' said Luc. 'He was dismissed from his previous post for excessive use of the cane and for drunkenness. He will never get another position at a decent establishment.'

Saskia's face turned ashen. 'Whatever have I exposed my poor children to?' she cried.

Felix covered her hand with his, suppressing the overwhelming urge to do more. 'One way or another you will soon be rid of him.'

'What action shall you now take, Felix?' asked Luc.

'Saskia will call upon her father tomorrow with my request for an introduction.'

'Are you sure you would wish to do that?' asked Clarissa, concerned.

'Perfectly! And it will not be tomorrow. I dislike procrastination. We shall return to Riverside House for luncheon and then, this afternoon, I will make the call.'

'Saskia!' Felix appeared genuinely alarmed by her precipitous intentions, a fact which did not escape either of his friends and which caused Clarissa to smile with delight.

'No, sir, my mind is made up.'

Felix sighed. 'Then in that case I shall drive you there.'

'There is no need.'

'Could you possibly imagine that I would allow you to go alone?'

Felix stood up and faced the other three, engineering an adroit change of subject, which ensured that the final word on the matter was his. 'Is Rosie with you?' he asked.

'Indeed she is,' responded Clarissa smiling.

'Then may I ask a favour of you, Luc?'

'Naturally.'

'When you depart for Western Hall tomorrow could I prevail upon you to take Saskia and the twins with you?'

'What? Hold on a moment!' Saskia leapt from her seat. 'What are you suggesting?'

'Saskia, listen to me.' He guided her to the other side of the room. 'Once I have set the ball in motion then nothing can stop the ensuing events. Your father,' he continued gently, 'will be desperate. He is unlikely to harm you when you simply call upon him and request that he sees me, but when he knows he has been exposed for the villain he is and that he can . . .' Felix hesitated. 'Well, that in all probability he can only look forward to a long gaol sentence at the very least, to say nothing of social ruin and public disgrace, he will use any weapon at his disposal to avoid that fate. A desperate man will do anything, Saskia, even use his own daughter and grandchildren to hide behind, if necessary.'

'But, Felix, what—'

'No, listen to me, please,' he continued forcefully. 'Despite your poor opinion of me, I could not confront him if I thought my actions would endanger you or the twins in any way. And, if something goes wrong and he escapes me, he will know that you were a party to the scheme and, from what you have told me of his character, he does not strike me as to the sort who would allow such treachery to go unavenged.'

'Felix is right, Mrs Eden,' said Luc, who had obviously overheard their conversation, in spite of the fact that it had been conducted in an undertone. 'But, Felix, perhaps Simms could escort the ladies and children to Western Hall. Surely you would wish me to stay and stand with you?'

'No, Luc, your sudden appearance would only complicate matters and I suspect your identity would not remain a secret for long. After all, you are registered here openly and besides,' he added flippantly, casting an envious glance over Luc's superbly cut coat, 'you are not in possession of the correct attire to play the part convincingly.'

'*Touché* !' Luc grinned at his friend. 'Yes, all right, I take your point, Felix, and with her permission I will be honoured to escort Mrs Eden and her children to Western Hall.'

'Saskia?' Felix looked at her expectantly. She had not, as yet, agreed to the scheme.

'I am not sure.' Felix could see that she was distressed by the prospect.

'Think of the twins.'

That seemed to do it and with another slight hesitation she agreed.

'Just one thing,' remarked Luc casually to Felix. 'If this Fothergill is in the pay of Mrs Eden's father, and also teaches her children, surely he will report their disappearance to Barker immediately.'

'Yes, I had thought of that. But I will forestall him by telling Barker myself, as soon as I have met him and have agreed to do business with him, that my concern for Saskia and the twins prompted me to send them away during our negotiations. I will play the love-struck buffoon who does not wish to appear before his lady love in a bad light.'

'I daresay the role must come as second nature to you,' remarked Saskia acerbically, turning away from him to hide the hurt in her eyes: but not quickly enough. Felix knew at once that his flippant remark had upset her, but this was hardly the time or place to try and put matters right.

'Is there anywhere that you and the children could reasonably be expected to travel to without exciting his curiosity?' he asked her quietly.

'You can inform my father that we have gone to Aunt Serena's late husband's sister in Norfolk. We have visited them on one previous occasion.'

'Perfect!'

'There is just one other matter, sir, of immediate concern. Will the earl and countess mind my descending upon them uninvited with two boisterous children in tow?' Saskia asked, in a deliberately casual manner.

'You are not uninvited, Saskia,' responded Felix, his voice a velvet caress as he forgot for a moment that they were not alone. '*I* have invited you and my father will be delighted to see you.'

'I see.' If Saskia noticed the omission of his mother's likely delight she made no mention of the fact.

'Good,' said Luc. 'At least one matter has been decided. Now then I—'

A door to an adjoining room opened and a little girl of about Amy's age entered, a large black shaggy mongrel limping at her heels. 'Papa, I . . .' She stopped as her eyes rested upon Felix. 'Uncle Felix!' All decorum deserting her, the child flew across the room and into his outstretched arms.

'Hello, sweetheart,' said Felix, swinging her round.

Saskia observed Felix as he placed Rosie back on the floor and, with lithe grace, crouched down to talk to her as naturally as he did to the twins, focusing all his attention on what she had to say to him.

Felix had warned her in advance that Rosie was an orphan from Whitechapel whom Luc and Clarissa had adopted. What she did not know was that he and Luc had founded that orphanage and still raised funds for its continuance. No more was she aware that Rosie had effectively saved Clarissa's life, thereby earning Luc's eternal gratitude and securing her own future into the bargain.

Chapter Eleven

LESS than half of his concentration on his horses, Felix constantly stole glances at his lovely companion as he drove her to Southview Manor that afternoon. Her face was devoid of all colour, but there was a steely glint of determination in her eye as she fought to maintain her equilibrium. Her rigidly erect posture lent proof to her resolve but she was unable to conceal the full extent of her nerves in so much as her hands were shaking. Felix covered them both with one of his own, attempting to infuse some of his own strength into her.

'Ready?' he asked, as they approached Southview Manor.

'Yes, I am prepared.'

'There is still time to change your mind. I wish that you would listen to reason and do so. I will find another way.'

'No!'

Halting the horses, Felix leant across and slid an arm around her shoulders. He tilted her chin with his index finger and looked directly into her eyes.

'You are without doubt the bravest lady I have ever met,' he told her, dropping his head and covering her lips with his own. He felt her stiffen, unwilling to meet his embrace at first, but Felix persevered, determined to elicit a response. Eventually her lips softened beneath his, her eyelids fluttered to a close and she returned his kiss with such tentative sweetness as to stir his blood and arouse his protective instincts to unheralded heights.

'I will be thinking of you every second of the time and shall return in an hour. If you do not appear immediately then I shall not hesitate to come in search of you. Smithers has several of his men secreted about the area. Just remember that you are not alone.'

'Yes, I do know it, and I take comfort from the fact.' She sighed and settled herself against his shoulder, luxuriating in the security it offered her for one precious moment, all antipathy towards him temporarily suspended. 'I shall go now before I lose my resolve.'

Felix alighted and assisted her to the ground. He kissed the hand which he held in his.

'God speed, m'dear.'

Saskia walked away from him and did not look back as she entered her father's driveway for the first time in six years. The maid who opened the door was unknown to her and politely asked Saskia her business.

'I am Mrs Eden. Is my father at home?'

The maid looked momentarily nonplussed, her eyes bulging with suppressed excitement as she consigned every last vestige of Saskia's appearance to her memory, the better to relate this stunning piece of news in the servants' hall later. 'I will enquire, ma'am. Would you care to wait in here?' She opened the door to the morning-room.

Saskia looked about a room that had not changed much in six years. It seemed strange to be here as a guest, though. She shivered, her nervousness increasing in direct proportion to the rapid beating of her heart. What if her father was not at home, or chose not to see her? They had not considered either of those possibilities.

Her fears were unfounded for the maid returned almost immediately and invited her to join her father in his study. As she entered, so her father rose slowly from behind his desk, regarding her in silence as she walked towards him, none of the hostility that had accompanied their last meeting apparent in his demeanour. She stopped several paces away from him and returned his gaze steadily, refusing to be intimidated into looking away first.

Her father had changed little, she observed. He had perhaps gained a little weight, his handsome face now sporting the beginnings of heavy jowls, his waistline a little thicker and his muscular form just beginning to run to fat. But she suspected he would still be able to coerce her as easily as ever. He still had that inexplicable air of authority about him, which in the past he had used to bend her to his will, playing on the deep-rooted sense of duty she was conscious of owing him. She vowed though that it would not happen today, knowing that if she showed the slightest sign of fear he would detect it and she would be lost.

'Good afternoon, Father.' She was astonished at her level, confident tone of voice.

'Saskia, you are come at last!'

'As you see.'

'You look well, my dear.'

His eye roved over her smart new travelling gown with obvious approval and Saskia was suddenly grateful to Felix for forcing her into it. He had been right about that, just as he had been right about so many things. She deliberately allowed a small silence to ensue before responding to him, something she would never have dared to do in the past.

'Thank you sir, I am in perfectly good health.'

'Come, my dear,' said Barker, moving round his desk. 'Please do sit.'

He ushered her to a large wing chair on one side of his fire, taking the one opposite for himself. Saskia perched elegantly on the edge of her seat, her head turned slightly to one side so that she was obliged to look at her father through the protection of the plume on her bonnet, making it impossible for him to read her expression.

'And how are my grandchildren?' asked Barker with ill-disguised covetousness.

'My children are in the best of health, I thank you, Father.'

'And so, my dear, to what do I owe this unexpected pleasure? Dare I hope that you have come to your senses at last and wish to return home?'

'Indeed not, Father. I am most comfortably settled with Aunt Serena.'

He scowled briefly, before moderating his expression, and Saskia understood then just how much it must be costing him to maintain an amiable visage. 'Then—'

The time had come to make her request. Saskia had decided that she would not beg or plead, knowing it would put her at a disadvantage. She had surprised her father with her visit and currently held the upper hand. It was a position she did not intend to cede and spoke to him now in a brisk tone.

'We have a new guest at Riverside House who has attracted my attention.'

'Indeed?' Barker's bland expression gave nothing away and Saskia was unable to deduce how much of the news she had to impart would come as a surprise to him.

'He wishes to be introduced to you.'

'And why would he wish that?'

'A matter of mutually beneficial business, so I am given to understand,' she responded, casually lifting her shoulders.

'This new guest must have made quite an impression upon you, Saskia, if you are willing to break your insolent silence of six years standing at his behest.'

Saskia forced herself to remain calm, knowing it would be a grave miscalculation if she were to rise to his bait. 'He is a gentleman, Father, a handsome and well-connected gentleman with charming manners.'

'Is he indeed! Well, perhaps that explains it. I am also given to understand that he is an excellent dancer.' Saskia remained demurely silent. 'You have become very beautiful, Saskia. You look more like your mother every day. . . .' His voice trailed away but Saskia knew better than to speak again and patiently waited him out. 'Does your gentleman have a name?' he asked eventually.

'He is Mr Felix Beaumont and he resides in Bristol.' Saskia paused, before dangling the carrot which she and Felix had agreed upon. 'He advises me that he is commissioned to undertake business on behalf of Lord Rydon, the Marquess, amongst others, although I am naturally ignorant as to the nature of that business.'

'Just as you should be.' Barker gave a nod of approval, as she had known he would, and it was all Saskia could manage not to smile.

Barker leant back in his chair. 'And why would I wish to discuss business with someone whom I do not know? What would I have to gain?'

'I know not, Father. Obviously that is a question that only you can answer. But when Mr Beaumont discovered that we were related he considered it to be a fortuitous coincidence, since it would appear that he came to this part of the country on purpose to seek you out. He intended to call upon you and make himself known, but when he discovered our relationship he simply requested that I facilitate the introduction. I did not wish him to know that we are estranged,' she added, with deliberate hesitancy. 'But no matter, Father,' she continued, making to rise from her chair. 'If you would rather not acknowledge him, I shall leave him to find his own way to you.'

'Not so fast, Saskia. You have changed, my dear, and are far more self-possessed than used to be the case.' He smiled. 'You have developed something of your mother's impatient nature as well.'

Saskia bit back the retort that sprang to her lips and contented herself with a casual inclination of her head.

'What do I stand to gain from all of this?' he repeated and this time she realized he was not referring to business acquisitions. There was a hunger, a glimmer of hopefulness in his eye, which he did not take the trouble to hide from her.

'My gratitude, Father,' she responded softly.

'Is that all?'

'For now.' She paused. 'I really do admire Mr Beaumont.' Her implication could not have been plainer, or more honestly expressed: not least because she spoke the truth.

'And if I see him will you, in return, bring my grandchildren to visit me?'

Saskia blanched. So Felix had been right about that too. He had anticipated that her father would use the opportunity to force his way back into their lives and had arranged it so that they would not be in the locality in the immediate future. She felt a sudden rush of gratitude for his foresight.

'When you have conducted your business, if you still wish it, I will do so.'

'I have wished for little else these past six years. Now then—'

The door flew open. 'Papa, I, oh . . . Saskia, is that you?'

'Hello, Elsbeth.'

'I did not know you were here, but I must say I admire your nerve after all the upset you have caused dear papa.' She scowled at Saskia before moving to sit on the arm of Barker's chair, seemingly intent upon making her territorial claim in front of the prodigal daughter. Barker was having none of it though and pushed her away irritably, not even bothering to glance in her direction.

'Get out, Elsbeth!'

'But, Papa—'

'Go!' he roared so loudly that she fled the room, bestowing a glance of pure vitriol on Saskia as she did so.

'Your Mr Beaumont may come to dinner tomorrow evening, Saskia,' said her father, 'provided that you also come yourself.'

Come herself! She had not bargained for that but she covered her confusion by dipping her head and taking refuge behind her plume. 'Very well, Father.' She stood and smoothed down her skirts. 'Thank you.'

'Saskia!' His voice stopped her as she moved towards the door. 'Welcome home, my dear. I think you can have little idea how much I have missed you.'

His possessive tone sent shivers down her spine and Saskia fled.

Johnson, alerted to Saskia's presence in the house, lingered in the hall. Barker had as good as promised his daughter to him in payment for services rendered way above and beyond the call of duty, services which had unquestionably saved Barker from the authorities. And now, at last, after all this waiting, she had come back. He had just known she was on the point of capitulation, had made it his business to be sure that she was, and now his patience was finally to be rewarded. He would hold Barker to his half-promise and she would be his.

Johnson had never met a woman with one tenth of her elegance and ethereal beauty and was hopelessly in her thrall. He groaned aloud as he remembered again the sight of her in her glorious emerald ball gown and savoured the anticipation of finally making her his. He would make her pay dearly for keeping him waiting though, for so callously cutting him in front of half the gentry. He had, after all, only wished to dance with her.

He stepped out of the shadows, startling Saskia as he called her name and attempted to take her hand. Appalled, she shook him off and fled.

Felix stepped forward and caught Saskia as she left her father's drive almost at a run, and fell helplessly into his arms, her eyes blinded by tears. She was shaking with the effect of delayed shock and appeared incapable of supporting herself. Felix closed strong arms around her, lifted her into his curricle and drove off at a cracking pace, leaving Southview Manor behind them in a matter of minutes. As soon as he was sure they were out of sight of her father's house, he brought the carriage to a halt on a lonely stretch of tree-fringed coast and pulled her close.

'Tell me about it? Was it terrible?'

'No,' lied Saskia unconvincingly. 'He was surprised to see me but he could not hide his pleasure at the thought of my capitulation and has invited us both to dine with him tomorrow evening.'

'Both of us? I had not anticipated that.'

'Nor I.'

'I will not put you through that, Saskia, I will find another way.'

'Oh no, we cannot stop now we have come this far.'

'No! Look at you. You are trembling all over. You have been more than courageous but enough is enough, I say.'

'No, no, I am fine!'

But to Saskia's utter horror she was unable to suppress a racking sob from escaping her lips. Felix's gentle concern did what her father's subtle threats had been unable to achieve and shattered the remnants of her fragile self-control. Felix pulled her closer, stroking her back and whispering soothing endearments as she sobbed uncontrollably against his shoulder.

And then, without warning, Saskia was not crying any more. Instead she was kissing Felix as greedily as he was kissing her, her hunger more than a match for his. Saskia's body felt as though it was melting into his: she was unable to tell where hers ended and his began and knew she should put an end to a dangerous situation that was likely to spiral out of her control. But her limbs appeared to have developed a rebellious streak and refused to obey her commands. In spite of her best endeavours her arms slipped round his neck, whilst her fingers at last buried themselves in the lush thickness of his curls. Brazenly she continued to return his kisses as though her life depended upon it. Fire streaked through her, wave after wave of pleasure attacked the outermost reaches of her body and all thoughts of putting an end to the interlude flew from her brain.

It was Felix who finally broke their last scorching kiss. Saskia suppressed a groan of protest and instead traced the outline of his cheek with her fingers, her mind delightfully dazed. If Felix's intention had been to divert her then he had succeeded better than he could ever have anticipated, for she soon discovered that she had lost the ability to think about anything except the exquisite feel of Felix's lips covering hers, the thrill that assailed her as his hands caressed her body with such tantalizing expertise, the desire in his melting brown eyes as he smiled down at her.

He gently removed her fingers from his face and kissed each one in turn, his eyes darkened by the intensity of the passion that gripped him. With his tongue he traced the line of her tears, still wet upon her cheeks, until they were all gone. She shuddered as a fresh wave of dizzying sensation gripped her and offered him a tremulous smile.

'You have a strange way of offering comfort.'

'Do you not approve?' His smile was a provocative challenge.

'Certainly not!'

'Hm, then I shall have to try to persuade you to my point of view.'

He kissed her again, more possessively still, and she thought she would die from pleasure as he forced her lips apart with his tongue, furrowing gently at first but then more assertively, demanding and receiving complete capitulation. It her current debilitated state it was quite beyond her to resist him and she abandoned her half-hearted attempts to do so.

'Still not good enough?' he asked her in mock irritation.

She shook her head brazenly, trancelike: unable to find her voice.

'I see. Well now, Mrs Eden, you may as well know that I am not about to be beaten.'

His ensuing actions lent proof to his words. Saskia could hardly believe the extent of her desire, the depth of her newly awakened passion, or the bolts of extreme pleasure which shot through her as she surrendered herself to his caress.

Felix kissed her one last time before reluctantly putting her aside and taking up the ribbons. He had forgotten that such an achingly acute degree of desire was possible; he was tormented to the point of insanity by the blatant need he could observe in her eyes and did not trust himself to remain alone with her for one moment longer.

Chapter Twelve

FELIX sent word to Luc that Saskia's departure with the twins would be delayed by one day, confident that Luc would understand the reasons why and be prepared to postpone his own departure accordingly.

As Saskia, looking breathtakingly beautiful in her new turquoise gown, entered her father's drawing room that evening for the first time in six years, Felix could only guess at the conflicting emotions she was enduring, since her features were composed in an impenetrable mask of self-assurance and it was impossible for him to detect her true feelings. He was proud of her air of composure, being all too well aware what effort of will it had taken her just to enter this room, but could offer her nothing by way of support, other than a tender smile of reassurance.

A man, obviously Barker, stepped forward and took his daughter's hand.

'Saskia my dear!' He studied her for what seemed like an eternity, before speaking again. 'So, you are really come.'

'Good evening, Father. May I present Mr Beaumont?'

The gentlemen had barely shaken hands before Saskia's older brother, Charles, stepped forward. He mumbled something incoherently beneath his breath, which already smelt strongly of liquor, and placed an awkward kiss on his sister's cheek. Gerald was far less circumspect and expressed genuine pleasure at seeing her. Saskia returned his warm embrace without reservation, just as she did that of his wife, Harriet.

Another lady approached them now: blonde hair piled high, watery blue-eyes and a doubtless once good body now veering slightly towards heaviness. She was wearing an embroidered white lawn gown, a colour which did not suit her pale complexion and did little to conceal the plumpness of her figure. The bodice was cut so low as to leave little to the imagination and her face was heavily coated with powder. Elsbeth, for it was she, pointedly ignored Saskia and reserved all of her attention for Felix, casting a look of unadulterated lust in his direction. Observing her, her husband gave a snort of disgust and turned towards the decanter.

Felix made eloquent small talk with Saskia's father. He named his aristocratic patrons frequently, incorporating such salacious on-dits into the conversation as he thought appropriate, intent upon impressing Barker with the depth of his social connections.

Saskia was deep in conversation with her younger brother and his wife, leaving Felix to Elsbeth's tender mercies. He would never touch such a woman in a thousand years but prided himself that no one could have guessed as much from the way that he responded to her overtly flirtatious overtures. Barker seemed amused, both by Elsbeth's display and Felix's reaction to it, causing him to wonder if Barker had ordered her to behave thus. He doubted that it had been necessary though, since she was the type to whom flirting came as naturally as breathing.

A man, who looked vaguely familiar, entered the room. His presence caused Saskia to tense and when he was introduced to Felix as Johnson, Barker's steward, Felix recalled that he was the man from the ball who had frightened Saskia so much. He left Barker and Felix with almost indecent haste in his eagerness to reach Saskia's side. Felix watched as she flinched away from the touch of his hand. It was clear that she was almost as frightened of this man as she was of her father and every bone in his body ached to rescue her. But he knew that he could not: he was being carefully observed by Barker and needed to concentrate all his efforts on tempting the man to fall in with his scheme. Even so, he cursed his stupidity in permitting Saskia to become so deeply embroiled in a situation she abhorred, silently vowing that, whatever the outcome this evening, she would not be permitted to intercede on his behalf a second time. The sooner she was safely ensconced at Western Hall, out of harm's way, the better he would feel.

Dinner was announced, which at least meant Saskia was rescued from Johnson, only to be replaced by her father, who offered her his arm. Felix forced himself to do likewise with Elsbeth, and sitting directly across from Saskia, blatantly flirted with the wretched girl for the duration of the meal.

Felix knew Barker would not raise the question of his business interests before the ladies withdrew but was surprised when he did not do so over the port. Instead he allowed the conversation to flow but remained mostly silent himself. Felix began to wonder whether he had underestimated the man when he found himself to be the exclusive target of Barker's silent scrutiny and would have given much, at that moment, to be privy to his thoughts.

When they rejoined the ladies Barker asked his daughter to play for him.

'It is a long time, my dear, since I last heard music of such quality in this room,' he observed a the end of her performance.

'Absolutely!' Gerald smiled fondly at his sister.

Elsbeth sulked, as Felix ignored her flirtatious smiles and joined in the praise being heaped upon Saskia.

'Come with me, Beaumont,' said Barker, rising abruptly. Unbidden, Johnson rose and followed them into Barker's library.

'Now, sir, my daughter informs me that you wish to discuss some matters of business.'

'Indeed I do,' responded Felix. 'I have the honour to represent the Marquess of Rydon. He requires certain commodities that I understand you are in a position to supply.'

Barker raised a brow. 'Indeed, and what might they be?'

Felix named large quantities of the usual merchandise: ankers of brandy, barrels of wine, tobacco and silk.

Barker looked confused. 'And why come to me for such mundane merchandise? Presumably these things are readily available in Bristol to one as well connected as the marquess?'

'Because, sir, the marchioness, it seems, has a fancy for a rather more, oh – exotic commodity, shall we say, with which, I believe, only you are in a position to supply her.'

'And that is?'

'Two Negro footmen.'

Felix did not miss the significant glance which Barker and Johnson exchanged. Barker however recovered quickly and offered Felix a blank countenance. 'And what makes you imagine that I could be of service to her ladyship in that respect?'

'Oh come now, Barker, I make it my business to know such things.'

'I am sorry, sir,' said Barker, after a prolonged pause, 'I fear you have had a wasted journey. I am unable to assist you.'

Felix would have been surprised if he had said anything else and simply shrugged his regret. 'Not wasted, sir, I do assure you, for I have had the good fortune to make your delightful daughter's acquaintance, which is more than enough compensation for a wasted trip.' Felix spoke casually, making the statement sound deliberately suggestive, causing Johnson to bunch his fists and take a step towards him. Barker halted him with a gesture.

'You will return to Bristol at once then?'

'It would seem that I shall have no alternative. I may however dally here for a day or two longer in search of compensation,' he drawled, looking fixedly at the closed door to the drawing-room. Johnson growled in frustration, but was obviously a well-trained henchman, for he did not move this time. 'Pity that,' continued Felix, 'her lady-ship would have been most grateful to you. She was most put out to discover that Lady Ballyman has a black retainer and is quite deter-mined to outdo her by securing two of her own. She would, doubtless, have invited you to Rydon Hall to demonstrate her grati-tude. No matter!' Felix made to leave the room. 'I thank you for your time, sir, and shall conduct my enquiries elsewhere.'

Felix sensed that the prospect of an invitation to Rydon Hall had succeeded where all his other enticements had spectacularly failed.

'Not so fast, sir.' Felix paused, hand on the door handle, and turned back to face Barker.

'It is possible that I could direct you to the person whom you seek. Pray, remain at my sister's house for a few days more and I will contact you there as soon as I have made the necessary enquiries.'

Felix bowed his thanks and left the room, smiling in satisfaction only when the door had shut safely behind him.

Felix and Saskia were preparing to take their leave a short time later when Saskia's father took her to one side.

'Well, Saskia,' he said, smiling. 'I have kept my side of the bargain and entertained your Mr Beaumont. Now it is your turn. When can I expect to see my grandchildren?'

'I must ask you to be patient for a week or two longer,' she responded evenly. Saskia and Felix had decided it would be better that he learnt of her impending departure from her own lips. They were aware that he would certainly hear of it from Fothergill and if she had not told him herself it would appear strange.

'Why?'

The one word was spoken with an air of imperious impatience, belying the artfully constructed attitude of the forgiving parent he had been striving to project that evening. It was a timely reminder that nothing had changed and Saskia knew that the moment he thought he had her and the twins back under his control she would no longer be her own mistress. More importantly, though, she would lose the right to control the twins.

Saskia forced herself to remain calm as she responded. 'Aunt Serena is arranging for us to visit Mrs James in Norfolk. She has been unwell and has expressed a desire to see the children again.'

Saskia watched her father's face as he battled with his natural instincts to forbid the visit, finally contenting himself with offering to place one of his own conveyances at her disposal.

'So much more comfortable for you than travelling post,' he suggested.

'Thank you, sir, but I believe Aunt Serena has already made the necessary arrangements.'

The finality in Saskia's tone made in impossible for her father to argue and risk this embryonic truce with his daughter.

Nothing further detained them and Felix drove away from Southview Manor at a rapid pace, pulling up in the same place as the previous afternoon. Saskia, seated beside him, was unable to stop trembling. Felix took her in his arms, sensing that tears were close. Sure enough they soon spilled from her eyes and ran down her face in rivulets, soaking her pelisse and Felix's handkerchief into the bargain.

'I am so proud of you,' Felix told her, as he stroked her back with long practised sweeps of his hand. 'You were magnificent!'

'God, how I hate him!' she cried passionately.

'Yes, but you did not allow him to see your fear. That confused him and left him wondering what he must do to persuade you back to him. He has never seen you in such a light before.'

'How do you know?' Saskia sniffed and tried to pull away from him. It did her no good though. His arms held her in a vice-like grip and her struggles made not the slightest impression upon him. 'You hardly looked away from Elsbeth all evening.'

'Do you not understand why?'

'No.'

'Because it was what your father expected me to do. Put yourself in his position. He wants you back and sees conducting business with me as a way to achieve your gratitude. If he thought I was as serious about you as you have pretended to be about me then he would not give me the time of day.'

'You should have said,' she snapped, averting her gaze in order not to reveal the extent of her injured pride. It was one thing to under-stand that he could never have a serious interest in her but quite another to hear him admit it with his own lips.

Felix's only response was to kiss her.

'I thought you realized,' he said gently.

'So that is why you patted Elsbeth on her. . . .' Saskia paused and blushed. 'Well, you know where you patted her!'

'Of course, why else? I thought it was a rather convincing touch. Your father noticed, of course, and roared with laughter, if you recall.'

She sniffed her disapproval. 'Yes, thank you, I observed more than enough.'

Saskia and Felix entered the kitchen at Riverside House, only to find Perkins waiting for them. Saskia blushed and pulled away from Felix's arm.

'Your pardon, ma'am,' said Perkins, bowing and grinning simultaneously.

'I must see to the children,' said Saskia, backing from the room.

'What do you want, Perkins?' asked Felix.

'Message from his lordship. Wants me to report back to him on your progress tonight and wants to know what time to expect Mrs Eden and her children tomorrow.'

'I see.'

'Oh, and one other thing I thought you should know. I popped into the Swyre Inn tonight. Fothergill was there, high as a kite and in great spirits because Mrs Eden had gone to have dinner with her father. He was so happy about it that he even appeared unconcerned that you had accompanied her. Well, m'lord, I decided it was too good an opportunity to miss and so I fell into conversation with him, keeping him well supplied with ale, naturally. When he was in his cups he confided in me that in return for his loyalty, Barker has promised him, Fothergill that is, marriage to Mrs Eden once she returns to him.'

'The devil he has!'

Chapter Thirteen

T HE following day was a Saturday and as the children did not
have lessons, it was Fothergill's custom to sleep off the
excesses of the week, usually missing breakfast altogether. Felix took
advantage of his tardiness and drove Saskia and the children away
from Riverside House very early. He hoped to deliver them into
Luc's care and return to Mrs Rivers's establishment before
Fothergill was about and realized the part Felix had played in facil-
itating their departure.

The twins were full of excitement, still believing they were to visit
Mrs James, of whom they were fond. Even the superior surroundings
of the Grand Hotel did little to diminish their enthusiasm, or to stay
their constant stream of chatter. It was only when they entered Luc's
suite and stared, open-mouthed, at the extravagant opulence that they
became temporarily subdued.

Luc and Clarissa stood to greet them, smiling in delight. Eyes as
large as saucers, the twins stood hand in hand, speechless with awe.
Felix made the introductions and Josh, belatedly remembering his
manners, executed an uncharacteristically elegant bow. Saskia knew
where she had seen it before and quietly despaired. Her son was
mimicking Felix! Amy, without the benefit of superior example,
managed her customary wobbly curtsy, almost dropping the
squirming Hoskins in the process.

Without hesitation Clarissa dropped to her knees, the better to address the children and exclaim over Hoskins, and that was all it took for the twins to overcome their shyness.

'We are twins—'

'—yes, and we're six—'

'—this is our dog, Hoskins—'

They were off! Felix and Luc stood together, watching indulgently. Rosie and Luc's dog, Mulligan, also joined the fray. The two little girls were drawn to one another and joined hands, disappearing together to examine Rosie's favourite dolls. Mulligan and Hoskins were more circumspect, prowling around one another tentatively, whilst Josh turned to Felix with a martyred sigh.

'I had better watch over them, Mr Beaumont,' he said, pretending an indifference he clearly did not feel as he hurried after the girls.

'Take good care of them for me, Luc,' said Felix *sotto voce*.

'Have I ever let you down?'

'No, but this is especially important to me.'

Luc silently regarded his friend, unable to miss the grim determination etched in his expression. 'I know,' he said softly.

Luc and Clarissa tactfully followed the children from the room, leaving Felix alone with Saskia. He wasted no time in pulling her into his arms.

'I will join you in a few short days.'

'Take great care, sir, my father is both dangerous and ruthless.' Her face was creased with concern. 'Do not make the mistake of underestimating him.'

'I appreciate the full extent of his malefice, have no fear. Smithers has the area swamped with his men, in readiness. Nothing can happen to me.'

'I pray to God that you are right!'

Saskia knew her mask of indifference was slipping but the realization that she might never see him again brought with it an acknowledgement that her feelings were of very little importance when measured against the greater scheme of things. Besides, it felt wonderful, just for a few moments, not to affect indifference.

'Saskia, I . . .'

Saskia, unnerved by his hesitation, looked at him in alarm. 'What is it?'

'Well, what I . . .' He released her and paced the room in agitation. Then he was back beside her, pulling her to him, his inexorable need for her far from sated. 'No, now is not the time. But when I return to Western Hall we must have a serious discussion.'

Saskia was perplexed, completely unable to account for his anxiety and lack of poise. 'If you wish it,' she said evenly, 'but what about?'

'You do not know?'

'No, I—'

There was a commotion behind them. Luc, making an unnecessary amount of noise, gave them early warning of his approach. Felix did not trouble to remove his arm from around Saskia's waist. Luc knew him too well to mind the indiscretion and besides, Felix was not about to have her anywhere except in his arms until the last possible moment.

'The carriages are at the side door, Felix.'

This was Luc's idea. Saskia and the children would enter Luc's carriage, with the distinctive Newbury crest on its doors, at the side of the hotel and out of sight of curious passers-by. All too soon they had done so. Luc, Clarissa, Saskia, three children and two dogs in the first: a maid, valet, governess and the luggage in the second. The procession moved off. Josh, Amy and Rosie leaned from the window and waved madly at Felix, who raised his hand to them in salute, feeling suddenly very isolated and alone.

Pulling himself together, he shook off his wistful mood, reminding himself that Saskia and the twins were now safely out of Barker's reach. He returned to his curricle and made the journey back to Riverside House, thinking of all the things he still had to do whilst he awaited Barker's summons.

It came just two days later in the form of a servant calling at Riverside House at eleven o'clock at night and asking Felix to accompany him: Mr Barker had requested his immediate presence. Felix cursed under his breath. He had expected to receive some notice from Barker, which he would have used to alert Smithers. But there was no help for it. If he declined to accompany Barker's man now, without good reason – and none sprang to mind – then it would raise suspicions. He would go with him and trust to luck that Smithers' men were still alert enough at this late hour to observe him being driven away. Either that, or Perkins, of whom he had seen nothing for two days – a good sign surely, as it must indicate his acceptance into the gang? – would know what the arrangements were and would somehow alert Smithers himself.

In truth, Felix was taken by surprise by his early summons. He, his father and Smithers had carefully constructed his cover, using the Marquess of Rydon's name with that gentleman's prior permission. They had assumed that Barker would look into Felix's bona fides before proceeding with such sensitive negotiations and had examined the ways in which he would be most likely to do so. Contacting the marquess direct was clearly out of the question for someone of Barker's lowly social status. Smithers suggested that Rydon should take his long-serving and completely trustworthy butler, as well as his equally faithful valet, into his confidence. Barker's men would undoubtedly travel to Rydon Hall, on the outskirts of Bristol, and ask about at the local inn. Rydon's valet or butler would take it in turns to be present, make themselves obvious to Barker's emissaries and drunkenly let slip their master's intentions.

Felix knew that they could not possibly have managed to do that in the two days since he had dined with Barker, and that gave him cause for concern. Was Barker aware who he, Felix, actually was, or was it merely that he had played upon his desire to improve his social standing to such a degree that ambition had caused him to become incautious? Or was he simply obliging Felix in order to curry favour with his daughter? Felix had seen with his own eyes that Barker was desperate to have Saskia back under his roof, answerable only to him, so was Felix inventing problems where none existed?

Felix observed that he was being driven by Barker's surly minion not, as he had anticipated, to Southview Manor but direct to Burton

Bradstock bay. He alighted briskly when the conveyance came to a halt and was greeted by Barker himself, along with Johnson, his son Charles and a few more of Barker's men. Felix was relieved to notice Perkins amongst their number, looking uninterested – and entirely at home.

'I apologize for the short notice, Beaumont,' said Barker, stepping forward and offering his hand, 'but I unexpectedly found myself in a position to facilitate your unusual request and did not suppose that you would mind the inconvenience.'

'Not in the least,' drawled Felix. 'But where. . . ?' He looked about him expectantly.

'Over yonder.' Barker indicated several large vessels anchored off-shore.

'Ah yes, but of course!' Felix cursed inaudibly. He should have anticipated the possibility. It could make things extremely tricky for Smithers's men.

Barker turned in the direction of a large wherry pulled up on the single beach.

'Shall we?'

Disguising his reluctance beneath an indolent pose, Felix inclined his head and followed Barker into the boat, which his men then pushed into the shallow water before clambering in behind them. Johnson took the tiller. Felix watched him impassively, wondering how the next hour would play out. For the first time since the start of this affair he no longer felt in full control and admitted to his appre-hension. Instinct told him that something about this business tonight was not right but it was impossible now to extricate himself from the danger.

As Barker's men silently applied themselves to rowing the wherry, Felix, fully alert and acutely aware of his perilous situation, thought he detected a tension about them. There was an air of expectancy, an indefinable something about their attitude which disconcerted him. He dismissed his fears, blaming the apprehension he had identified in himself earlier as their cause, and sought reassurance in rational thought. With the exception of Perkins, all the men in the boat were totally loyal to Barker, armed to the teeth and more than ready to use their weapons. This knowledge did little to quell his concerns, especially since he was unarmed himself, but he could do little for the moment, other than to pray that Smithers and his men had him in their sights.

Silence prevailed within the wherry, as the men put their backs into their rowing. The full moon, which had served Felix so well a week before when he had dined *al fresco* with Saskia on the beach, was now on the wane. All the same, it still cast sufficient light for Felix to be able to make out Perkins's reassuring outline, hunched over his oars, intent upon his task, a sight which reinforced his sense of purpose. An image of Saskia sprang unbidden into his head. Barker was engaged in a despicable trade, a trade which had to be stopped. He was also a tyrant and a bully. If Felix failed tonight then Saskia and her children would eventually be forced to return to a life beneath his rapacious control. This thought served to strengthen his resolve, his determination not to be bested. Saskia, the twins, Mrs Rivers, his father – they were all depending upon him to put a stop to this evil business and bring Barker to justice. His own sense of duty, as well as an awareness of what he owed to them all, would *not* permit him to fail them.

They had reached the side of a new and fast looking cutter, the name of which it was too dark for Felix to detect. A rope ladder was lowered and Barker invited Felix to ascend first. He had no choice but to comply and was relieved when the rest of the party followed him swiftly over the side. Felix could detect only two members of the crew on deck but had to assume that more were below. Barker was beside him once again and invited him, with a gesture, to precede him towards a companionway leading to the lower deck and thence to a ladder, descending towards the hold.

Felix hesitated for the first time and looked enquiringly at Barker. Neither of them had spoken since leaving the shore, both aware how acutely sound is amplified over water at night. Barker broke that silence now.

'The captain of the vessel can hardly display his cargo on the deck,' he explained softly.

'I see.'

Felix did see, far too well, and every bone in his body warned him not to enter that hold. His earlier feeling that all was not well had intensified tenfold and his instincts screamed at him to find a way to avoid making a blind descent into the unknown. He searched his mind, frantically trying to come up with a plausible reason why he should not enter the hold, but his brain remained indifferent to his plight and no form of salvation presented itself.

Barker and his men were now standing behind Felix in a menacing semi-circle. They were shuffling their feet with impatience and Felix, recognizing that procrastination was a luxury no longer available to him, placed his foot on the first rung of that ladder which he was now convinced could only lead him to his doom.

A dim light emanated from the gloomy space below him as Felix slowly descended. That there was at least one lantern illuminating the space was Felix's last conscious thought as his feet hit the deck and, simultaneously, something heavy hit the back of his head, knocking him out cold.

Felix came to with an agonized groan. His head was pounding mercilessly: surely his skull must be broken? He attempted to sit up but found that he was securely bound hand and foot. He did not know how long he had been in the hold but through the one grimy port-light within his line of vision he could detect fingers of dawn light, shrouded by curling mist, above the flat surface of the sea. So he must have been here, unconscious, for several hours then? He listened but could detect no sounds at all, other than the creaking of timber and sawing of ropes as the boat rocked gently on her anchor.

Making a monumental effort, Felix eased himself into a sitting position by putting his elbows to good use against the hard bunk beneath him. He waited for the swimming sensation in his head to subside before looking about him. That he was still in the hold of the boat was obvious. There were several dubious-looking sacks piled forward and assorted seafaring detritus lying about in a haphazard manner. Felix absently concluded that it was not a well-run vessel: such slipshod seamanship would never pass muster on one of his father's ships.

A sound behind him caused him to turn his befuddled head sharply, an action he instantly regretted as the pain behind his temple intensified. He found he was nose to face with a large rat, which he had clearly disturbed, and which was now anxious to resume the search for its breakfast. The rat cast him a disdainful look and disappeared.

Felix forced his disorientated brain to assess his hapless situation. That Barker knew he was not who he purported to be could no longer be disputed. But was he aware of his true identity and purpose for being here and, if he was, how had he made that discovery? Perkins's loyalty was beyond question and only two of the Customs men, besides Smithers, knew of the scheme. Both had been in the service for years and were personally vouched for by Smithers himself.

Trying to reason out how Barker had discovered him proved to be too painful and Felix abandoned the attempt. Instead he turned his still protesting brain to the far more pressing matter of his current predicament, and how he was supposed to escape it. That Perkins was not in the hold, bound hand and foot as well, must surely be a bonus, since it implied that they did not know about him. But, that being the case, why had Perkins not attempted to affect his rescue? Perhaps because they did know about him after all but were holding him elsewhere? Or had already killed him? After all, the life of a mere valet would not be worth a farthing to these ruthless men, whereas his own. . . ?

No, that could not be possible. The thought that Perkins could be no more, all due to Felix's arrogance in believing that he could tackle these people alone, was far too depressing to contemplate. He was now acutely aware that he had blithely persuaded his father to allow him to investigate the matter, without taking seriously his warnings as to the inherent dangers. He had been bored and had wanted to escape far too keenly to consider his actions properly. Well, he was certainly paying the price for his folly now: as no doubt was Perkins. But still, he refused to believe that he would never see the audacious Londoner again and forced himself to adopt a more positive frame of mind.

Slipping gingerly to the edge of the makeshift bunk, Felix painstakingly drew his legs up until he could manoeuvre them over his hands, which were currently bound behind his back. It took forever but at last Felix managed to get them in front of him. Apart from being more comfortable, this small victory made him feel much better about his situation. Now perhaps he could work on the ropes that bound his wrists so viciously? He had already discovered that this was a poorly run ship. Surely there must be something lying about in this untidy hold that he could use to cut through his bindings?

Although he could not hear any sounds from the crew, he was under no illusions and assumed that several men must have been left on board. Still, if he could just move about quietly and not alert them as to his wakeful state, perhaps a solution would present itself? Prevented from walking because of his bound feet, Felix moved on his knees, making almost no sound, and conducted a systematic search of the hold. It was slow, painful work but his patience was eventually rewarded when he happened upon a short metal pipe, designed as a handle for winching ropes. It was broken off sharply at one end, accounting for its presence amongst the rubbish in the hold no doubt, and was by no means the ideal object for his purpose. Still, there was nothing better available to him and Felix considered that as long as he had sufficient time undisturbed, then perhaps it just might do the job.

He sat back on the bunk and, holding the handle firmly between his knees, commenced the painstaking task of pulling the thick rope binding his hands back and forth, like a saw, across the sharp end of the handle. It seemed he had hardly started with this work though, and made little impression upon the rope, before the sound of heavy feet on the ladder caused his slim hopes of escape to dissipate as swiftly as the earlier sea mist. Felix only just had time to conceal his prized winch handle behind him before the door opened and Barker stood there, flanked by his son Charles and by his steward, all three of them displaying irksome smiles of triumph. With a sinking heart Felix detected the sound of at least two more men on the deck above.

'Good morning, your lordship,' said Barker, still smirking. 'I trust you slept well?'

'Damn you!' responded Felix contemptuously.

'Come, come now, Lord Western, where are those pristine manners that have set all the ladies' senses reeling?' Barker roared with laughter at his own clumsy attempt at wit, his son dutifully joining in. Johnson contented himself with an acrimonious glare. 'There is no need to look so venomous,' continued Barker, recovering himself. 'Do you suppose me to be entirely stupid? Perhaps so, you would not be the first! But you might be interested to learn that I have known your true identity since the second day of your arrival at my sister's house. Do not imagine that I leave my daughter and grandchildren there unprotected?' At Felix's blank expression, he could not resist further boasting. 'You were recognized by an acquaintance of mine.'

Felix was about to ask him what he intended to do with him, but realizing the futility of such a question just in time, wisely remained silent.

'I am however grateful to you. I was wondering what you were doing in the vicinity, staying somewhere as lowly as my sister's establishment, but you saved me the trouble of having to find out by coming to *me*: and bringing my daughter back to me in the process.'

'Do you imagine that she would ever live beneath your roof again?' Felix spoke in a lazy drawl but there was no mistaking the disdain beneath his words.

'Of course! She was close to giving up her foolish quest for independence before you came along. You have merely been of service to me by bringing her back a little sooner than I had anticipated.'

Felix gave a derisive snort. 'You would be well advised not to count upon it!'

'Oh, she will come back, do not trouble yourself on that score. She and my grandchildren will live beneath my roof, where they belong, and do as they are told!'

His voice resonated with confidence and the steely glint of determination in his eye forced Felix to concede that he had underestimated the man. All other thoughts were, at that moment, literally knocked out of his head by Johnson, who reached out and put all of his considerable weight behind a hefty punch, which caught the unprepared Felix squarely on the side of his face.

'That was for having the nerve to dally with Mrs Eden,' he growled.

The blow cut Felix below his eye and caused his already throbbing head to erupt with a thousand new pains. But he was damned if he would reveal the fact to Johnson and took satisfaction from his perplexed expression when he simply shook his head and grinned.

'I believe Mrs Eden enjoyed dallying with a gentleman,' he remarked, with deliberate provocation.

Johnson roared like a bull and made to strike Felix a second time, but Barker stayed him with a look. 'All in good time, Johnson, all in good time!' He strutted about the hold, clearly enjoying his moment of triumph. 'Now then, Lord Western, before I decide what is to become of you, perhaps you would like to tell me why you are here and what you hoped to achieve by it?' He looked expectantly at Felix.

'Since you clearly intend to kill me, Barker, why would I give you that satisfaction?'

'Ah, but then there are so many ways to die. Slowly and painfully, as I am sure Johnson here would be only too happy to demonstrate to you or, there again, swiftly and in the manner of a gentleman.' Barker's eyes, so gentle when they had regarded his daughter two nights previously, now wore an expression of icy determination and Felix did not doubt for a moment that he was quite capable of ordering his murder, without a second thought, if it suited his purposes to do so.

'I ain't letting him die like a gent until I know what he did to Mrs Eden!' declared Johnson belligerently.

'A gentleman never kisses and tells, Johnson,' responded Felix languidly. 'But then, I suppose you could not be expected to know anything about gentlemanly conduct.'

Once again Johnson lunged at him and managed another aggressive punch before Barker had him pulled off. This time though Felix anticipated him and managed to avoid the worst of it.

Barker growled at his steward. 'What's the matter with you, man?'

'But, sir, he has treated your daughter, my future wife, with disrespect. He must be made to pay!'

'Your future wife? What in the name of Hades are you talking about?'

Johnson's face was a study of incomprehension. Felix watched with satisfaction as his confused expression gradually gave way to one of suspicion, before realization finally penetrated his slow brain.

'You promised 'er to me,' he growled aggressively. 'I've waited all this time 'cos of what you said. Don't think to go back on yer word now! You owe me and you know it.' His face was puce with rage. He was a giant of a man and his aggressive demeanour would doubtless have terrified the bravest of opponents. On Barker though, who was used to having Johnson obey his every dictate, it appeared to make no impression whatsoever.

'And you believed me?' he sneered contemptuously. 'Are you mad? You think I would let an animal like you anywhere near my precious girl?'

'What the—'

'Promised her to Fothergill as well, didn't you, Barker? Not above using anything you consider to be yours to get what you want.'

'Yer didn't!'

'How the hell—'

Barker and Johnson spoke at once, glaring at each other with a mutual dislike that neither felt any further need to conceal, and Felix recognized the means of escape that should have been apparent to him at the commencement of this altercation. Divide and conquer! Charles Barker had watched developments, but so far had not spoken a word. Felix considered it the height of bad manners to exclude him and addressed him direct.

'Your father likes to make free with what he considers to be his, is that not right?'

'What do you mean?' The words were slurred and spoken reluctantly, as though he could anticipate what Felix was about to say but had no wish to hear it.

'Oh come now, Barker, I know it all from your sister. Your lovely wife, it seems, prefers the intimate company of her father-in-law to that of her husband.' Felix raised a brow, challenging him to demur. 'And, what is more, I gather she considers your father to be more of a man than you will ever be.'

Felix lapsed into a satisfied silence, waiting to assess the damage he had inflicted. It was a long time before Charles broke that silence. That he knew of his wife's dalliances was obvious. What was equally clear was that he could live with that knowledge, provided no one publicly commented on her indiscretions or his inability to control her. Discovering that a comparative stranger was conversant with the matter was not a factor he had bargained for and appeared to tip him over the edge. But Felix was well aware that old habits die hard and seeing his father's belligerent glare, the outraged light left his blood-shot eye as quickly as it had arrived. Charles was still unable to think or act for himself.

'She's just a whore!' he eventually muttered.

'Is she indeed!' Felix was almost enjoying himself.

'Ignore him, Charles,' ordered Barker tersely, 'and concentrate on the matter in hand.'

Barker had miscalculated: Felix could see that at once. Charles was prepared to bury his head in the sand when it came to his wife's behaviour, but his father's assumption that he could still order him to do his bidding, with casual disregard for his feelings at such a humiliating moment, was altogether another matter. It was that, Felix suspected, which finally roused Charles from his drink-induced lethargy, causing him to let out an anguished bellow as years of suppressed frustration finally gained release. He crossed the deck and punched his father with all of his considerable strength. He stood over his sprawled figure, legs firmly planted apart, fists still raised, panting from his exertions. His eyes glistened with satisfaction as he saw his father's shocked expression and a flickering of fear in his eyes as, for the first time in his son's life, Barker was unable to direct his actions or anticipate his next move.

It was just the opportunity that Felix had been awaiting. As Johnson turned, confused, to watch the fray, Felix grabbed his winch handle in his bound hands and awkwardly thrust it with all of his might into the centre of Johnson's bulbous stomach. The man had been standing close to Felix and in spite of its awkwardness the attack caught him unawares. But not for long. He screamed a string of vitriol and was upon Felix in seconds, raising something in his hand and bringing it down hard towards the defenceless Felix's face. Felix, expecting such a response, held up his bound hands and the blow fell across his left arm.

Johnson had attacked him with a dagger. It had sliced through his clothing and penetrated the fleshy part of his upper arm. Blood was flowing copiously but Felix ignored it. The pain was intense but Felix focused hard on quelling the dizziness that assailed him: aware that if he weakened and lost consciousness he would be doomed.

Johnson kicked hard at Felix's prone body, whilst Barker and his son continued to grapple. It was then that the door burst open. Felix had never been more pleased to see Perkins in his life: especially when he raised his smuggler's bat and brought it down across the back of Johnson's head with all of his strength. Barker and son ceased the scrap and appeared ready to rejoin forces against Felix and Perkins but again Perkins was ready for them. He was younger and faster than both men and casually raised his bat a second time, on this occasion making Barker his target.

Assimilating events with a speed that surprised the helpless Felix, Charles held up his hands to Perkins, dropping his own bat in the process. He was carrying no other discernible weapons.

'I have no intention of swinging for him!' he said with surprising dignity, indicating the prostrate figure of his father, 'and, what's more, I'm through with doing his bidding.'

'Untie his lordship then,' ordered Perkins.

Charles did so, leaving Felix to massage his bruised limbs and attempt to staunch the flow of blood from his wounded arm.

'Thank you, Perkins!'

'It was my pleasure, my lord. I would've come sooner but—'

'Later!' Felix held up a precautionary hand. 'Let's get these three tied up. What about the rest of the crew?'

'Dealt with.'

Fifteen minutes later Perkins rowed the two of them back to shore.

Chapter Fourteen

TWO days later Felix and Perkins left Riverside House in the earl's barouche, bound for Western Hall. As soon as word reached the earl of Felix's entrapment, and the fact that he had survived only thanks to Perkins's quick-wittedness, he was apoplectic with rage and blamed Smithers for leaving his son thus exposed. Upon learning that Felix had been injured into the bargain, only the assurance that he was not in mortal danger but instead intent upon returning home, prevented the earl from travelling to Swyre and collecting him in person. As it was he contented himself with sending his fastest, most comfortable and best-sprung carriage – together with a decent set of clothes.

The activity, following Felix's escape, had been intense. Upon their return to Riverside House, Felix and Perkins found Smithers and his men assembled there, summoned by an anxious Mrs Rivers when Felix had failed to return. Their relief at seeing both men in one piece was palpable. It appeared that the two men whom Smithers had set to keep Riverside House under observation had assumed the household to be settled for the night and left their post for the purpose of visiting Swyre Inn. Smithers had promptly put them under guard for dereliction of duty.

A physician was summoned to attend to Felix. The cut on his arm was deep but had not severed any ligaments and merely required stitches. The cut below his eye was considered superficial but would leave Felix in possession of a black eye and ugly bruising for some days. He had two broken ribs, now restricted by a vicious bandage, which caused him some discomfort. There were deep marks and bruising around his hands and ankles, where he had been bound so tightly and for so long, as well as to his chest, thanks to the attention it had received from Johnson's boot.

But by far the worst injury Felix had sustained was to his pride. He knew he had behaved with breathtaking arrogance, walking into what now seemed such an obvious trap without so much as a dagger about his person, casually endangering not only his own life but that of his valet too.

Mrs Rivers informed him, with satisfaction, that as soon as Fothergill had heard of Barker's arrest he had visibly paled, packed his few possessions and left the house without a word to anyone. Mr and Mrs Jenkins, outraged to find themselves at the centre of such an unseemly scandal, had expressed their intention of leaving the following day. No one attempted to prevent them. Captain Fanshaw and Miss Willoughby would be Mrs Rivers's only remaining residents but, as Felix was able to assure her that her income from her late husband's estate would soon be restored to her, she had no concerns on that score.

Southview Manor was taken over by Smithers's men, searching for evidence to reinforce Barker's guilt, since he was refusing to admit to any wrong doing. The absence of any illegal natives on his boats currently in the harbour made it difficult to prove their case and thus far the only crime they had to lay at his door was that of kidnapping Felix.

At last their carriage turned into Western Hall's immense, tree-lined driveway and started the long haul towards the house. As they neared the lake, Felix saw his father and Luc fishing there, together with a very familiar red-headed child. Ordering the coachman to pull up, Felix alighted and walked towards them. His father saw him approaching almost immediately, but took a moment to collect himself and conceal his horror at Felix's appearance, before stepping forward to greet his son.

'Felix!' Lord Western was thoughtful enough not to clasp his son's shoulder in his usual robust manner. 'Are you all right?'

'Never better, Father! Fear not, it looks far worse than it is.'

Lord Western regarded his son's battered face with a mixture of horror and amusement.

'God alone knows what your mother will make of it all. I told her you have been involved in a carriage accident.'

'Very sensible,' said Felix, with a rueful grin. 'But tell me, Father, how has she responded to Saskia and the twins?'

'You know your mother! But I have to say, Felix, that I have been thoroughly enjoying their company. The children are a delight.' He settled a shrewd glance on his son's face. 'And Mrs Eden is a refreshing change from the predictable norm.'

Before Felix could respond, Luc joined them and shook his friend's hand.

'Knew I should have stayed with you,' he remarked, hiding his own horror behind a mask of casual amusement.

Once again Felix was prevented from responding as Josh joined the group.

'Hello, Mr Beaumont,' he said brightly, too full of his own news to notice Felix's battered state. 'Their lordships have been helping me to fish but the girls did not care to join us and have gone walking in the woods with her ladyship and mama. They are picking wild flowers.'

Felix smiled and ruffled his hair. 'Hello, old chap! How many fish have you caught?'

'Only two so far. Do you want to help us?'

'Tomorrow, perhaps.'

'Good!' And he trotted happily back to his rod, which was being held by a footman.

Lord Western told Felix and Luc all he had learned from Smithers. It seemed that none of the people whom they had captured was prepared to admit to any knowledge of importation of slaves aware, naturally, that the penalties for any involvement would be severe. Even Johnson and Charles Barker were keeping quiet on the subject, although they were willing to supply any amount of information on Barker's other illicit activities.

'Unless we are prepared to offer them immunity in return for their intelligence then I think they are unlikely to talk. But I, for one, would be reluctant to take such a step when it is obvious that they have been fully involved themselves.'

'I agree, Father, but what other option do we have?'

'Well, we can prosecute them on the smuggling charges and, of course, for your kidnap. But again, you see, they will attest that you entered that ship with criminal intent. It is something of a farrago, I fear.' Lord Western rubbed his chin in agitation. 'Barker's operation in Burton Bradstock is over, that is for sure. No one will risk dealing with him now and no one of significance will wish to receive him. But there is still nothing to prevent him from starting up again elsewhere.'

'What sentence can we expect him to receive from what we can prove against him?'

'Hard to say. Doubt that we have enough though, as things stand, even to get him transported.'

'So I have failed.' Felix was unable to hide his bitter disappointment. 'All these risks have been for naught.'

'No, Felix, not failed, I—'

'Felix, whatever has happened to you?' Clarissa, Saskia and the children had silently joined the group. 'Oh my dear, how are you?' Clarissa appeared openly horrified.

'Pray do not concern yourself, Clarissa, it is nothing.' He kissed her cheek fondly before holding out his hand to Saskia, who accepted it without hesitation.

'Are you sure you are all right?' she asked him quietly. 'We have been so worried about you.' Her lovely green eyes, full of concern and, Felix fervently hoped, something more, assessed his injuries with a horrified shudder she did not attempt to conceal.

'I am perfectly all right,' he assured her. He peered round the ladies and grinned. 'And who have we here, I wonder?'

Rosie and Amy ran to him. Ignoring the protests from his injuries, he bent down to speak to them both. 'Hello, sweethearts, did you pick those flowers for me?'

'Do gentlemen like flowers, Mr Beaumont?' asked Josh doubtfully.

'He's not Mr Beaumont any more, Josh,' Amy reminded her

brother. 'Mama explained it all to us, remember? He is a "lordship" too!'

'Well,' said Felix easily, 'this lordship likes flowers very much if they are picked for him by his favourite girls!' Rosie and Amy, both now beaming broadly, offered up their wilting posies and Felix gravely accepted them.

'I have an idea, girls!' said Clarissa brightly. 'Why do we not seek out Miss Adams and see if she will show us how to press the flowers? Then Uncle Felix will be able to keep them forever.'

Two little girls, two dogs and even Josh, fishing abandoned, loped off towards the house, Clarissa scurrying to keep pace with them. Lord Western and Luc diplomatically returned to their fishing and left Saskia and Felix alone. They regarded one another for several minutes without speaking. It was Saskia who finally broke the silence.

'Thank you,' she said simply. 'Without your courageous interference there can be little doubt that I would have been forced by necessity to return to Southview Manor. As it is, my aunt and I should be able to run her establishment now without any external sabotage.'

'But, Saskia, surely you realize that will no longer be necessary? Your aunt's stipend will be restored to her and there should be something for you as well from your late husband's estate. Luc's brother, Anthony, is an attorney and is looking into the matter.'

'That is very obliging of him.' Saskia smiled her appreciation. It was a smile that lit up her huge eyes and it took all of Felix's willpower not to sweep her into his arms and kiss her until she begged for mercy.

'Well,' she said brightly, unaware of the nature of Felix's concupiscent thoughts, 'at least now I shall be able to return home and not concern myself with thoughts of the future. I think we will leave tomorrow, if it can be arranged.'

Felix was aghast. 'Please stay!'

'No, sir, I think it would be for the best if we left.'

'You have not enjoyed your stay here?'

'Indeed, yes! How could one fail to appreciate such a beautiful house? But I would not wish to outstay our welcome.'

Felix was alive to her slight hesitation, her careful choice of words, and understood her problem immediately. His mother had doubtless made little attempt to disguise her disapproval. He cursed inaudibly before addressing her again.

'Please stay a little longer. I promised to fish with Josh tomorrow and, besides, we must still find a moment to have that conversation, remember?' He offered her a curling smile; one that crinkled the corners of his eyes, exasperating his injures, but somehow making him appear even more attractive. Added to his sensually persuasive tone and the gratitude she was all too aware that she owed him, it was an impossible combination to deny.

'All right, since you wish it, but only a day or two more. My aunt will have need of me.'

'Thank you!'

He patted the hand, which now rested on his arm, and together they turned on to the lawns, only to find all of the ladies seated there taking tea. As one they turned in Felix's direction and all conversation was momentarily suspended. Just as quickly they all started talking again at once, several of them rising to their feet and covering their mouths in alarm at the sight of Felix's injuries. Lady Western dashed forward to meet him, closely followed by her daughters and, inexplicably, Lady Maria Denby. Lady Maria had never before demonstrated initiative of any sort and was far too timid to put herself forward without encouragement: proof positive of his mother's less than subtle hand.

Lady Western declared that their own apothecary should be summoned at once, since she would find no peace until she had been personally assured that her son's injuries were not life threatening.

Felix was pulled from one lady to another, soon to be swallowed up within their midst, all contact with Saskia broken. As if that were not bad enough, Felix became conscious of a lady at the edge of the group staring fixedly at him, her expression concerned but otherwise entirely predatory. Felix's supply of exasperated sighs was inexhaustible that afternoon, it would appear, and he could not prevent himself from expelling yet another. Angelica Priestley, beautiful yet deadly in cream-coloured muslin, had him firmly in her sights. He was appalled that she should be here, now, of all times and watched as she tilted her parasol by way of greeting and sauntered away.

Felix, impeccably turned out by Perkins, entered the drawing-room that evening to find everyone already gathered there. His eye immediately searched out Saskia. She was wearing her changeable silk gown and was seated beside Clarissa. That particular gown had looked so spectacular at the ball in Burton Bradstock and, to Felix's eye, was just as lovely in this setting. He could tell though by the openly scathing looks which were being cast upon her by some of the other ladies present that his opinion was in the minority.

Anxious to reach her side, Felix could scarce conceal his frustration as he was waylaid at every step with enquiries as to his injuries and requests for first-hand accounts of how they had been sustained. Punctilious as ever, Felix answered with every appearance that his questioner was holding his complete attention and thus it was sometime before he was able to reach Saskia.

Finally managing it, he lifted her gloved hand and brushed it against his lips.

'At last!' he breathed quietly. 'Good evening, Mrs Eden, you look ravishing.'

Saskia responded with something resembling a snort.

'M'dear,' he responded, correctly interpreting her reaction, 'you put them all to shame! I wish I could tell you what I—'

'Lord Western.'

Felix frowned and turned slowly, well recognizing the voice that had the audacity to interrupt his hard-earned conversation with Saskia.

'Lady Towbridge.' Felix bowed slightly, but for once even his exquisite manners were insufficient to conceal his irritation.

And so it went on. Naturally his mother engineered it so that he escorted Lady Maria into dinner. He noticed, with relief, that Luc had placed himself at Saskia's disposal, both escorting her in and ensuring that she was entertained for the duration of the meal. He felt impotent, seated close to his mother and deliberately, he felt certain, as far away from Saskia as the table would permit. The meal appeared endless and was an agony for him. His mother and sisters lost no opportunity in promoting Lady Maria to him and treating her as though she were a part of the family, their union a foregone conclusion. Felix's jaw set in a stubborn line: his mother was in for a disappointment.

What Felix could not know, however, was that there was one other person at the table, watching his mother's efforts with interest, determined to assist the match in any way she could. Angelica had been in a dither of excitement when she received her prized invitation to this house party, having deliberately befriended Lady Western for that precise purpose. Working on the assumption that absence would make the heart grow fonder she had supposed Felix would be delighted to see her again and had been devastated by his thinly veiled guise of indifference. She was unaccustomed to failure and the fact that Felix was less than enamoured by her presence only served to make her want him more. Now, if he were to marry that silly Denby girl, then all would be well between them again. One such as she could not possibly hold the attention of someone with tastes as exotic as Felix's for more than five minutes, and then. . . ?

Conscious that her husband's curious gaze was focused upon her from across the table, Angelica suspected that she had momentarily permitted the burning desire she entertained for Felix to become apparent. Collecting herself, she offered her husband a dazzling smile, but continued to brood. Felix had clearly acquired a *tendre* for that little red-haired hussy, the one with those awful freckles and home-made gowns. But Angelica could not bring herself to believe it would be lasting and dismissed Saskia from her mind as an irritating insignificance: no threat to her plans whatsoever.

The meal did finally come to an end. Felix was torn between dragging out the port and delaying the gentlemen's return to the drawing-room, where his scheming mother was sure to be hatching further stratagems for his entrapment, and an equally urgent desire to rejoin Saskia at the earliest possible moment.

When they did return to the ladies one or two of them took little persuading to play for the company, Lady Maria conspicuous amongst them. After the third indifferent performance, Lord Western remarked to Saskia that he understood she played: would she oblige them? Felix observed the outraged expression on his mother's face, which was quickly replaced by a calculating look and a sweet reiteration of her husband's request. They were the kindest words he had thus far heard his mother utter to Saskia and Felix knew it was because she assumed Saskia would not be equal to the task of performing before such august company. She would either demur, which would make her appear impolite and ungracious when the earl had specifically called upon her, or she would be so nervous that her performance would be abysmal, thereby showing her up for the inconsequential nobody his mother clearly considered her to be. Felix's lips twitched and he contained his mirth only with the greatest difficulty.

Felix rose with effortless grace and offered to escort Saskia to the instrument. She declared that she was disinclined to play, unwittingly playing into his mother's hands. One look in her direction confirmed the fact. She was maintaining a polite façade but could not help exchanging smugly satisfied looks with her daughters. Felix was not about to have Saskia fall prey to his mother's spite and smiled a silent entreaty into her eyes. Seemingly aware that every pair of eyes in the room was trained upon them, and possibly surmising as well that Felix was more than capable of maintaining such an indiscreetly intimate expression until he bent her to his will, Saskia nodded once and rose to her feet with a grace to equal his own.

Saskia chose Bach again this evening and Felix almost laughed aloud at his mother's horrified expression. The applause for Saskia was prolonged, led by Lord Western, Luc and, of course, Felix. Basking in Saskia's success he offered his mother a raised eyebrow and ironic little smile, to which she responded with an irritated frown.

None of the other ladies who had planned to play now wished to do so and the party broke up into smaller groups: several people strolled out on to the terrace, an example which Saskia, feeling the need for escape, was not slow to imitate. Nonchalantly Felix followed her from a different door a short time later. At last he would have her to himself and they could talk properly.

He had not progressed ten paces across the deserted side terrace though before a familiar perfume assailed his nostrils. A well-manicured hand reached out and touched his shoulder.

'Looking for me, darling?' asked Angelica sweetly.

'Not with your husband about,' he responded more dismissively than he had intended.

'That did not appear to concern you at our last meeting.'

A shadow crossed her lovely face as she spoke, demonstrating the extent of her hurt and causing Felix to feel rather ashamed at his treatment of her, for he was well aware that he had used her badly. She had not been given her *congé* and had every right to assume that she was still his mistress. A mellowness, in direct proportion to the guilt he was experiencing, engulfed him. He rested his good arm against the wall behind her, smiled properly at her for the first time that day, and asked her how she had been.

Saskia, temporarily alone on the main terrace, cursed herself for being such a fool. She should have stuck to her guns and insisted upon returning home tomorrow. She knew all too well that she was not really welcome in this house: Felix's mother had made that abundantly clear in hundreds of not-so-subtle ways. With the exception of Clarissa, all the other ladies had shunned her, looking down upon her and succeeding in their efforts to make her feel inconsequential. Her triumph at the piano half an hour ago had offered her a brief respite from her feelings of inferiority. She would never forget the horrified look on Lady Western's face, or the tenderly proud smile on Felix's. But it had been a petty victory, a much needed but transitory boost to her failing confidence.

Saskia looked about her with true regret. She would have liked to remain a little longer and enjoy Felix's company – albeit from afar. And Lord Western's behaviour was nothing less than courteous and charming. She could tell that he enjoyed the twins' company as well, his attitude diametrically opposed to that of his wife. There were also six unattached gentlemen at this house party and all of them appeared to find her company diverting. They singly, and as a group, sought her out at every opportunity. She had not experienced anything like it before and would be fooling herself if she pretended that she did not find their attentions flattering. She knew some of the other ladies had noticed their preference for her, possibly accounting for their hostility. She wanted to scream aloud that they had nothing to fear from her. She was not interested in any of them – except Felix. But ever since his true identity had been revealed to her she had been sensible enough to realize there could be no future for them.

She gazed up at the velvety sky and sighed. She would keep her word to Felix, she owed him that much, and stay for the two days more that she had promised. Then she would take the twins back home. Things would be easier now that their monetary problems were at an end. She could arrange a good school for Josh, a governess for Amy. She recalled yet again that this was only possible because of Felix's endeavours. She would seek him out, tell him of her decision, thank him once more and leave him, with a clear conscience, to enjoy Lady Maria's blushes. She was obviously the lady his family intended for him and Saskia could not bear to stand by and watch it happen.

Turning the corner of the terrace, still deep in thought, she was conscious of being no longer alone. A gentleman with thick brown curls had his back towards her. He was talking to someone. She heard his deep, amused laughter ring out, echoed by the more delicate, mocking tones of a lady. It was Felix, of course, but before she could make her presence known, he dropped his head and kissed his companion lightly on the lips. The lady, Saskia realized with horror, was Angelica Priestley – one of her foremost critics. Saskia didn't realize that she had permitted a horrified gasp to escape her lips, but she must have done so for they pulled guiltily apart and looked in her direction. She was too quick for them though and escaped in the direction from which she had come before they realized who had discovered them.

Saskia only slowed to a walk when she saw a gathering of other guests nearby. She forced herself to adopt a carefree expression, ignoring the feelings of anguish which appeared intent upon ripping her apart. Felix was, of course, free to kiss whomsoever he chose and Saskia was well aware that a lady's marital status was unlikely to deter many gentlemen of his class. There was nothing between Felix and herself and never could be. Had she not just told herself that? So why these feelings of betrayal and humiliation?

Oh, what was the use of pretending? She knew why! She remembered the feel of Felix's experienced hands as he caressed her so tenderly and made her body come alive that afternoon on the dunes. She would never forget the intensity in his eyes as they burned passionately into hers, or his gently spoken, loving words and the softness of his lips; a softness which had become hard and demanding as his passion escalated.

What a fool she was! She had dared to hope, for a short time, that his admiration for her was sincere. But it was all so obvious now! He had been alone in Swyre and unusually bereft of female company: not a situation he was accustomed to, from what she had observed since his return home. She had been there when he had been in need of a diversion and had temporarily filled that void. There was nothing more to it than that.

Saskia's admirers were strolling towards her. Were they looking for her? She smiled at them brightly and for once did not demur at their outrageously suggestive remarks. One returned to the drawing room to fetch her a glass of champagne, whilst a second was sure she must be cold and begged permission to fetch her shawl. A third requested the privilege of being allowed to hear her play again – in private. He was taking an outrageous liberty in even suggesting such a thing, for he could hardly have made his intention plainer, but Saskia, far from setting him down as she should, simply batted her emerald eyes at him and agreed to consider the matter.

'What is going on?' Saskia did not need to turn round to know that it was Felix who had joined their group.

'Carstairs here is trying to persuade Mrs Eden to play for him again – in private!'

Felix looked enquiringly at Saskia, a pleasant smile still gracing his battered features. There must be some misunderstanding, surely? But Saskia simply shrugged, turned away from him with a dismissive nod and asked Lord Carstairs which composers he favoured.

She turned from one gentleman to another, playing them off gently against each other: acutely aware that Felix was frozen rigid with disapproval. Good, let him see how it felt! She did not even look in his direction as she accepted Lord Shorter's arm and agreed to stroll the terrace with him. She walked past Felix as though he were a statue, not once acknowledging his presence. But she was unable to mistake his furious glare, the rigid set to his features and the unquestionable fact that he was struggling to contain his temper.

Saskia, having decided that Felix had merely been amusing himself at her expense whilst in Swyre, was surprised to observe that her behaviour had shocked and upset him to such an extent. She could almost bring herself to believe that he was jealous. Almost. She tossed her head, a defiant gesture designed to cover the fact that she was already a little ashamed of her brazen behaviour.

Saskia felt Felix's flint-like gaze focused on her retreating back and retaliated by squaring her shoulders and moving imperceptibly closer to a delighted Lord Shorter. Her petty scheme to bolster her wounded pride by engendering Felix's jealousy was working better than she could have anticipated. This realization did not bring the elation she had expected though and instead left her feeling inexplicably wretched.

Chapter Fifteen

T HE evening dragged to a dilatory close and Felix could finally escape to his chamber. He did so with ill-disguised relief: at last able to give full vent to his towering rage. Sensing his master's mood, Perkins went about his duties with his usual efficiency and for once did not attempt to regale Felix with the latest gossip from the servants' hall.

Alone, Felix moodily lit a cigar. What in the name of Hades had got into Saskia to make her behave so improperly? Was everything she had told him about her past when they were in Swyre just a fiction? No, of course not! Felix had met her father and seen for himself how he behaved towards his daughter and how scared she was of him. Even so, he stubbornly dismissed the image of her reaction after her first meeting with him for six years, when he had held her in his arms as she sobbed bitter tears of humiliation against his chest. Felix had no wish to dwell upon the tender protectiveness her behaviour had aroused in him. At that precise moment he was feeling anything but tender and could cheerfully have throttled her.

Where had she learned to flirt so efficiently anyway and why did she appear to take pleasure in doing so in front of him? Once or twice, when she had been temporarily alone, he had observed an expression of genuine anguish on her face and could sense her deep despondency. She had looked so vulnerable then that he had momentarily forgotten just how angry he was with her and, had she but approached and offered him one of her intimate smiles, effectively excluding the rest of the world, then he knew he would have forgiven her everything in a trice.

Felix knew also that Saskia was not a natural flirt: that it was all new to her. She had been in his father's house for three days already, mixing with very superior society. She was not used to such opulence and he was uncomfortably aware that she had been made to feel unwelcome by many of the ladies present, who took their lead from his mother.

For the past three days she had been surrounded by females who were far more adept at the art of flirtation than she and never wasted an opportunity to hone their talents. Unaccustomed to inactivity, Saskia doubtless wished to alleviate the boredom which he knew many ladies complained of at house parties, when they were left to their own devices for hours on end. That being so, perhaps all the attention she had received from the gentlemen had turned her head? She had been forced into marriage at sixteen and had not been given the opportunity to experience true admiration before. She would be less than human if she was not enjoying the experience.

Realizing that, in his desperation, he was dredging up pathetic reasons to excuse her behaviour, Felix's anger returned tenfold. Surely she had sufficient sense to know that she was going too far? She was behaving like a member of the muslin company and even some of the other ladies present, hardened flirts all of them, were starting to look at her askance.

Had she forgotten that he wanted a private conversation with her? It was almost the last thing he had said to her before she left Weymouth but although several opportunities had arisen during the long evening for them to escape for half an hour unobserved, Saskia had remained deaf to his silent entreaties.

The temptation to seek her out now and clear the air was almost overwhelming but Felix knew he could not risk it. For one thing he doubted that he would be able to keep his temper in check. It was already at boiling point and if she started defending those damned popinjays to him then he would be powerless to control his reaction. The very thought of her harbouring feelings for any one of them caused such acute pangs of jealousy as to make him feel physically ill.

For another, he knew that with the house as full as it was, he was unlikely to avoid detection. He was also well aware that, however angry he was with her, being alone with her anywhere near a bed could only end in one possible way. He wanted her with an intensity that he had long ago forgotten was possible, leaving him in a permanent state of frustration and, for that reason alone, he definitely could not risk going in search of her.

He longed to point out to her that as a young widow, she would be considered 'fair game' by all the gentlemen present and, what was more, they would assume she was aware of it and demonstrating, by her behaviour, that she was not unwilling. Carstairs and Shorter, both disreputable rakes, appeared to be competing for her favours and were unlikely to misinterpret her signs of encouragement.

Felix clenched his fists in a futile attempt to control his anger. He was entirely certain that Saskia did not understand what she was about. She had to be warned. But, Carstairs and Shorter aside, Felix reserved the bulk of his concern for Lord Bingham. He was not much older than Saskia herself but immensely wealthy and in a position to choose a spouse wheresoever he wished, both his parents being long since dead. Felix half thought that his mother, forever scheming on behalf of her offspring, had invited him in order that he might have sight of his youngest sister, even before her presentation next year. Bingham was a respectable man who, unlike some of the other gentleman present, was not in possession of tendencies that veered towards debauchery.

Bingham did not appear to show any particular favour towards Felix's sister and was merely polite to her. There could be no question however that Saskia intrigued him. Felix had seen him pursuing her with quiet determination: a situation which was driving his mother demented. Had Felix been less involved he would have been diverted by the fact. His grin was devoid of all humour though as he acknowledged that he was almost more concerned by gentlemen with honourable intentions towards Saskia than those with a more salacious purpose.

Pouring himself a substantial measure of cognac, and accepting that he must wait for the morrow to talk with Saskia, Felix continued to brood for another two hours.

The following morning Felix strolled towards the lake. From his superbly attired appearance no one could have guessed what a sleepless night he had endured. His neckcloth was folded in a perfect mathematical, his boots polished to an impossibly high shine, his breeches clung to him like a second skin and his green superfine coat was displayed to perfection by his broad shoulders. Josh was impatiently awaiting his arrival for their promised fishing expedition and Felix was happy to oblige him, confidently expecting Saskia and Amy to be lurking thereabouts, for she was never far from her children's activities. He was acutely disappointed and his mood not improved in the slightest when Luc and his father appeared, informing him that all of the ladies had gone into Plymouth to pursue the shops.

In Josh's ebullient company it was impossible for Felix to brood, or to dwell too much upon the happenings of the previous evening. Several of the other gentlemen joined in the fishing and Felix decided that a morning spent in congenial masculine company was just the thing to restore his good humour. By the time he detected the sound of carriage wheels on gravel, announcing the return of the ladies, he was in a much better frame of mind but more determined than ever to find a way to engineer his meeting with Saskia that afternoon.

Easier said than done, Felix decided moodily as luncheon was cleared away and he still had not had a moment alone with her. Felix observed her as she strolled across the lawns, surrounded by her devotees. She was wearing a new gown of amber Swiss mull, which did little to conceal her charms and much to agitate Felix. He had asked Clarissa to take her to the local modiste upon arrival at Western Hall, well aware that she had little in her present wardrobe that would pass muster in his father's house. Felix now regretted his thoughtfulness, since *he* was supposed to be the only gentleman to enjoy the results.

The warmth of the sun and post-luncheon lethargy caused general drowsiness amongst the party, and only half-hearted attempts were made at entertainment. Targets had been set up at one end of the lawn and Felix allowed his temper full rein as he observed Carstairs and Shorter fighting one another for the privilege of showing Saskia the *only* correct way to draw a bow. Carstairs, damn him, was almost touching her body as he leaned far too closely over her shoulder, placing his hands over hers, as together they pulled the bow taut and released the arrow. He listened, disgusted, to their ringing laughter as the arrow missed its target completely and other gentlemen jostled to take Carstairs's place.

Felix was obdurate in his bad humour. He could go into the house and leave Saskia to enjoy her suitors without his brooding presence or he could remain where he was and suffer. He knew very well though that he would not budge and contented himself by working his way morosely through a decanter of madeira, whilst making desultory conversation with the gentlemen who were sprawled on the lawn nearby. Even Luc had deserted him, for Clarissa had declared her intention to rest. He knew what that meant and felt a brief stab of jealousy. Then he sat a little straighter as an idea occurred to him. Clarissa was indefatigable; she never felt the need to rest during the day . . . unless? Felix smiled for the first time in hours as a delightful possibility crossed his mind.

All thoughts of Clarissa's possible condition rapidly left Felix's head as he noticed Saskia, alone, strolling towards a path that led to the woods: a path that Shorter had taken not five minutes before. God in heaven, surely she had not agreed to meet with the man in the woods alone? He was on his feet in seconds. He caught up with her at the edge of the woods and grasped her elbow in a grip of steel. She swung round, surprised, and looked straight into his outraged eyes.

'What the hell do you think you are doing?' he demanded furiously.

'I might ask you the same question,' she countered, unsuccessfully attempting to pull her arm free, before giving up the struggle with an imperceptible shrug.

'Attempting to prevent you from doing anything foolish,' he answered her, his voice colder, more hostile than she had ever before known it to be.

'Lord Shorter knows of a badgers' sett on the edge of the woods. He said he would show it to me, kindly thinking it would be of interest to the twins.'

Felix's nostrils flared in anger. 'And you agreed to go with him? Alone?' He was incredulous.

'Why not?' Her tone was belligerent but Felix could now detect a note of uncertainty.

'Saskia, even you cannot be that naïve!'

'I beg your pardon!'

'Come with me.' It was not a question and, with his hand still firmly gripping her elbow, he turned her decisively away from the woods and in the direction of the lake.

'I wanted to see the badgers! The twins would love them.' Her voice was indignant still, but her protest was half-hearted and she allowed him to lead her away.

'And immolate your reputation in the process?'

'What do you mean?'

'Saskia, did you really imagine that Shorter wanted to show you only badgers?'

'Yes, of course!'

'Well, I am glad to hear it, but I am unsure how he hoped to achieve it.' Felix paused before adding, in a scathingly mocking tone, 'Surely you are aware that badgers are nocturnal?'

Saskia glared at him with a mixture of embarrassment and anger but said nothing.

'I can assure you, m'dear, his mind was on anything but badgers! And did you imagine that your sojourn alone in the woods with a gentleman would go unobserved?'

'No, well yes, I mean, that is . . . oh, I know not what I mean! You are intent upon confusing me,' she finished in an accusatory tone.

'Saskia.' He stopped dragging her along at his previous furious pace and turned her to face him. 'If his intentions had been so innocent why did he go ahead of you instead of escorting you to the woods himself?'

'He did not wish for me to be inconvenienced if they were not there. He said he would look and then wait for me at the edge of the woods if I gave him a five-minute start.' She paused, before slanting a sideways glance at Felix from beneath lowered lashes. 'I suppose I have been rather stupid,' she admitted ruefully.

'Just a little!' agreed Felix, feeling his temper slipping away, only to be replaced with a very different emotion.

He tucked her hand into the crook of his arm and recommenced walking, at a more leisurely pace, content now to bide his time. They reached a bench on the far side of the lake and Felix seated her. As he took his place beside her she reached up and gently traced the line of his bruised face.

'Are you in a great deal of pain?' she asked him with such tenderness as to dissipate any remnants of his anger.

'Only at the thought of being unable to kiss you in such a public place,' he responded lightly, lifting her hand to his lips and kissing each finger gently in turn.

'But I thought such behaviour would cost me my reputation.'

She had meant to tease him back into good humour, he realized when he thought about it later, but the jealous wounds she had inflicted with her bold behaviour were still raw and he reacted instinctively, without recourse to proper thought.

'That depends upon the situation you find yourself in and with whom,' he informed her portentously. 'Shorter has an appalling reputation. There can be no doubt what he intended when he got you alone.'

Saskia paled under his austere gaze. 'I had no notion.'

'I know that but he does not and, more to the point, nor did any of the people watching you from the lawns – and the house. Your reputation would have been beyond recall if I had not intervened.' He paused, warming to his theme. 'And what is more, Saskia, you are not entirely blameless in the matter. You might have acceded to his request in all innocence, but the gentlemen here know you are a widow, the mother of twins and supposedly well versed in the ways of the world. In accepting his invitation you were agreeing to a tryst with him, however unwittingly.'

'Thank you for your informative discourse, my lord,' said Saskia in a tone that Felix had never heard her employ before. 'It is fortunate that I have one as experienced in these matters as you are to set me straight.'

'Indeed it is!'

He offered her a gentle smile, fully expecting it to be reciprocated. He was not angry with her any more. How could he be? At last he had her to himself and had already forgiven her for her transgressions. After all, amongst these predatory and experienced wolves, she was as innocent as a baby. So lost in pleasant thoughts about the outcome of their much-postponed conversation was he that it took a moment for Felix to realize that far from returning his smile, Saskia was glaring at him with open hostility.

'Something wrong, m'dear?'

'Not a thing,' she responded mellifluously. 'I was merely reflecting upon the disparity between the sexes.'

'Were you now!' Felix's chuckle hit a wicked note and he moved a little closer to her, his inexorable need for her company overcoming his sense of propriety. They could be clearly seen from the lawns, and therefore could not be faulted, but were also not close enough for anyone to see how tightly they were seated. Felix suppressed acute feelings of frustration as he wondered how much longer a man could be expected to go on, in the face of such extreme temptation, before surrendering to his passions.

'Indeed I was, my lord. How is it, I was wondering, that a gentleman can take whatever liberties with a lady that she will permit and only enhance his reputation in the process, whilst any lady foolish enough to succumb to a little sincerely expressed flattery is immediately branded as a muslin, or worse?'

It was only when Felix looked into her face that he realized the lightness of her tone belied a fulminating anger.

'Saskia, what's troubling you, m'dear? What can I do to put it right?'

'Hmph, it is a little late for that.'

'Saskia, not all gentlemen behave in the way that you have described.'

'Do they not?' she asked him in a pleasantly conversational tone. 'How very informative! And you, sir, if you do not mind my remarking upon it, seem to be very well acquainted with many of the ladies present at this party.'

'Saskia, they are members of the *ton*. I have known most of them for years.'

'How well?'

'Saskia, why the inquisition?' Felix, detecting that something was seriously amiss, was starting to feel distinctly uncomfortable.

'I was merely trying to discover the acceptable parameters for behaviour in good society. You must remember that I have never before been exposed to it. When, for example, may a gentleman kiss another gentleman's wife?'

'He cannot, other than in the most chaste way: such as I would kiss Clarissa.'

'I see! Thank you. And so you would never kiss another gentleman's wife's lips?'

'Certainly not!'

'Not even one as beautiful as Lady Towbridge?'

Realization dawned at last. 'Ah, I see! That's what this has been about. You observed me with Angelica last night? It was you?'

'Yes.'

'There is a perfectly rational explanation.'

'I have no wish to hear it: it means nothing to me.'

'You have spent the last twenty-four hours flirting with every man available and making a thorough cake of yourself in the process because you saw one innocent kiss—'

'Innocent? Huh!' She tossed her head, her expression telling him more than he cared to know about the workings of her mind.

'—one innocent kiss between old friends,' continued Felix, angry again and not prepared to counter interruption, 'and yet rather than simply asking me for an explanation you prefer to risk your very reputation? My, my, Saskia, I am delighted to discover that you hold me in such high esteem.' His words ripped into her, remnants of his anger from the previous evening spilling over, making his tone more acerbic

179

than he intended. The abject look on her face, which she seemed powerless to disguise, tore at his heart, twisting and tearing at his insides and causing his anger to dissipate as quickly as it had arrived. He had hurt her by laying her jealousy open to his disdain. He hated himself at that moment and wondered what it was about her that made him continually act in such an uncharacteristically crass manner. 'Saskia, I'm so sorry m'dear, I did not mean to—'

She stood and looked down at him as he belatedly rose in her wake. Unshed tears rimmed her compelling eyes but she refused to permit them to fall whilst still in his odious presence. She twisted her parasol over her shoulder, using it to shield both her face and her hurt expression from his penetrating gaze. Then, having no further use for words, she walked away from him, shrouded in a quiet dignity, in the direction of the house.

Felix watched her go, knowing it would be useless to pursue her. How could he have behaved so clumsily? Instead of reassuring her and taking the opportunity to say the things that were in his heart, he had adopted an opposite stance: mocking her inexperience and emphasizing the social chasm between them. But damn her, she had not even given him an opportunity to explain about Angelica. Not that he could have explained: not really – but still, that was not the point.

Frustrated beyond reason, Felix thumped his hand against the bench and roundly cursed the whole of womankind. He enjoyed the pain which shot through his injured arm. It suited his mood perfectly and was, he belatedly realized, no more than he deserved.

Chapter Sixteen

STORMING into the house, Saskia was too angry to care that she might have slighted some of her fellow guests by ignoring their invitation to join them for tea. She disregarded their startled expressions and did not even care that Lady Western was wearing a smug, '*I-told-you-so-but-what-else-could-you-expect-given-her-background*?' sort of expression as she watched her less than welcome guest commit several social *faux pas* simultaneously.

Saskia headed straight for her room. She flung her bonnet on the bed, attempting to rein in her raging temper and think more rationally about what had just occurred. It was true that Felix had saved her from herself: she accepted that much. How could she seriously have believed Shorter's story of the badgers' sett? Now that she thought about it, it did sound ridiculous and, belatedly, she understood the brief smirks that had passed between the gentlemen present when Shorter had first mentioned the matter and she had expressed so keen an interest. Felix was right: she had been a trusting fool. She could still hear the taunting lilt in his voice as he had goaded her, '*Badgers are nocturnal, surely you were aware of that*?' The memory prompted a string of most unladylike epithets in respect of his arrogant superiority. That he happened to be in the right did not excuse his high-handed attitude, or the withering condescension in his tone.

She had been pleased when he had followed her to the edge of the woods. She had known he was there long before he took her elbow – she did not need to be able to see him in order to detect his presence – but her pleasure evaporated when she observed the sinisterly wrathful expression on a bruised face that was twisted with anger.

Saskia paced the room, allowing her indignation and humiliation free rein. What gave him the right to treat her so disrespectfully? He was not her keeper. She was sure she would have been able to handle Lord Shorter without his interference. Too fired up with anger now to accept still that he had saved her from ruin, Saskia mutinously placed the blame squarely at Felix's door. How dare he tell her not to flirt after the way she had seen him behaving? Huh, she would show him!

Thoughts of Felix and Angelica Priestley brought her up short. Her anger drained away and was replaced by a mood of bitter reflection, only to be succeeded by a deep melancholy. She had developed a *tendre* for Felix; she had known it since he insisted that she and the twins leave Swyre, demonstrating the extent of his determination to protect them. After she had left him alone to face her father she had tried to convince herself that it was merely concern for his safety that was causing her such unease but, in her present mood, she was now ready to admit the truth. Although far too level-headed to believe that anything could ever come of her feelings for Felix, seeing him paying court to another woman – and a married one at that – had been more than her heart could endure. That he could not have comprehended her true feelings was her only source of comfort. Knowing he could never be hers was punishment enough: at least let her be left with her dignity intact.

Saskia threw herself onto the bed and fell into a troubled doze. She was woken by Lizzie, the young kitchen-maid whom Lady Western had reluctantly allocated to look after her when she recovered from the shock of discovering that Saskia had no maid of her own. Lady Western had spitefully appointed the youngest and newest girl in the house, presumably thinking that Lizzie would be incapable of turning Saskia out to her best advantage. But in that she had seriously miscalculated, for Lizzie was delighted to be given this unexpected opportunity to play lady's maid. She loved beautiful clothes and seemed to know instinctively how to make the best of them, adding clever and unusual accessories that Saskia herself would never have considered. She looked after Saskia's meagre collection of gowns lovingly and was good at dressing hair; although thus far had been unable to persuade Saskia to any elaborate style.

Well, Saskia decided, as she gratefully sipped at the scalding tea which Lizzie had thoughtfully woken her with, tonight would be different. If Felix thought her to be an irresponsible flirt then she would not disappoint him.

Clarissa had persuaded Saskia to purchase two further day dresses and one lovely evening gown as soon as she arrived at Western Hall. She had been saving the evening gown until Felix joined the party, knowing it became her well and foolishly hoping to impress him. It was of the finest pale pink silk, which somehow managed to enhance her hair colouring rather than clashing with it. It was woven with strands of gold, which reflected the light from all angles as she moved. The bodice was cut daringly low and Saskia would never have countenanced such attire had Clarissa not been there to persuade her that if she could not wear such a bodice then nobody could. They had laughed together and suddenly it had seemed all right. The tiny sleeves just capped the tops of her arms and the bodice was cinched tight beneath her impressive breasts with a curling gold ribbon. The skirts fell straight and floated about her as she moved, ending in flounces of gold, before tapering at the back to a small train.

Lizzie had looked hopefully at the gown each evening but Saskia had just smiled and shaken her head. But tonight was different. She would wear it and Felix could think whatever he chose.

'Will you trust me to dress your hair for you, ma'am?'

'Yes, Lizzie, do whatever you think best.'

Half-an-hour later Saskia looked in the full-length pier glass but did not recognize the elegant image reflected there. For a ridiculous moment she thought that another person must be in the room, wearing the same gown as her. This other lady also had red hair but it could not be her for this one had her tresses piled high, gold ribbons which Saskia had never seen before entwined elaborately within the curls, and long ringlets falling about a lovely face that shone with expectation.

'Lizzie,' said Saskia, smiling at the nervous expression on her little maid's face, 'you are a wonder!'

Lizzie beamed in delight, handed Saskia her fan and dropped a respectful curtsy.

Saskia made sure she was late entering the drawing-room. If she was going to do this then she might as well do it properly: she would make a grand entrance. The only problem was that the drawing-room doors were open to the terrace and the evening was so fine that everyone was already outside. So much for making an entrance!

But all was not lost. As she paused in the doorway to the terrace, so one of her admirers happened to turn in her direction and exclaimed with pleasure. Slowly every head turned her way also and a hush descended. Saskia attempted an impervious expression but knew she was blushing furiously. Flaunting oneself was obviously not as simple as other ladies made it appear, but, determined not to be intimidated, she plastered a smile on her lips and dropped a curtsy for Lord Shorter's benefit.

Almost to a man the gentlemen moved towards her to offer compliments: almost all but not quite. The one gentleman in whom she was most interested remained just where he was, speaking with Clarissa and Luc. She knew he had seen her, for she had been watching him closely from beneath her lashes and had the satisfaction of observing his surprise and, she felt certain, a spark of appreciation at her appearance. She was no longer so sure though because he was totally ignoring her now, and carrying on an animated conversation, his back towards her.

Saskia hid her devastation beneath a round of blatant flirting, thinking all the while that her heart would break. She knew she could never look better than she did tonight and if her best efforts were insufficient to make any impression upon the suave Felix then any foolish, lingering hopes she might secretly still harbour as to his partiality for her were well and truly dashed. She accepted her third glass of champagne in half an hour and turned to Lord Carstairs, a dazzling smile on her lips, as he recounted the particulars of an amusing escapade for her entertainment.

Tonight's proceedings lacked the customary formality and the gentlemen were free to escort whomsoever they wished into dinner. Saskia cynically assumed that Felix's mother had relaxed her vigil because matters between her son and Lady Maria had been privately settled. The pain that this expectation produced was crippling but, determined not to permit it to show, she took comfort from the fact that every unattached gentlemen in attendance was now surrounding her, each one noisily proclaiming that only he should be entrusted with her care. Saskia smiled at them, not caring in the least which one she selected but already deciding that it might as well be Lord Shorter, if for no other reason that to vex Felix, when she sensed a familiar presence at her side.

Felix bowed and offered her his arm. 'I believe the honour is to be mine, Mrs Eden,' he said, his face devoid of the prerequisite smile.

The other gentlemen grumbled but good-naturedly gave way to their hostess's son. He appeared so confident that she would accept him that she was, for a moment, devilishly tempted to turn her back to him and accept Lord Shorter instead, the only one of her admirers not to have ceded his place at her side in deference to Felix. But no, even she would not dare to defy him so flagrantly in front of the entire company, especially after all he had endured in bringing her father to justice. But still, his arrogant manner was most irksome and she made a point of hesitating before placing her hand on his proffered arm. She did not utter a single word in response to his presumptuous request, nor did she offer him so much as a ghost of a smile.

This elegant rake, whose complex personality she could not fully comprehend, never failed to surprise her. He did so once again now as he leaned towards her, his mood switching without warning from morose to mellow, the expression in his eyes soft and full of approval. He spoke quietly so that only she could hear him.

'You look stunningly beautiful this evening, m'dear!' And this time he did smile his appreciation, that special raffish smile of his that caused her heart to flip in a most disconcerting manner. He must have sensed her confusion for he spoke again in an even softer voice. 'Am I forgiven?' he asked her so humbly, that she had to bite her lip to prevent herself from laughing aloud, a mixture of relief and happiness flooding her.

She tried to look stern, but it was no good: she just couldn't resist him. He was a curious combination of penitence and devilment and for the next couple of hours she would have him more or less to herself. She could not bring herself to ruin that time by indulging in pettiness or sulking: such behaviour was not in her nature. She would simply enjoy his company and not concern herself with his reasons for singling her out.

'The incident is entirely forgotten but,' she added graciously, something preventing her from absolving him altogether, 'I am now on my guard so there was no necessity for you sacrifice your evening by escorting me.'

'That is where you are mistaken.'

'You take a lot upon yourself, sir. May I enquire as to why?'

'Because you are my responsibility.'

'How tiresome for you,' she remarked scathingly.

'Indeed,' he responded, grinning roguishly, 'but you know what a slave I am to duty.'

'Let us hope then, for both our sakes, that your mother has a short dinner planned for this evening.'

'I fear that must be a vain hope,' he exclaimed, with such apparent insincerity that Saskia was giggling as he held a chair for her which was, she noticed, as far away from his mother's position at the foot of the table as he could manage.

'Thank you.'

'My pleasure!' He picked up her hand and kissed the back of it, mindless of his mother's ferocious stare. 'Some wine, m'dear?'

Saskia was already feeling giddy, partly due to the large amount of champagne she had consumed but also, she suspected, due to another kind of intoxication. The kind that came in a superbly fitted black coat, blue-striped silk waistcoat and pristine buckskin breeches: the kind that had melting brown eyes and that wretchedly enticing smile. She nodded her head mutely in response to his question, unwilling to divert her greedy gaze from his features. Felix waved the hovering footman away and poured the wine for her himself. She observed his long, elegant fingers as they wrapped themselves around the bottle and shuddered as she imagined them caressing her skin, as they had so expertly done once before. For a moment she was mesmerized by the thought but shook it off and made an effort to face him with equanimity. Far too many of the ladies at this house party, she had observed, spent their hours following him dreamily with their eyes: she had no intention of behaving so transparently.

They were seated with Luc and Clarissa and Saskia was reminded once again just how comfortable these two elegant noblemen were with one another. Luc was ribbing Felix unmercifully about his injured face, declaring that his looks had improved as a consequence. Clarissa tapped her husband's arm playfully and told him to behave.

'He is just enjoying himself because he is more handsome than you for once, Felix!'

'My dear, how could you suggest such a thing?' Luc grinned, a devilish light in his eye. 'But what is your opinion, Mrs Eden? Do you not agree that Felix owes the man who inflicted his injuries a debt of gratitude?'

'Indeed I do, my lord,' she said with spirit, casing a mischievous sideways glance at Felix. 'He looks rather like a gypsy. Perhaps it is his intention to set a new fashion?'

'That is indeed what I intend,' said Felix, leaning towards her and sporting that familiarly wicked smile of his, warning an amused Luc that trouble was brewing. 'What say you, m'dear? Shall we run away together, join the gypsies and live a bohemian life?'

'Not this week, my lord, for I fear I have other more pressing engagements. But pray do not let me deter you from your purpose. And I am sure that Josh would be delighted to accompany you. He seems to have developed a marked preference for purely boyish pursuits since being admitted to your company.'

'So I should hope! Ah well, if you are heartless enough to deny me my simple request then I suppose I shall have to seek another companion to join me in my adventures.'

'Lady Towbridge, perhaps?' suggest Saskia sweetly, causing Felix to choke on his wine and Luc to grin broadly.

*

When the gentlemen rejoined the ladies, it was immediately obvious to Felix that his mother was not to be outwitted for a second time. The opportunity to escort Saskia into dinner had been as welcome as it had been unexpected. His mother's disapproval had been easy to ignore, and a small price to pay for the pleasure he exacted in having Saskia to himself for a few hours, and the opportunity to repair their faltering relationship.

Dinner had passed far too quickly for Felix's liking. Sitting with Luc and Clarissa, Saskia at his side in that becoming gown, had seen the restoration of his good humour, and he had put his best efforts into entertaining her, driving any lingering thoughts of the other men in the room from her head, he sincerely hoped. By the time the ladies left the table she was smiling and laughing with him as naturally as she had done in Swyre.

To Felix's eye, and to that of every other gentleman in the room if he was not mistaken, Saskia had never looked lovelier than she did tonight. When she had appeared on the terrace, wearing that revealing gown, his first reaction had been instinctively appreciative, soon to be replaced by annoyance when he saw the effect it had upon the rest of the assembly. Still, he would have overcome that had she but looked in his direction and made some effort to apologize for her abrupt departure that afternoon. He thought he had made her see the folly of her ways but instead of thanking him she had stormed off in a high dudgeon.

She had made no effort to seek him out when she stepped on to the terrace but instead appeared to make a point of curtsying low to Shorter. After all his warnings, she was still determined to associate with that scoundrel, had drunk champagne faster than any lady ever should and openly flirted with the men who surrounded her. Her behaviour disgusted Felix and left him fuming with impotent rage. But when his mother unexpectedly relaxed her rigid rules, Felix was no longer able to control his desires and knew there was only one lady whom he wished to escort. If she was so determined to flirt then let it be with him!

Now that the party was once again assembled in the drawing-room, many of the gentlemen applied to Saskia for music. But Lady Western cut them short. She had no wish to see Saskia shine again and abruptly announced that she had other plans for the evening. Noisy games of chance were to be played and Felix was not surprised to find that he was needed at a table far away from the one occupied by Saskia. It concerned him that Saskia had consumed so much wine and that many of the gentlemen now surrounding her were also aware of the fact.

Felix fared badly at cards, mainly because he was more concerned with keeping half an eye on the distant table occupied by the lady whom he intended to have as his wife. A great deal of noisy laughter came from that table, as many of the gentlemen loudly encouraged Saskia to be bold and wager her all. Felix's jaw set in a rigid line as he sat across the room, powerless to do anything to protect her from their audacious intent.

One by one the games came to an end and the occupants of the drawing-room milled around, some seeking the cooler air on the terrace. Felix, frustrated by being at a table still playing, was unable to follow Saskia in that direction. The gentlemen who had been her gaming partners were not similarly restricted though. Silently he fumed, but so elegant were his manners that even Lady Maria, seated beside him, could not have known it. Constantly she leaned towards him and asked him for his advice, which he gave charmingly, his mind only one-tenth occupied by the demands of his pretty companion. His mother however, misinterpreting his conduct, sighed with satisfaction.

At last Felix could escape and go in search of Saskia. He could wait no longer! They would have their conversation tonight and he would reveal his feelings to her. Heartened by this decision, he gained the terrace before his mother could think of further excuses to delay him. Clarissa and Luc were already there and he had supposed that Saskia would be with them. She was not and Felix felt the first stirrings of alarm when they said they had not seen her since leaving the drawing-room.

Felix strode around the side of the terrace, but it was deserted. Where else could she be? She could not have returned to her room.

To do that she would have had to pass through the drawing-room and he would have seen her. So where?

His question was answered for him when he heard a familiar masculine voice coming from the direction of rose garden. His blood froze. It was Shorter and by the sounds of things he had Saskia there with him. Alone.

'Come on, you little tease,' he heard Shorter encourage. 'You have been offering yourself to me all week. Now is not the time to become coy.'

'Unhand me, sir!'

'Oh, so that is how you want to play it, is it?' drawled an amused-sounding Shorter. 'Well, I have no objection to a little sport.'

'I . . . I do not understand your meaning.' Felix could hear the panic beneath Saskia's coolly spoken words and broke into a run to cover the distance still separating them.

'Enough! Now are you going to come to me voluntarily or must I come and get you?'

As Felix rushed headlong towards them he heard the sound of a hand slapping hard against flesh. What in God's name was Shorter doing to her now?

'You little wild cat, you will pay for that, you whore! No, do not consider screaming. If you do you will only succeed in bringing everyone on top of us. They have all seen how you've been playing up to me and will know you asked for it. Your reputation will be ruined. Do not imagine they will accept the word of the likes of you rather than me. Now just relax and let me—'

'N-oo-oo!'

'Come on now, sweetheart, just a little fun!'

'The lady said no, Shorter!'

'Felix, thank God!'

'Nothing for you to concern yourself about, Western,' drawled Shorter, unperturbed. 'This is a private matter between the lady and myself.'

Felix walked up to him, seemingly relaxed and self-assured, refusing to allow his anger to determine his actions. He was half-ahead taller than Shorter, considerably younger and far more muscular and was thus able to intimidate him easily, in spite of his injuries. Shorter, at last sensible to the threat that Felix posed, eyed him with suspicion. Felix stood mere inches away from him and spoke in a deceptively mild tone.

'If you lay so much as one finger on the lady, Shorter, then so help me God I'll pulverize you, regardless of the fact that you are my mother's guest. Is that understood?'

Shorter paled beneath the intensity of Felix's unwavering stare and the steely timbre of his quietly spoken words.

'Of course, Western, I was not aware that you have a prior claim,' he said with a meaningful smirk. 'I will just leave the field to you then, shall I?'

Without waiting for an answer Shorter backed away. Felix would have smiled at the sight of him tumbling over a rosebush and landing in an inelegant heap, had he not been focusing all of his energies upon keeping his blistering temper in check.

'Oh, Felix, thank you!' said Saskia in a grateful rush.

Without speaking he grabbed her elbow for the second time that day and steered her around the side of the house.

'Where are we going?'

'We are going nowhere,' growled Felix from between clenched teeth. 'You, on the other hand, are going straight to your chamber. We will talk tomorrow.' She flinched slightly at his hostility. 'Are you hurt?' There was a note of concern in his tone now, which gave Saskia courage.

'No but, Felix, I could not help what happened just now! It was not my fault. He duped me into going with him.'

'Saskia, I am in no mood to hear it now. If I do not get you safely back into the house then it is possible that I might cause you permanent harm. You have clearly learned nothing from our conversation this afternoon.'

'I do not see—'

'Be quiet!' He roared the words at her, still too angry to look her in the eye.

191

They had reached the side door to the hall and Felix opened it. None too gently he steered her up the stairs and opened the door to her room.

'I trust you will find nothing to tempt you in here, madam. Good night.'

Without another word he turned on his heel and left her staring at the closed door.

Chapter Seventeen

HALF an hour later, Lord Western, searching for his son, found him slumped in a chair in the library, an enormous glass of brandy in his hand, an angry scowl doing nothing to improve the appearance of his already bruised face. Wordlessly, the earl helped himself to his own share of the brandy and sat down opposite Felix.

'Your mother wondered what had become of you?'

'Did she indeed? And whom would she have me dance attendance upon now?'

The earl paused, phrasing his next question with care. 'Have you spoken to her yet?'

'Who, Mother?' The earl regarded his son steadily but did not speak. Unsettled by his father's penetrating gaze, and well aware of the true nature of his question, Felix settled for candour. 'What's the point? I thought I understood her character but obviously I was mistaken.' Felix finished his drink in one swallow and moodily reached for the decanter.

'And your solution is to get thoroughly foxed?'

'Why not? It seems to work for her.'

'What happened just now?'

'I found her in a compromising position in the rose garden with Shorter.'

The earl grimaced. 'But you saved her?' Felix nodded morosely. 'And you blame her?'

'Of course! I advised her this afternoon that her behaviour was not up to the mark. I might as well have saved my breath.'

Felix's father merely smiled. 'And what was Mrs Eden's explanation for being there with Shorter?'

Felix hesitated, looking slightly less sure of himself. 'She did not say.'

'She did not say or you did not give her the opportunity to explain?' Felix's lack of response told the earl all he needed to know. 'Do you have so little faith in her? Felix, you know how it is with Shorter: he has the scruples of an alley cat. If he had set his mind to getting her alone, it would be the work of a moment for him to come up with a plausible way in which to do so. One does not need to be a genius to see through Saskia's façade of sophistication and glimpse the naïvety that resides beneath it.'

Felix hesitated again and the earl remained perfectly relaxed whilst his son gathered his thoughts. 'Maybe, Father, but that being the case, why has she been flirting so blatantly with Shorter, and all the others for that matter, for the past two days? What can she imagine she will achieve by such behaviour?'

Lord Western answered his son's question with one of his own. 'Was she doing so when you first arrived?'

'Not that I could detect,' conceded Felix slowly.

'Then what has changed?'

Close as he was to his father, Felix could not bring himself to admit she had observed him in intimate conversation with Angelica. 'I know not,' he muttered shortly.

The earl was not deceived but did not pursue the matter. 'Felix, allow me to speak frankly and enquire what feelings you entertain towards Mrs Eden.'

He already knew the answer to his own question but wondered if his son did. He could recall the look on Felix's face when he first returned to Western Hall and Saskia joined them by the lake. Suddenly there was no one else in Felix's world: his attention was for her alone. He had waited a long time to see that expression on his son's face. This stupid misunderstanding between them must be rectified before it was too late and the earl was not about to let his son's pride stand in the way of his resolving their differences.

In a state of semi-inebriation Felix saw no reason to prevaricate and answered his father's question now with straightforward honesty. 'When I saw her for the first time, even though I thought her to be in league with her despicable father at the time, something changed inside me and I was powerless to help myself. I cannot really describe the feeling adequately, but it was as though I had discovered something important that I was not even aware I had been seeking but which had been eluding me for my whole life. She was so strong and determined, Father, I wish you could have seen her,' continued Felix, standing to lean against the mantel and smiling slightly as he warmed to his theme. 'She was proud, in spite of her straightened circumstances, and resilient enough to find the strength to overcome the problems constantly thrown into her path. Some days she was almost dropping with fatigue and yet still managed to find time for her children, and to play hostess to the guests at Riverside House with astonishing poise.

'She is totally unaware of her beauty, and the effect it has upon people, and that is part of the attraction for me. I am so used to *tonnish* women, who are just the opposite. I will never forget the look on her face either when she spoke of her resolve to facilitate my introduction to her father. She was petrified of him but not for one moment did she permit it to show. She was magnificent!'

The earl smiled at his son. 'And so, at last, you have found your destiny?'

Felix's soft expression was replaced by an angry scowl. 'I thought I had but now, after the episode this afternoon and then again this evening, I'm no longer quite so sure.'

'Felix, do you still not comprehend the folly of jumping to conclusions? Perhaps you should listen to her explanation first?'

Felix looked at his father in amazement. 'Father, I know what Mother's reaction to my choice is likely to be, and in spite of our difficult relationship I will be sorry to cause her pain. But it was the thought of disappointing you that was causing me to hesitate. Saskia is, after all, merely the daughter of a Cit; not quite *the thing*, as no doubt the tabbies will enjoy reminding one another. And if that is not bad enough, when her father is finally prosecuted and the truth regarding her background comes out, who in good society will wish to receive such a person?'

'And that bothers you?'

'Not in the slightest! But I was rather afraid that it might be of concern to you.'

It was the earl's turn to leave his seat and pace the library. 'Felix, we will ensure the world knows that Saskia played a leading part in bringing her father to justice: that she distanced herself from him years ago. If that, or the strength of our position within society, is not sufficient to withstand a little scandal, then I shall be delighted to turn my back on the world.

'I think Saskia is a spirited and imaginative young woman: everything that Maria Denby is not. She would stand up to you and keep you on your toes: just as she has been doing for the past few days.' Felix looked up at his father in surprise. 'Well, is that not the truth? I have never seen you so distracted. Excellent, excellent!' chuckled the earl. 'And anyway, even if I did have reservations about her suitability, any lady who can make the sort of music that she does would always be welcome in my drawing-room.' The earl turned towards Felix and grinned. 'And as for those twins of hers, well I can hardly wait to become their step-grandpapa.'

'You mean it, Father?' Felix was stunned. He knew his father to be a fair-minded liberal but could never have expected such wholehearted approval of his choice of bride, a choice that he was well aware would heap far more censure on the family than his father pretended to realize.

'Indeed I do! Felix, I would not have countenanced your betrothal to the Denby girl, even if your mother had somehow persuaded you to it. I want to see you happy. You are the most important person in the world to me and I have no wish to see you being forced by circumstances to live your life in the same manner as I have been obliged to live mine.'

Felix was too stunned to speak. He knew his father was referring to his own unhappy union and the resulting necessity to seek happiness with his mistress, something that had never been discussed openly between them before.

Seeming to understand Felix's confusion, the earl continued in a brisk tone. 'Talk to Saskia in the morning. Send word to her first thing, before she gets embroiled with the rest of the ladies, and allow her the opportunity to explain herself. I will keep your mother at bay and give you time for the interview. But do not waste any time,' added the earl, with a devilish grin, 'for Bingham is behaving like a love-sick puppy and could well beat you to it.' Felix's answering scowl caused the earl to roar with laughter.

'I am grateful to you for your support, sir, but what of Mother? She will be scandalized.'

'Your mother,' said the earl emphatically, 'will do as she is told for once.'

'Thank you, Father.'

'You are entirely welcome, my boy. Now come on, you need to have your wits about you in the morning for I doubt that your feisty intended will let you off lightly.' This caused Felix to scowl for a second time. 'Oh, and Felix, about Angelica. . . .'

'Yes, Father, I know what I must do there.'

Saskia was surprised that she had managed to sleep at all but supposed she had the champagne to thank for that. Now, this morning, her head was thumping and her throat parched. She drank her third glass of water in ten minutes and tried to gather her thoughts. She could stay at Western Hall no longer: she was at least sure of that much. Matters between her and Felix had come to such a sorry pass that remaining in the same house as him was now an impossiblity. A fresh wave of anger washed through her as she thought of his arbitrary attitude of the evening before. How could he imagine she would deliberately put herself in a compromising position with Shorter, especially after his warning of that afternoon and the splendid time they had passed together at the dinner table? What did he think she was? Well all right, it was obvious enough what he thought of her character, but that being the case, why should he care what she did and, more to the point, why did her conduct make him so angry?

Saskia was exhausted with playing the games of the indolent rich, the rules of which were incomprehensible to her. She thought of Riverside House, and its orderly routine, which allowed her no time to reflect upon her feelings. Its familiar presence called to her and she would not ignore that call: she would return to Aunt Serena's comforting presence. She would summon Lizzy to pack her meagre wardrobe, seek out the earl and request transport as far as Plymouth, from whence she and the twins would travel home by post.

Unaware that Lizzy had silently entered the room, Saskia started violently at the sound of her voice.

'Sorry to disturb you, ma'am, but I have a message for you.' Lizzy handed Saskia a note, which she read rapidly, annoyed that her heart leapt with pleasure at the sight of Felix's signature. Damn it, he requested an interview with her at her earliest convenience, and she knew that manners forbade her from leaving his house until she had at least confronted him. For a moment she considered simply penning a line or two saying that she had been called away. But no, that was the coward's way out. She would face him and see what he had to say for himself but, if he adopted that puritanical attitude with her again, she rather suspected he might finish up with one or two more bruises than he currently sported. Heavens alone knew, after the way she had seen him behaving he was hardly in a position to adopt the moral high ground.

Bolstered by her resolve not to be intimidated, Saskia rose from her bed and permitted Lizzie to assist her with her toilette. Half an hour later she tapped at the library door and complied with Felix's request that she enter. He stood and smiled at her, appearing to be his usual elegant self again; no residual traces of anger in evidence.

'Good morning, Saskia. Thank you for coming so promptly.' He took her hand and sat her on a couch in front of the fire, taking the place beside her. Saskia noticed that he did not ask her if she had slept well and from the ravages evident on his own face she took comfort from the fact that his repose had clearly been as inadequate as her own.

'Good morning,' she responded guardedly.

He poured coffee for them both, his expression unfathomable. 'I suspect that we are both in need of this.'

'Indeed.' She did not intend to make this easy for him. She owed him an explanation, it was true, and perhaps an expression of gratitude, but he most definitely owed her an apology first.

They sipped their coffee in silence, a silence which Saskia obstinately refused to break. The atmosphere between them almost crackled with tension, the sound of their breathing in the silent room unnaturally loud, but Saskia was not about to make the first effort to ease matters. Once again though, Felix surprised her by reaching into his pocket and producing a gold chain. He held it in front of her.

'What is that?'

'A locket,' he said, with a mischievous grin. 'It contains an amulet.' When Saskia looked at him in confusion, he explained further. 'It is purported to possess magical powers; to ward off evil spirits. I thought you might gain comfort from wearing it when in my company.'

He looked so penitent that, in spite of her best intentions, Saskia burst out laughing and the tension between them evaporated.

'It is beautiful, sir, and highly unusual but obviously I cannot accept such a gift.'

'Then regard it as a loan to keep you safe from my quick temper whilst you are in this house,' he responded easily, having no intention of allowing her to return the trinket. 'I am so sorry I was so raddled with you, Saskia!' His hands moved to her neck and he fastened the chain about it. Best not to tell her yet that it had belonged to his grandmother and he had kept it forever, always intending it for his bride.

'I suppose you had a right to be angry, but still. . . .'

Felix drew a deep breath. 'You wanted to explain last night. If you still wish to, I would like to know what that coxcomb said to you to persuade you to go with him.' He saw a combination of anger and uncertainty creeping back into her expression and hastened on, 'I have had time to reflect and I know it was not your intention to become embroiled in a compromising position with him.'

'Thank you, that is most magnanimous of you.' There was only the merest trace of sarcasm in her tone and her accompanying smile had the effect of dissipating even that. 'You see, after the card games broke up I wandered outside, along with everyone else. Lord Shorter came on to the terrace from the side of the house and said that an abigail was looking for me urgently: one of the twins was asking for me. He said he would take me to her. He behaved in such a gentlemanly manner, and appeared so genuinely concerned, that I did not doubt him for a moment.' She observed Felix's incredulous look and shrugged her shoulders. 'I know! I can see now how silly I was but as you can imagine, just the thought of one of the twins feeling anxious in this strange house was sufficient for me to forget that his lordship might have ulterior motives.'

'Yes, of course it would be.' Felix knew better than to add that the twins had both Miss Adams and his old nurse to watch over them or, indeed, that any servant looking for a guest would have entered the drawing-room for that purpose, not come skulking around the side of the house. His truce with Saskia was still too fragile to confront her with the full extent of her foolhardiness. 'I am only glad that I set out to look for you. I shudder to think what he might have done to you had I not arrived when I did.'

'He would not! You see, he made the mistake of assuming that I cared about my reputation. Rather than permit him to take liberties I would indeed have screamed.' A devilish light flared in her eyes. 'And put my knee to good use at the same time!'

Felix's expression was a mixture of pride and admiration as he threw back his head and roared with laughter. 'Good for you! But I am pleased that it did not become necessary for you to resort to such measures.'

'I think Lord Shorter might have benefited from a put-down of that nature. I suspect that in his case one is long overdue.'

Felix paused. He did not wish to break the mood of intimacy that had once again sprung up between them but he had to know the truth, or he would go out of his mind.

'Saskia, all of those popinjays who have been seeking you out this week, do you find them agreeable?'

'I do not understand your meaning?'

'Well, what I mean is, oh hell, Saskia, come here!' He pulled her to her feet and as closely into his arms as his protesting ribs would permit. 'What I mean, my love, is that I want to know if any of those rogues have captured your heart?'

'Of course not! Why do you ask?'

'Why?' It was obvious that she didn't have a clue as to the true nature of his feelings and was not expecting his declaration. Her curious expression as she regarded him, her modesty and comparative innocence fuelled his ardour and he kissed her passionately. 'Why? You ask me why? The reason why, my fiery little vixen, is because I want you for my wife.'

'What!' Saskia pulled away from him so fast that she almost tripped over her skirts. Felix reached out to steady her.

'I had no notion you felt that way,' she muttered in a dazed tone.

'Why do you think I have been behaving like a jealous lover whenever I have seen any of that *canaille* anywhere near you?'

'Ah yes, that would explain it and really I am truly honoured but . . .' She ran out of words and looked helplessly up at him.

'But what?' He brushed her lips with his own, causing ripples of pleasure to cascade through her.

'Felix.' She pulled herself up to her full height. 'I can't possibly marry you.'

'Why not?'

'Because your mother wants Lady Maria.'

'Then let my mother marry Lady Maria.'

'Felix, be serious!'

'I have never been more serious in my life.'

'Your mother would be devastated.'

'She will recover.'

'And your father would expect you to marry someone with a better ancestry: certainly not the daughter of a convict.'

'Not only does my father approve of my choice but he cannot wait to play the part of grandpapa to the twins.'

Saskia tried to smile but looked truly astonished. 'You have discussed me with him? And he approves?' A slow smile graced her features. 'He does me great honour.'

'No more than you deserve. Can you not see yourself as mistress of this house one day?'

'Frankly, no.'

Felix sat back down and pulled Saskia on to his lap. She traced the line of bruises which showed on his wrist below the snowy white frills of his cuff, whilst he set about the arduous task of kissing some sense into her. She leaned slightly closer to him, causing him to wince and her to move her position immediately.

'Did I touch your arm? Sorry, I thought the injuries were to your left side.'

'It is of no import.'

'You have other injuries?' she declared accusingly.

'Nothing of consequence.'

'Tell me!'

'I would prefer to show you,' he countered wickedly.

'Felix!'

'Oh all right, just a brace of broken ribs.'

She tried to move from his lap but Felix grasped her waist and pulled her back again. 'Oh no, you are going nowhere until you have given me an answer.'

'I believe that you are serious about this mad notion,' she said slowly.

'Oh yes, never more so. I want you for a wife and the twins as the start of our family . . . but only the start, mind. You can rely upon my full co-operation in producing many brothers and sisters for them.'

Saskia tried to frown at his forwardness but found herself smiling instead.

'What do you say?' Felix was looking at her, his expression serious and sombre. She was starting to believe that he really did want to marry her and her heart soared. But it was all too much. The enormity of the situation struck her like a thunderbolt. She needed time to think about it and told him so. If he was disappointed not to receive an immediate answer he gave no sign, contenting himself with kissing her as thoroughly as she would permit.

'Take all the time you need,' he assured her, as he peppered her neck with delicate kisses designed to send her senses reeling, 'just so long as I have my answer by this time tomorrow!'

'Felix!'

'Now then, little vixen, my mother is planning a *ridotto al fresco* this evening. There will be twenty more guests for dinner and another thirty or so neighbours to join in the dancing after that. And tonight, madam, you will remain exclusively at my side.'

'That will not be possible, surely? We will excite unnecessary interest and, besides, what about your mother's plans for you?'

'Forget her. I am not prepared to suffer another evening of agony watching you with those shallow coves. Besides, the house will be full this evening and my mother's attention will be elsewhere.' Felix reached up and touched the locket around her neck. 'Wear it for me tonight,' he commanded, this time trailing a tantalizing line of kisses across her muslin-covered breasts, before reluctantly letting her go.

Saskia spent the rest of the day in a daze, scarcely knowing what she did and whom she spoke to. Everywhere she went Felix appeared just behind her, catching her eye and smiling. She could not help but be flattered by his attentions but also felt a little overwhelmed by the obvious depth of his feelings. She took the earliest opportunity after luncheon to escape to her chamber: the need for solitude and quiet reflection had never been greater.

That Felix wanted to marry her; that he was prepared to defy his mother and probably the view of the majority of the plutocracy into the bargain, was an honour that it was impossible for her to ignore. And quite simply, she desired him, more than she could ever have imagined possible. But could she do it: was she being fair? The advantages for the twins were unarguable: and for herself too, for that matter. But when things settled down, would he regret his rashness in offering for her? Would they spend the rest of their lives hating one another? Saskia lay on her bed, too exhausted to think further and drifted into a dreamless sleep.

That evening she appeared in the drawing-room, only to find Felix patiently waiting for her at the door. He looked approvingly at her changeable silk gown. She was intuitive enough to realize that he would not appreciate seeing her in her lovely creation of the previous evening: that he would associate it with Shorter and that rose garden. The changeable silk, on the other hand, and the amulet which nestled comfortably between her breasts, was for him alone.

Felix offered her a contagious smile, and his arm. 'Ready, little vixen?'

'As I ever will be.'

Luc and Clarissa materialized and the four of them spoke to virtually no one else until dinner was announced. Felix's mother was about to invite Felix to escort Lady Maria but before she could do so the earl stepped in front of his son.

'Allow me to pull rank,' he said to Felix jovially. And then, to a startled and thoroughly frightened-looking Lady Maria. 'You and I have not had an opportunity for a private conversation since you arrived in my house, m'dear. May I have the honour?' He offered her his arm and she placed her hand upon it so timidly that it appeared she might at any moment lose her courage and run for cover.

It was all done with such charming grace that Felix could see his mother was completely taken in, believing that her husband had at last come to be of the same mind as she on the matter of Lady Maria's suitability for Felix. It was only when she noticed a brief glance exchanged between father and son, the look of gratitude in Felix's eye, that she realized she had been duped, but by then it was too late.

The evening was one of sweet agony for Felix. He had Saskia to himself, but only in the midst of this crowd. He put his heart and soul into entertaining her, holding her gaze for far longer than he should, touching her hand at every opportunity, not caring that he was being observed with varying degrees of curiosity by the people about him.

Felix was able to plead his injuries as an excuse for not performing a country dance with Lady Maria, and took the opportunity to stay resolutely beside Saskia, his predatory stance warding off any gentlemen who entertained notions of inviting her to dance.

Felix felt the full force of his mother's glare when the first waltz struck up and he swept Saskia into his arms. Well, why should he not? He had not, after all, declared that he was unable to dance: merely that he was not up to the rigours of a country dance.

Felix was too swept up with the dizzy satisfaction of being with Saskia to notice that she was being openly shunned by some of the party: that clusters of guests were looking at her strangely and speaking about her in whispers as she passed them.

Saskia did notice though, finding it strange at first and becoming increasingly more uncomfortable, unable to understand the reason for it. She considered, briefly, mentioning the matter to Felix but eventually decided against it, having no wish to mar their time together by introducing a discordant note.

But still, as the evening wore on and snubs became increasingly marked, Saskia became seriously concerned. During a brief respite from Felix's sedulous attentions, the reason why she was being ostracized was explained to her by a gleefully vengeful Lady Western, who kept her gaze focused, in seeming fascination, on the locket around Saskia's neck as she addressed her.

The following morning Felix sent a message to Saskia, inviting her to walk in the grounds with him, but by then she had already left Western Hall for good.

Chapter Eighteen

Iᴛ was only as Saskia leant back against the comfortable velvet squabs in the earl's barouche that she realized she still wore Felix's locket about her neck. In the mayhem that had preceded her hasty departure she had forgotten to return it. Ignoring that niggling problem she attempted instead to concentrate upon what the twins were saying to her. She was mightily glad of their company, for it obliged her to make the occasional response to them on the rare occasions when they paused with their excited account of activities at Western Hall for long enough to permit it. She reminded herself repeatedly that the welfare of her children mattered to her above everything and it was that thought alone which prevented her from sobbing aloud with the pain of her shattered heart.

As soon as she had learned the truth from Lady Western the previous evening she knew straightaway that she had no choice but to leave Felix's home immediately. Doubtless that was Lady Western's purpose when she had taken the trouble to enlighten her as to the nature of the on-dits currently circulating the room and causing such consternation amongst her guests. She adopted a sympathetic attitude and claimed to regret being the bearer of such distressing tidings. Saskia might have revised her opinion of Felix's mother, had it not been for the fact that her eloquence was in direct variance to her unmitigated glee.

She had sought out the earl early that morning and requested that he supply transport for her as far as Plymouth. She implied that she had received an urgent summons to return to Riverside House. The earl had regarded her closely, seeming as though he wished to dissuade her from her purpose, but did not attempt to do so. He contented himself with saying that he would be heartily sorry to see her go and insisted that she travel the whole way home in his barouche, complete with no less than two coachmen and two footmen up behind. The twins appreciated travelling in style and were wide-eyed with excitement. Saskia only hoped that they were not becoming accustomed to it.

If Saskia had been undecided about her response to Felix's proposal, then the revelations made to her last night had confirmed the impossibility of the match. It would be a *mésalliance* in every sense of the word and she would be the ruination of Felix. She loved him with a singularity that caused her acute physical pain. It was because of that love that she was taking the only course possible to her and setting him free.

Later, when the pain was less raw, perhaps she would be able to examine their brief relationship with equanimity and be grateful that she had, however fleetingly, been truly and completely in love. She would lay down her life for Felix without a second's hesitation. As it was, all she could do to demonstrate the extent of her devotion was to release him. One day, perhaps, he would learn to be grateful to her for her selflessness.

Saskia shuddered as she thought of the brief note of explanation she had left for him. She had agonized over the wording for half the night and considered that, after twenty false starts, she had got it right. But now she realized how hurt he would be by her brusqueness, and by the fact that she had run away and not even told him of her decision in person. She sighed deeply, knowing that had she faced him, he would have somehow managed to talk her out of her decision. He would have taken her into his arms and forced her reasons for wishing to leave from her, before casually dismissing them as unimportant. But Saskia knew better: in the end such things always mattered: more than love, more than anything.

By now he would have read her note. She tortured herself by imagining his reaction. His face would light up at the sight of her hand.

Then his brow would crease with incomprehension and slowly the truth would dawn upon him. His fading smile would give way to the furious glare she had seen so often over the past few days. She had left him and did not intend to return. Not only would she not marry him but she would not even discuss her reasons with him for not doing so.

The children's excited chatter recalled her attention and she realized, with surprise, that they were already approaching Riverside House. Her aunt, brother Gerald, and sister-in-law, who were currently residing with Aunt Serena, had come out to see who was calling upon them in such a fine equipage. Seeing Saskia being assisted from the carriage by one of the footmen they descended upon her in delight.

At dinner that evening Saskia kept up a stream of cheerful chatter, confident that she would appear in every way the same as before she had left. She was aware of her aunt's gaze frequently resting upon her and did not realize that her carefree demeanour was no match for an old lady's perspicacity. She did not comprehend that she was talking far more than usual, and in an artificially bright voice. She seemed unaware that there were dark shadows beneath her eyes, which were listless and lacking in their customary sparkle: that her brittle smile was dispossessed of warmth. She did not notice comprehension dawn in her aunt's expression either as she struggled constantly not to turn towards the chair which had always been occupied by Felix when he dined at Riverside House.

Felix stormed through the house in search of his father, running him to earth in his dressing-room. Taking one look at his son's distraught face, the earl dismissed his valet and suggested to Felix that they repair to the library. Once there, Felix waved Saskia's note under his father's nose.

'Where is she, Father?'

'Gone.'

'I was able to comprehend that that much, but where?'

'Home to Swyre.'

'Why?' The bleakness of his son's tone, the desolation in his expression, tore at the earl's heart.

'She gave no reason that rang true.' He held up a hand to silence the protest that he sensed Felix was about to voice. 'Or rather she did not when she came to me early this morning requesting transport to Plymouth.'

'She has only gone to Plymouth then?' Felix's face lit up with a combination of relief and hope, only to be dashed by his father's reply.

'No, Felix. She has returned to Swyre. She informed me that she had received an urgent summons from her aunt, which she could not ignore. I did not believe her but thought her decision was more than likely the response to yet another spat between the two of you. I deemed it better not to interfere but insisted that she travel all the way in the barouche.'

'Why did you not inform me before she left?'

'I tried to but you were not about. And Saskia was in such a rush to leave that I ran out of ways to detain her.'

'I went out riding early,' said Felix, slapping the crop he still held in his hand against his boot in frustration. 'I could not rest until I received Saskia's answer, which she had promised me today.' He paused, before adding bitterly. 'It seems that I now have it.'

'Should you have been riding, with your injuries?'

Felix, an expert horseman, shrugged. 'Perhaps not, although not for the reasons you are implying.'

'I think I have found out why she left.' As the earl had known it would, this comment engaged all of Felix's attention.

'Tell me!'

'Did you not notice last night that she was less popular than hith-erto?'

'No, I cannot say that I did. I was enjoying her company too much to take much notice of anything else. I did see that fewer people were seeking her out, but I thought I was the cause of their discourage-ment.'

'Not exactly.' The earl stood up, taking the time to choose his next words carefully. 'I'm afraid the blame lies with Shorter.'

'What!' Felix shot to his feet.

'Calm down, Felix, and let me tell you it all. As soon as I had seen Saskia and the twins safely on their way, I determined to discover what it was that had frightened her away. I had, by then, ascertained by her demeanour which, by the way, was exceedingly bleak, that it was not anything you had done to upset her. But from an idle remark she made I got the impression that your mother was somehow behind it all.'

'What, but you just said that Shorter. . . ?'

'I know, just be patient and listen, Felix. I went in search of your mother and asked her if she had said anything to frighten Saskia away. Of course, she claimed ignorance but could not hide her satisfaction at the turn events had taken. I was not in the mood for her nonsense this morning and insisted that she enlighten me as to the substance of the conversation she shared with Saskia last night.

'Shorter, it seems, desired more than an idle dalliance with Saskia. He had developed quite a *tendresse* for her over the course of the week, was confident that she returned his feelings and would agree to be set up as his mistress.'

'The bastard!'

'Easy, Felix. You know very well she would never have agreed.'

'Indeed not!' Felix thought for a moment. 'But, Father, I thought Shorter was on a repairing lease?'

'He is obviously not as badly placed as the rumourmongers would have us believe. But, as I was saying, his wish to have her under his protection accounts for his determination to get her alone. He wanted to convince her that he would take responsibility for her and her children.'

'And he told Mother all of this?'

'No, of course not! But,' added the earl grimly, 'he told me, in not so many words, when I sought him out this morning, after gaining your mother's intelligence. It seems that when you interrupted him in the rose garden, it dawned on him for the first time just how much he wanted her, and was furious that she had the audacity to reject him.' The earl paused, choosing his next words circumspectly. 'When

Smithers was here a couple of days before you came home, Shorter came upon us when we were discussing the events in Burton Bradstock. There being no further need for secrecy, I did not mind Shorter knowing some of the particulars. But what I did not realize was that he had made the connection between Saskia and Barker.'

'Dear God!' Felix's head fell forward into his hands.

'Indeed! And during the dance last night he spitefully put the word about that Saskia was the daughter of, and in league with, a smuggler of slaves. He doubtless hoped to put an end to your obvious attraction to her and leave the field free for himself.'

Felix paced, too angry and agitated to stand still, whilst the earl remained silent, allowing Felix time to digest all he had just heard.

'But why did she just go like that? She knew I wanted to marry her and that her background did not matter to me.'

'She probably thought she was being noble: saving you from your own impetuous nature. I am afraid that your mother, although she is reluctant to admit to the crime, took great delight in informing her of the rumours that were circulating. It would have brought it home to Saskia just what an alliance with her would do to your family's social standing and she presumably considered that you would not now wish to make the sacrifice.'

'Oh no, I must go after her!' Felix looked almost relieved: confident that it could all be sorted out, now that he was aware of the nature of the problem.

'Indeed you must, but not yet. There are two more days to go with this wretched house party. See it through and allow Saskia time for reflection.'

'Must I?'

'I think it would be for the best. Apart from anything else, Saskia may see things differently when she has been back in familiar surroundings for a few days.'

'Maybe.' Felix sounded unconvinced. 'But you cannot seriously expect me to spend a further two days in Shorter's company? I told him what would happen if he attempted to interfere with Saskia.'

'Shorter,' responded the earl, with a grim smile, 'suddenly remembered that he had urgent business elsewhere, after our discussion this morning. He left half an hour ago.'

'I see! Well, all right then, I will stay provided I am not expected to be civil to Mother.'

'It would have helped, Felix, if you had not given Saskia your grandmother's locket until things were formally settled between you. If your mother had been merely concerned about your infatuation before, then seeing that about Saskia's neck undoubtedly made her imagine that she had been gulled.'

'Yes, I suppose so, but I wanted Saskia to have it so much that I just did not think.'

The next two days crawled by. Felix could not have said afterwards how he occupied his time. Barely on speaking terms with his mother, he allowed himself to be manipulated into escorting Lady Maria into dinner, playing cards at the same table as her, driving her and her mother about the grounds. He squired her in a perfunctory manner, his mind on anything but his fair companion. But watching him, Lady Western could detect none of his inner feelings and was completely taken in by the seemingly fastidious attentions he paid towards Lady Maria. She tolerated her son's bad humour, sure that it was a transitory affair, and now that the dreadful Eden woman had left she was confident that her son would finally come to his senses, see reason and do his duty by his family.

Finally the last carriage, carrying Lady Maria and her mother, left Western Hall. Lady Western was profuse in her expectations that they would see Maria at their home again very soon. She looked smugly pleased with herself as she exchanged a knowing smile with Maria's mother and waved the carriage away.

First thing the following morning Felix was in the box seat of the fastest travelling chaise that his father owned, four prime goers between the shafts. He was, of course, on the road to Swyre but this time he did not even take Perkins with him. The business which he had to conduct did not require the attentions of a valet, any more than he required a distraction from his purpose.

Saskia hesitated on the landing, hand on the door to the bedroom she had not entered for over six years. She was in Southview Manor: alone. Her brother Gerald had driven her over and offered to stay with her but she had sent him away. She had something she wished to do and she needed privacy in which to do it.

The Customs men had thoroughly searched the house, their less than careful attention to their duty obvious everywhere she looked, but they had been unable to find any evidence linking her father to the ghastly trade of slave smuggling. Saskia did not know whether to be relieved or angry by their lack of success. As it was she had been granted permission to call at the house and collect a few of the personal possessions which still remained in her old room.

Most of the staff had been dismissed, some taking up the offer of employment at Riverside House, and only the housekeeper remained. Saskia had chosen to call on a day when she knew that the old lady, once so well known to her, would not be in the house. The effort of maintaining a cheerful attitude at her aunt's establishment was starting to tell upon her and the temptation to steal a few hours by herself had been irresistible.

There were two Customs men guarding the front of the house, but she had been permitted to enter and could now enjoy the solitude she had sought. She felt the stillness of the house closing around her and shivered, expecting her father at any moment to burst upon her and demand to know what she thought she was about. Shaking off such gloomy thoughts she opened the door to her chamber and stepped inside.

It was much as it had been when she left it, except for the obvious signs of the recent search. She felt confident however that they would not have found her secret hiding place and was proved to be right when she heaved the table beside her bed to one side and lifted the corner of the rug. It was the work of a moment for Saskia to remove the still familiar loose floorboards and grope gingerly about in the gap below, searching for the hessian bag which she prayed would still be concealed there.

Relieved at locating the sack without difficulty, Saskia hauled her prize on to the bed and sat down beside it, a smile of satisfaction on her face. Her hiding place had been the only secret she had ever been able to keep from her father, and she had treasured it. Opening the sack reverently, Saskia withdrew a packet of letters, tied together with a ribbon, written to her at various times during her childhood by her mother. The sight of her mother's elegantly curving hand caused Saskia's eyes to mist with tears, but she dashed them away impatiently and put the bundle of letters firmly to one side. She would take them back to Riverside House and read them again when she was feeling less sensitive.

Next she extracted a thick pouch and poured the contents on to the bed. Pieces of jewellery given to her over the years spilled forth. Some had belonged to her mother and, although of no intrinsic value, were precious to her. She allowed the strands of beads to slide through her fingers, dust motes hovering above the shiny facets, and smiled at the memories the sight of them invoked: happy memories for once. Her mother, laughing as she danced with her father the year before she died, these very same crystal beads sparkling about her neck. Her mother smiling indulgently, wearing that mother-of-pearl brooch, as Saskia failed in her attempts to master the finer intricacies of embroidery.

A bundle of her childhood diaries tumbled from the sack next. She recalled painstakingly recording every detail of her daily routine in a childish hand, encouraged by her mother. The habit had never left her and she kept a diary still, even to this day.

There were items of baby clothing, which had been the twins' first garments. Assorted other treasures brought memories flooding back. Her first music books, scraps of lace retained from gowns long since outgrown, a handkerchief made for her by her mother. The tears flooded her eyes as she handled each memento lovingly, wishing now that her childhood – the idyllic part before her mother's death, that is – could have lasted forever.

Saskia dried her eyes and pulled herself together. This would not do. She was ridiculously relieved that her treasure-trove had remained intact: safe from her father's all-seeing eyes. Knowing that she had scored this one little victory over him bolstered her confidence. Crying had helped too, but she was unaware whether she crying for the lost innocence of her youth, for the heart-rending regret that was Felix, or simply because she felt sorry for herself.

Bundling the last of her treasures back into the sack, she encountered a small ledger, bound in black leather, which was not familiar to her. She opened it and exclaimed aloud. It was filled with her father's scrawled handwriting. It was impossible for her to say what the book contained for her eyes were once again full of tears: but this time they were tears of rage. So after all, even her secret hiding place had not been safe from him. Irrationally she felt as though he had just violated her all over again.

Calm at last and determined to banish all thoughts of her father's tyranny, Saskia continued to reacquaint herself with her treasures. So intent upon the task was she that she did not realize she was no longer alone, until a voice from the open doorway made her start violently.

'You, Mrs Eden, are one devilishly difficult lady to catch up with!'

Looking up, Saskia gasped, 'You!'

'Who else were you expecting?' asked Lord Shorter, strolling into the room. Taking Saskia's silence as a sign of encouragement, he continued. 'Not Western? You do not imagine that he had a serious attachment to you, surely? Western is known for his peccadilloes: Angelica Priestley is just the latest in a long line.' He saw the shock on Saskia's face and laughed nastily. 'Oh, do not take offence, m'dear, I am sure he found you attractive enough. But even if he was serious he could hardly offer for you now the truth about you is out, could he?' Shorter was prancing, cat-like, across the expanse that separated them, his eyes shining with very obvious intent and Saskia was suddenly afraid. To be alone in a bedchamber with him, after everything she had learned about his character: the consequences did not bear thinking about.

'Why did you do that to me?' she enquired haughtily.

'Tell the truth about you, do you mean? You left me with no alternative, m'dear. Had you but listened to my proposition in the rose garden it would not have been necessary and so, you see, you brought it all on yourself.'

As Saskia looked up at him her spine tingled with fear, a fear which slowly crept through the rest of her body. There was something about that look in his eye, about the confidence beneath his studied nonchalance, that made her realize this time it would not be so easy to reject his advances. She knew he was dangerous, accustomed to getting what he wanted, and there could be no doubting that, for some reason, what he wanted was her. The naked hunger in his eye was all the proof she needed to confirm her fears.

Saskia's room was at the back of the house. Even if she screamed, the Customs men out front would not hear her. Her only way out was to talk to him, she supposed, and to try and charm him into being reasonable.

'Well, I am listening now, my lord. What did you wish to say to me?'

'That's more like it!' He stopped if front of her and tilted her chin upwards, compelling her to look into his face. The feel of his fingers on her skin was abhorrent to her but she made herself ignore it. 'Now, m'dear, when I first saw you I had in mind just a short dalliance but your spirited resistance is a challenge I am unable to ignore and has endeared you to me. Now, what I propose is that I set you up in London with a nice house, money and education for your children.'

'Why would you do something so kind?'

Lord Shorter looked at her askance, attempting to detect sarcasm in her tone, only to discover there was none to be found. She honestly did not understand his meaning! It increased his already monumental attraction to her tenfold. 'M'dear, you are charming!' When she still stared at him blankly, he smiled, shrugged in amusement and explained. 'You will be under my protection.'

'Nooooo!' Saskia couldn't help it. She was shocked and appalled by the very suggestion and the outraged denial slipped from her lips before she could prevent it.

Shorter's attitude changed to one of soft persuasion. 'Come, come, m'dear, don't imagine you can increase the stakes by pretending to be shocked. Besides, what is your alternative?'

'To live here, just as I have always done.'

'What, in this backwater? I do not think so, that would be such a waste.' His voice was a soft purr as he took a step closer. 'Just think of the splendid life you could live in London: all the time you continue to please me, that is.'

'Never!'

The disgust, the contemptuous vehemence of Saskia's tone engendered another abrupt change of Shorter's mood. How dare this inconsequential chit turn him down! In a blind rage he lunged for her but Saskia had been expecting something of the sort and was ready for him. She employed her knee, just as she had told Felix that she had intended to do in the Rose Garden, and at the same time gouged her nails across his hateful face as viciously as she could manage.

He howled with pain and stumbled towards her. 'You little bitch!' Then, inexplicably he smiled slowly at her. 'Is that the way you want to play it? All right, have it your way.'

He continued to advance upon her, his eyes never leaving her face, his expression one of lustful anticipation. The floorboards that Saskia had removed to access her treasures were still out of place and Shorter, mindless of where he was walking, for his eyes remained steadily focused upon Saskia, placed his foot plum into the centre of the hole. He pulled it out with a howl of rage and splintering of wood, but ignored his pain and continued to advance upon her, seemingly more aroused than ever by her continued resistance. Saskia, who was now backed helplessly against the wall, looked frantically about her but accepted, with a sinking heart, that there was nowhere else for her to go.

Felix's unexpected arrival at Riverside House caused quite a stir. Upon learning that Saskia was alone at Southview Manor he determined to follow her thither; relieved that they would be able to conclude their long overdue conversation, free from interruption.

He was annoyed to be told by the Customs men on guard that Saskia already had a visitor. Whoever it was, Felix decided as he ascended the stairs two at a time, had best be brief for he was in no mood to he hospitable, or to share Saskia with anyone else.

Still not sensing danger, Felix followed the sound of voices to the back of the first floor. Entering the room in question, the scene which greeted him caused him to stop dead in his tracks. Discovering that Shorter was there before him caused his blood to run cold. He had Saskia pinned on the bed and was attempting to rip her bodice open with one hand, whilst holding her down with the other. She was putting up a spirited fight and in the split second that Felix stood motionless she managed to land the index finger of her right hand in Shorter's left eye. He swore profusely and slapped her face. Hard.

Felix sprang forward and grabbed Shorter by the back of his coat. Swinging round in surprise, his mouth gaping open stupidly, Felix punched him squarely on his jaw. Staggering from the force of the blow, Shorter half-heartedly tried to retaliate, but even had he been prepared for the confrontation, he would have been no match for Felix, even in his injured condition. Felix landed a second blow to the side of Shorter's head. His legs crumpled beneath him as he fell to the floor. This time he wisely stayed down.

Felix was at Saskia's side in a second, helping her to sit up.

'Are you all right? Did that bastard hurt you?'

Saskia looked at Felix for several moments before responding. She had imagined him appearing like this so often over the past couple of days that she could still scarce believe that he was actually here. She reached up to touch his face, reassured by the sight of the now fading bruises. He really had come for her! Her senses soared and just for a moment she permitted herself to forget the impossibility of their ever being together.

'I am all right,' she said slowly. 'And thank you for coming to my aid. You seem to be making a habit of it, but I can assure you that on this occasion I did nothing that could be construed as encouragement.'

'You are entirely welcome and I know that you did not.' Felix smiled at her and her insides melted at the sight of the soft expression in his liquid eyes. 'But still, I should have anticipated this,' he said, almost to himself, his features now set in a grim line.

'What?'

'Never mind. Just give me a moment to get rid of this mess,' he said, indicating the prostrate Shorter, 'and then we will talk.'

It took no time at all for Felix to summon the guards from the front of the house. They unceremoniously bundled the semi-conscious Shorter into his carriage and ordered his coachman to take him home immediately, before charges could be preferred.

Returning to Saskia's room, Felix took her hand and looked at her for a long time without speaking. Only after a delay of several minutes did he steel himself to ask the inevitable question, using a brisk, no-nonsense tone to disguise his anxiety.

'Now, what was that ridiculous note you left me all about?'

'Was it not self-evident?'

'Not to me.'

Saskia withdrew her hand from his and sat a little straighter. 'I cannot marry you, Felix,' she said, looking at him but not quite meeting his eye.

'Because of that ridiculous rumour that Shorter put about?'

'You know about that?'

'I do now, but I would have known a lot sooner if you had told me yourself.'

Saskia accepted the mild rebuke calmly. 'I could not: you would have dissuaded me.'

'Of course I would! Saskia, I told you that your connections do not matter to me, or to my father. We would have overcome that.'

'But your mother?'

'She would overcome it too,' said Felix shortly.

'And society?'

'Hang society! It is you I want and if they cannot accept who you are then it is their misfortune.'

Saskia stood and moved away from him but even though she turned her back she could still feel the intensity of his gaze and imagine the determination in his expression. Somehow she had to convince him that she was right and that she was not just doing this for his sake. She sensed that only then would he let her go.

'Felix,' she said, turning to face him and meeting his eye for the first time, 'I do not love you and I do not wish to marry you. It is as simple as that.'

As she spoke, knowing that she was hurting him and being deliberately cruel, Saskia could imagine any number of responses from Felix, other than the one that he provided her with – a burst of relieved laughter followed by one dismissive word.

'Nonsense!'

'I beg your pardon?'

Felix crossed the room to join her, but did not, as she thought he would, take her in his arms. Instead, he stood a foot away from her, smiling, relaxed and confident.

'I said nonsense! You'll have to do better than that.'

'You really are the most infuriating man! What do I have to do to convince you?'

'I am hardly likely to tell you that, am I now?'

'Felix, it is worse than we thought. The Customs people have found no direct evidence against my father. He has enough influence to wriggle out of the charges already pending against him and then he will be out for revenge. And you will be his first target.'

'Your concern for my welfare is touching but you do not really imagine that your father has more influence than my family, do you?' He did reach for her now and drew her close. 'He cannot touch you any more, sweetheart. You have nothing to fear.'

Saskia pulled away from him, knowing that if he held her close or kissed her, then her resolve would crumble. She sat back on the bed, next to her pile of treasures. Felix watched her, smiling. 'Is that what you returned here for?'

'Yes. There are letters from my mother and some of her jewellery.'

'And the Customs men did not find it?'

'No. I was confident that no one would ever find my hiding place.' She paused before adding bitterly, 'But my father did. Not even that was to be mine alone. Look.' She held up the ledger. Felix took it from her and, flipping through it casually, his whole demeanour suddenly changed.

'This is it!' he exclaimed. 'This is what Smithers' men missed!'

'What do you mean?'

'We knew that he must have a record of his transactions somewhere, and this is it. Smithers' men turned your father's study upside down thinking it must be concealed in that room, but your father was too clever for them. He hid it here instead, right under their noses, and they missed it! Look! Names, dates and amounts of money that changed hands.' When Saskia still looked blank, Felix stood up and swung her round. 'We've got him, him and all of his vile customers. And we will ensure that the world knows you found the evidence that convicted him. You will be a heroine, Saskia. You will be fêted everywhere you go. Now, tell me again just why it is that you cannot marry me?'

They were the last words he spoke before he finally kissed her, tenderly at first but then with a hunger and passion that left Saskia giddy with desire and happiness. Slowly, and then all in a rush, it dawned on her that there now really was nothing stopping her from marrying him. Except for one thing! She pulled away from him.

'Angelica Priestley,' she said, averting her gaze from his face.

'Ah yes, well. That was what I was doing when you observed us on the terrace: ending our relationship. But how did you know?'

'Lord Shorter took great delight in informing me,' said Saskia tightly.

'Well,' said Felix, reaching for her again, 'you have nothing to fear from that quarter.'

'Maybe not,' she said, avoiding his grasp, 'but what of other ladies. How can I be sure there are no others?'

'You have nothing to fear on that score either.'

'Huh, that is easy for you to say.'

He clasped her firmly by her shoulders and she did not attempt to evade him. Felix could sense a lessening of her uncertainties and hurried to press home his advantage.

'Luc and I were, er . . . well, let us just say infamous in our time,' he said, with sufficient embarrassment to cause Saskia to giggle. 'But you have seen him with Clarissa: he is a changed man. He knew he had met his heart's desire in her, just as certainly as I know I have met mine in you. Do you believe me now?'

Without waiting for a reply he gave in to the urge to kiss her again. When he finally stopped long enough for her to speak she told him that she would marry him.

She would never forget the look of happiness, the unmitigated relief that suffused his features. He kissed her again, fleetingly, gently. Saskia was surprised, having expected more urgency on his part, now she had finally succumbed.

'We have plenty of time,' he explained, in response to her confused expression, wincing as he released her.

'You're hurt again,' she said with concern.

'It is nothing.'

'Let me see. Take off your coat.' Her voice brooked no argument.

'With the greatest of pleasure!'

Saskia gasped as she saw blood on the sleeve of his shirt.

'It must have opened up when I hit Shorter.'

'Take off your shirt, let me see to it.'

Sighing, but unable to resist, with one of his wolfish smiles, Felix complied, only remembering when it was too late the dreadful bruises still on his chest.

Saskia was appalled and Felix could not help using the fact to his advantage, pretending a giddiness, as her fingers gently and tenderly probed his injuries.

'You look faint,' she said, concerned as she redressed his arm. 'You should lie down.'

'Only if you lie with me,' he said, rolling onto his back and pulling her on top of him.

'Felix!' she exclaimed, trying to sound shocked, 'I declare you to be a fraud!'

'Hm, is that so!' He sounded abstracted as he showered kisses across her neck and shoulders.

Saskia felt happier than she had ever believed it was possible to be. As his hands greedily explored her body she felt a heat building within her. Her mouth was dry and her pulse was racing. So this was desire! At last she understood.

Felix reluctantly pulled away from her, pleased that the withdrawal of his attentions produced an indignant protest from Saskia. He wanted to make love to her so desperately that he would not be able to stop himself from doing so if he did not release her right now. He wanted their first time together to be something special and knew this was neither the right time or place. This room held too many unpleasant memories for her. It was here, in this chamber, that she had endured her husband's selfish advances, had been beaten by her father and attacked by Shorter. Now that she had agreed to be his he could wait: at least for a little longer.

'Come on, m'dear, your aunt and the twins will wonder what has become of us.'

He drove her back to Riverside House, one hand on the ribbons, the other possessively clasping hers, the black ledger safely in his pocket. Not a word was exchanged between them but they smiled broadly and constantly turned to look at one another, as though neither of them could quite believe the turn events had taken.

As they crossed the lawns at Riverside House they heard two familiar voices speaking in unison to an amused Aunt Serena.

'It is very difficult, Aunt Serena—'

'—and we are unsure what to do—'

'—you see, Rosie calls him Uncle Felix—'

'—but we call him Mr Beaumont—'

'—but now,' they finished together, their tone accusatory, 'we are told that he is a "lordship" too—'

'—what should we do?'

Aunt Serena was about to make a soothing reply when she espied Felix and Saskia approaching and smiled in delight.

Joining the group, Felix sat Saskia on a bench and took his place beside her. He pulled Amy on to his lap and put an arm around Josh's shoulder. Felix's smile was for the children, but encompassed Aunt Serena and Saskia as well.

'I would feel very honoured,' he said gently to the twins, 'if you would consider addressing me as Papa.'